Ghosts of the Green Swamp

Ghosts of the Green Swamp

A Cracker Western

Lee Gramling

Pineapple Press
Palm Beach, Florida

Pineapple Press

An imprint of Globe Pequot, the trade division of
The Rowman & Littlefield Publishing Group, Inc.
4501 Forbes Blvd., Ste. 200
Lanham, MD 20706
www.rowman.com

Distributed by NATIONAL BOOK NETWORK

British Library Cataloguing in Publication Information Available

Library of Congress Cataloging-in-Publication Data available

ISBN 978-1-6833-4304-2 (paper : alk. paper)
ISBN 978-1-6833-4326-4 (electronic)

∞™ The paper used in this publication meets the minimum requirements
of American National Standard for Information Sciences—Permanence
of Paper for Printed Library Materials, ANSI/NISO Z39.48-1992.

Dedicated to the memory of
Gamble Rogers
preeminent Florida storyteller
and continuing inspiration

Central Florida 1877

Contents

1

"IF YOU SO MUCH AS MOVE A EYELASH, Barkley, I'm going to blow your guts all over this country-side!"

Well, that fellow with the slouch hat and the two-barreled shotgun who was standin' in the road in front of me sounded like he meant exactly what he'd said. And the fact I'd never in my life set eyes on him before didn't appear to make a awful lot of difference to his thinkin' neither. I kept my hands easy on the saddle-horn and nodded just a hair to show I understood.

"All right, Jube!" he called, glancin' over towards the stand of oak and hickory what run alongside that little stretch of sand road there between Newnansville an' Lake City. "C'mon and take his shootin' iron away from him. And see you do it careful!"

When I'd had a look at Jube out of the corner of my eye, I kind of swallowed hard and sucked in my breath. He was the biggest colored man I'd ever seen. The biggest man of any color. Seven foot an' upwards if he was a inch. And I didn't expect he'd run a heap shy of four hundred pounds if anybody was able to get him up on a wagon scales to weigh him. Them overalls he was wearin' was a deal too small, so the pants legs stopped a good ten inches above his big bare feet. And the muscles bulgin' from his shoulders an' arms looked ready to bust clean out of his faded cotton undershirt just any minute.

I mean it was enough to give me pause, and I ain't exactly no half-growed runt of a feller my ownself. I reckon I plumb near forgot the other gent's shotgun for a second there, when that live oak in man's clothing come stridin' out of the woods towards me.

He moved right swift for a big man, too. Never took his red-rimmed eyes off me for a instant while he stepped up and yanked my Dragoon Colt from its holster an' throwed it on the ground. Didn't even bother unhookin' the leather thong from around the hammer before he done it. Just snapped it in two like a piece of ole rotten thread.

I'd a mind to say somethin' about that. But I didn't hardly get the chanct before I felt myself bein' lifted up off my ole roan horse and tossed down in the dirt on the other side away from my six-shooter. And it come right close to makin' me mad.

"Look-a here," I said, rollin' over and spittin' sand out from between my teeth. "What the dag-gone Hell do you-all think you're . . ."

That's 'bout as much as I got to say before Jube crossed behind the Roan and swung a mighty kick from the hips, bruisin' a couple ribs and leavin' me all curled up an' croakin' whilst I tried to get my wind back. Them feet of his was rock hard from goin' without shoes for what I expected was prob'ly his entire life. And he was aimin' a second one at my head when the man with the shotgun took a step closer and got his attention.

"Hold on there, Jube. Think about what you're doin'. We don't want him so bad messed up that he can't make it back to the hammock under his own steam. Be way too much trouble to tote him."

The big Negro nodded thoughtfully. Then he set up an' smashed another powerful kick to my ribs, instead of my head. I hadn't got enough breath left over from that to swear good. But I was a-thinkin' it.

The man with the shotgun come up and stood lookin' down at me.

"You led us a merry chase, Barkley. Over a hundred mile from where we started out at. And nigh onto two weeks beatin' through the brush a-lookin' for you. But I reckon Mister Ravenant'll be pleased to see you onct we get back. Ain't many big an' strong as you, what can stand up to the life an' still do the work of a couple men." He glanced across the road to where my roan horse stood, nibblin' at some leaves with his ears pricked and a watchful look in his eyes.

"Wonder you was able to find yourself a hoss and a outfit like that, shape you was in when you lit out. Stole 'em from some homesteader, more'n likely." He shrugged. "Don't matter a' awful lot I reckon. They'll belong to Mr. Ravenant after we bring 'em home to him."

I was beginnin' to get my wind back a little bit now, and I still had a couple, three things to explain to these fellers if they'd give me half a chanct. One of 'em was that Ole Roan an' me had seen a good big piece of the country together, and I didn't cotton to no Mr. Ravenant nor anybody else settin' hisself up to appropriate him for his private use. And what was more important at the moment maybe, was how clear it was to me that they'd got me plumb mistook for some other gent named Barkley.

I eased myself up onto one elbow with a effort, keepin' a eye on Jube and his partner's shotgun both whilst I was doin' it. Then I tried to make 'em understand the way things was, in as reasonable a voice as I could manage. Which come out right then to be a kind of a whisperin' croak.

"Look here," I said, "I reckon maybe you-all made some kind of a mistake. See, I ain't . . ."

Well, it was clear neither one of them gents was in much of a listenin' mood. 'Cause the man with the scatter-gun looked up at Jube and nodded. Then that big Negro reached out and smacked me acrost the mouth with all his might, forward and back, usin' a hand what felt like it was made out of spring steel. I noticed he was missin' a couple joints from his fingers when he done it, but that didn't hold him back a bit when it come to rattlin' my brain cage from here to yonder.

When I'd shook the sparklin' lights out of my eyes enough to where I could cuss, he did it again.

"Shut up," the shotgun gent said mildly, whilst I spit blood and felt around a couple loose teeth with my tongue. "If we want any talkin' from you, we'll ask for it."

I looked from him to his colored compadre and back again, thinkin' real particular thoughts about what I'd a mind to do to both or either of 'em whenever I got the chance. And I hoped I would. But for the time bein' it 'peared a whole heap smarter to just keep my ideas to myself.

"You got him, Purv?" There'd been this sound of a horse

comin' up the road behind me for a little while now. But I hadn't paid it much mind till that voice spoke up, followed by a swish of linen skirts as the rider jumped to the ground. "You didn't hurt him bad, did you?"

I jerked my head around and come right close to bitin' through my tongue when I'd got a look at who the speaker was. She was one of the prettiest little things I ever did see. Maybe nineteen or twenty, with long black hair an' shinin' dark saucers for eyes, her cheeks all flushed an' pink from the ridin' and the way she run up so quick to kneel down beside me.

If I was some surprised at seein' anything that fetchin' in the company of Mr. Shotgun and big Jube, it weren't nothin' to what I felt a minute later, when she grabbed holt of my ears with both hands and leaned forward to plant a big wet kiss right square on my lips. Afterwards she backed off real fast and looked me up an' down mighty peculiar for a long minute.

"It ain't him," she said finally, turnin' to the man with the shotgun, the one she'd called Purv. Her voice had got awful cold durin' that couple seconds she was starin' at me. "You big dumb lunker!" she went on, spittin' out the words like she was spittin' out snake venom, "You cotched the wrong man!"

"Huh?" Purv come a step closer, his shotgun still steady on my brisket. "Damnation, Lila. You certain?" He squinted up his eyes and cocked his head over to one side, peerin' down at my face as though he was seein' me for the first time. "This-un surely does favor him. Though when you mention it he do seem a couple pounds heavier than what I recall. And maybe a tad shaggier 'round the ears, too. . . ."

Lila answered him with a word I didn't think a lady'd ought to know. Then she got up and walked on back to where her horse was restin' three-legged in the shade. "Don't you 'spect I'd be able to tell if'n it was him? You think I wouldn't recognize any man what . . ." She broke off and spun round on her heel.

"You just go ahead an' take my word on it. It ain't him. Now what are we goin' to do about it?"

The man with the shotgun shifted his feet kind of awkward-like, glancin' at Jube. "Take him along with us?" he asked, not sounding terrible certain. "He's a big-un. Could make a right powerful field hand onct we got him broke in right."

"You know the rules. We don't take nobody back yonder what might have kinfolks or friends anywheres about this country. It ain't worth the trouble." Lila was lookin' at me kind of thoughtful now. Reminded me of some li'l green frog on a lily pad eyin' a blue-tail fly. "Uncle's awful partic'lar about his rules bein' broke. Myself, I'd hate to be the one to explain it to him."

"We don't know nothing 'bout this gent," Purv answered, a mite peevish it seemed to me. "Prob'ly ain't got no folks hereabouts nohow. 'Pears to be just some kind of a low-ridin' drifter."

Lila smiled a sort of a half smile. "Why don't you ask him?"

"Ain't nobody else in this whole wide world but me," I said. "'Less'n you count my daddy an' eighteen brothers. Ever one of 'em's half man an' half gator. With another half piney woods rooter throwed in for good measure."

I was lyin' pretty broad, of course. And I reckoned they

all knowed it. But on t'other hand, they couldn't be real sure what was the actual truth neither. And that there was the general idea.

"Well," Purv says, lookin' at me all disgusted with his bottom lip poked out, "I reckon we better just kill him then and be done with it. Jube can bury him so deep in these woods them eighteen brothers'll spend the rest of their natural days lookin' for a bone big enough to use as a toothpick!"

Lila nodded and glanced at me in a way that made me think she'd a little rather do the deed herself as let Purv at it. And judgin' from the .38 Colt in that holster at her waist, I'd a idea she wouldn't have no trouble managin' it if she took the notion. But then she frowned and shook her head.

"Too many folks hereabouts to take a chanct on shootin'." She almost sounded disappointed. "I passed a farm house not more'n a half mile back. And they's a settlement a couple miles further on, this side the river. Never can tell who-all might hear the sound of it and come snoopin'. Likely before we could even get out of the country good."

"Well . . ." Purv lifted his eyes up to Jube, who was standin' over me with his big fists restin' on his hips, and I saw Lila nod in agreement.

"Jube, honey," she said, all sweetness an' smiles. "We need you to kill this man for us. Without no fuss nor callin' out, but just as quick an' quiet as you can with your two bare hands."

I didn't waste any time lookin' up at Jube. Weren't no doubt in my mind he'd do what he was told. Instead, I made a sudden lunge for the gent with the shotgun. Figured if I was to have to die anyhow, I'd at least try an' fix it so it weren't neither quiet nor easy for 'em. Just some part of my natural-

15

borned cussedness, I imagine.

Only I didn't come half as close to layin' a hand on Purv as I thought I would. When I said that Jube was quick for a big man, I didn't tell the half of it.

I hadn't got more'n a foot off the ground when his big paw come down on my right shoulder, clampin' up so tight I felt my arm turnin' numb. Then he yanked me back and upwards, throwing his left arm acrost my throat so's I didn't even have a chanct to cuss or yell out.

I'd played at this game a time or two my ownself, though. So I turned my head and tucked my chin into my chest almost without thinkin'. But when Jube grabbed a big fistful of hair with his free hand and started in to pull, it hurt so fierce I almost couldn't keep my wits about me. Just barely managed to kick back with a spurred boot heel and grind it down onto his bare foot.

That colored man was a heap better at followin' orders than I'd of been at a time like that. 'Cause he didn't hardly yelp or cry out a-tall. Just made a little sound like a wheezin' grunt whilst he stepped back an' throwed me to the ground, usin' his grip on my hair for leverage. I felt a bunch of it come loose in his fingers 'bout the same time my nose bored into the dirt. A instant later the breath was bein' crushed out of me by a big heavy knee in the small of my back.

Jube let me have a whoppin' left and a right to the ears with his open palms, purely out of meanness for the hurt I'd caused him. Then he got his fingers round my throat and started in to squeeze.

I mean I was in some sorry shape at that moment. My mouth was fillin' up with sand so's I couldn't take a breath. Couldn't hardly twitch my arms or legs, much less turn over with that four hundred pounds of meat an' gristle pressin' down on top of me. It weren't too much longer before my eyes begun to roll up, and I could see orange an' silver flashes against a real deep shade of velvet black.

After another minute there wasn't even that. Only a kind of a helpless fallin' feeling, like I was slippin' off into some bottomless hole without no way of catchin' myself.

I reckon I must of faded out there for a pretty good while, what with Jube's big fingers shuttin' off my windpipe and his weight pressin' the air an' life out of me. If he'd waited another half second before gettin' up from what he was doin', I expect I'd of been ever bit as dead as I prob'ly appeared to him an' Lila right then. But luck was with me, 'cause somethin' they'd heard was makin' 'em skittish and anxious to leave out before they could be real certain the job was finished proper.

None of this come into my head right away, you understand. It weren't until I felt a woman's fingers goin' through my pockets real quick and thorough that I begun to even halfway recollect where I was. Then I could hear Lila's harsh whisper as she called out to the others:

"Mount up and let's ride! That buggy'll be showin' itself over the rise yonder in just another couple minutes!"

It didn't take no partic'lar effort for me to keep lyin' real still like the corpse they thought I was. Her voice got fainter when she stood up and moved off into the road. "Purv, you got a lead rope on that roan? All right then, let's be travelin'!"

While the sounds of their harness an' hoofbeats faded out to the south, I decided to see could I drag my hands up underneath me and push my shoulders a couple inches off the ground. Turned out that weren't near the easy job it appeared at first glance. Took me a couple, three tries to manage it, and then it seemed like my head wasn't stayin' attached to my body the way it was accustomed to a mite earlier. I couldn't hardly keep my eyebrows from scrapin' the dirt.

After another minute I gagged an' coughed up a mouthful of earth and sandspurs. Then I rolled real slow over onto my back.

The sky was a pale robin's egg blue, with only a couple fleecy clouds away off in the distance. It was a right pretty sight, and I just let myself lay there, breathin' kind of shallow and thinkin' how lucky I was to look up an' see any kind of a sky one more time. Finally I begun to notice the clip-clop an' rattle of some kind of a rig movin' down the road towards me.

When it got up close enough to make stirrin' worth the effort, I turned my head to find out who my new visitors was.

What I seen was this brand new lookin' surrey, all shiny black with fringed tassels an' black leather seats, being drawed by a high-steppin' charcoal gelding what had these red ribbons tied in its mane an' tail. I got a real close look at that outfit when it slowed down for a couple seconds to steer past where I was sprawled there in the sand.

"Hey!" I croaked, tryin' to push myself up onto one elbow but not quite able to manage it. "Hey, mister!" The voice what come out of my crushed windpipe weren't hardly much stronger than a whisper.

This gent in a white straw hat an' broadcloth suit peered back over his shoulder at me, his face all twisted up like he'd just finished a big old dinner of lemon seeds an' pickles. Then he turned round and whipped his gelding into a trot, mutterin' something real spiteful 'bout "drunken

Southern trash" to the woman on the seat next to him. Just before they went out of sight round the bend up ahead, I heard her answer him with a couple remarks of her own, what had to do with "in-breeding," and somethin' sounded to me like "Miss Seegy Nation."

And there I was again, all by my lonesome an' feeling helpless as a new-hatched sparrow in a yard full of chicken snakes. I figured it was gettin' to be a plumb miserable world whenever a hurt man couldn't even expect no help nor sympathy from passin' travelers.

After a little while I got up the strength to hitch myself into a sittin' position, with my arms hugging my knees and my chin restin' on top of 'em. I sat there for a time longer, takin' in a couple deep breaths what made me want to yell out from the pain in my ribs, before finally openin' my eyes. When I'd had a quick glance up an' down the road, I begun to take stock.

2

NOT THAT THERE WAS so awful much left to take stock of. My Ole Roan horse was gone, which was bad enough. But along with him was just about my entire outfit: a big Texas saddle with some good years of use left in it, a bedroll and saddlebags what carried a week's worth of provisions that I'd bought only the day before yesterday when I got paid off from that cow-hunt an' cattle-drivin' job up to Lake City. And worst of all, my Winchester .44 in the saddle boot with a couple hundred rounds of spare ammunition.

My pistol belt had been stripped off too, along with the Bowie knife in its sheath at the side; and I knew there weren't no point to go lookin' for my Dragoon Colt now, what Jube had took and throwed on the ground. With them weapons missin' I felt about as naked as if they'd done stole my pants an' boots at the same time they was stealin' everthing else.

Speakin' of boots, I realized of a sudden I wasn't wearing any. A quick look around showed 'em both layin' off to the edge of the road next to my hat. So at least them no-counts had left me that much. But then I remembered somethin' else had happened before Lila an' them others rode away, and I started checkin' through the pockets of my shirt and britches real careful-like, gruntin' and cussin' ever time I come acrost a bruise or some other hurt Jube had give me.

When I got done, I took my time and did a more thorough job of cussin'.

That Lila had cleaned me out en-tire, from my Barlow knife and whetstone to even the cigarette makin's in my shirt pocket. 'Course there wasn't no sign of the money I'd had left from what I bought in Lake City. And when I crawled over to fetch my hat an' boots, I realized she'd found the gold double eagle I'd had hid inside there too.

Now, that made me mad. I'd been holding onto that gold coin special, meanin' to pay back a loan from a certain lady over to the Gulf coast soon as I could make it up there again. Stealing from me was one thing, and it done a pretty good job of gettin' my dander up all by its ownself. But takin' something I'd thought of as belonging to a partic'lar good friend of mine was just addin' insult to injury.

There was goin' to be some settlin' of accounts over this here business today, or my name wasn't Tate Barkley. And it ain't ever been anything else since my Mam an' Pap brought me into the world.

It's a name folks in some circles has found reason to fight shy of here an' about. I been spoke of all the way from Arizona to the Florida panhandle as a feller what can become mighty unsociable once his toes get stepped on hard enough. And I could feel my corns startin' to pain me, right about now.

Some might of thought it foolish for me to be havin' ideas like that, considerin' the shape I was in just then. And maybe they'd be right. Good sense ain't never been commented upon as a partic'lar Barkley trait.

But on t'other hand, stubbornness is. And they's only one way I ever heard of for a man to get from here to there, no matter where "here" an' "there" turn out to be. That's by hitchin' up his galluses and startin' in to set one foot before the other.

So once I'd put on my hat and stomped back into my boots, I just pointed my nose in that southward direction where them bushwhackers rode off after they got finished leavin' me for dead, and I set out to walkin'.

If I passed that settlement Lila mentioned this side the river, I never did see it. They was a few scattered cabins here an' about, most of 'em well back off the road. But nothin' what struck me as lookin' anything like a town. And no folks I could see close enough to holler to.

Not that it concerned me a awful lot right at the moment. I wasn't in no mood for idle conversation, and there weren't anything I wanted to know about them outlaws what couldn't be read in the sand road at my feet. Their sign was plain enough, 'specially since Jube 'peared to be ridin' a mule. And I'd of recognized the tracks of my Ole Roan horse anyplace.

I reckoned it was maybe nine or ten o'clock in the morning when Purv first stepped out from the trees with his shotgun to get my attention. And I didn't figure the whippin' and the robbin' I'd got took much over half a hour afterwards. By the time I'd passed by the store at Old Leno and started makin' my way south 'crost the Natural Bridge of the Santa

Fe River, the sun had climbed up to where it was pretty near direct overhead.

I was some grateful for the coolness of the deep woods all around me 'bout then, 'cause that late September sun was hot enough to make the sweat run down into the cuts an' hurts ole Jube had put on my face, which didn't give me much pleasure a-tall. And Lila hadn't even left me with a kerchief in my pockets to sop up the worst of it with.

The hills an' ravines northwest of Newnansville was beginnin' to get my feets' attention too before long. I'd already covered maybe six, seven miles by the time I reached 'em, and those western boots I wore wasn't exactly made with walkin' comfort in mind. My earlier thoughts about achin' corns was startin' to take on a more realistic meaning as I imagined them blisters on my toes an' heels beginnin' to grow larger with ever step.

Weren't much I could do about it though, since I'd a mind to keep close an' steady on those bushwhackers' trail as long as I was able. You never could tell when it might cloud up to rain in this Florida land, which would wash out their tracks completely.

I might of took off my boots and gone barefoot. But seemed like ever time I'd a thought about doin' that, I'd come acrost a big patch of sandspurs or poison ivy or somethin' else along the road, like a fresh snake trail windin' through the sand, which just had a tendency to change my mind.

I managed to keep from dwellin' on my present miseries so much by lettin' my thoughts roam back over what-all was said an' done there amongst Purv and Lila an' Jube after they'd jumped me — things I might not of paid real close attention to the first time around. I knew pert' near anything

I could recall would be a help in runnin' 'em to earth, 'cause it trackin' ain't so much a matter of readin' sign on the ground, as it's knowin' where to look for the sign in the first place. And that means understandin' the ways of whatever critter it is you're huntin', be it animal or bird or human.

Some of that talk back yonder I couldn't hardly make no sense of. Like how come Purv had called me "Barkley" right off when he seen me, and what Barkley he thought I was that I turned out not to be. It ain't a uncommon name, I reckon. But I didn't know of no others in this Florida country my ownself. My folks been dead quite a number of years now, and the only brother I had took off from home pretty soon after Pap was killed back in '63. Last time I heard from him was just after the war, when he was on his way to California with a deck of cards, a fast horse, and high hopes.

Anyhow, it seemed like that Barkley feller they'd mistook me for was somebody they knowed right well once upon a time — leastways Lila had — and they wanted him back mighty serious now, wherever they come from. What was it Purv had said? 'Bout leadin' 'em a merry chase for more'n a hundred miles? I thought that over whilst I stopped by the side of the road and pulled out my shirt-tail to try dabbin' the sweat away from my eyes with it.

Tell you the truth, I didn't know my way about the central an' south part of this Florida peninsula worth a hoot, for all that I was born an' brought up in Taylor County and spent my first eighteen years of livin' in the state. That cow hunt down to Otter Creek a couple weeks ago was the furthest south I reckon I'd ever been. Right now I was tryin' to picture the rest of it in my mind, from travelers' talk and a occasional peek at a map in some general store or railroad depot here an' there.

'Peared to me a hundred mile ought to put the place them three started out from somewheres north of Tampa Bay on the west coast, or between Mosquito Inlet and Cape Canaveral in the east. That still left a heap of country to go huntin' round in if I happened to lose sight of their tracks. But it could of been worse. I reckoned it was near four hundred miles from where I stood right now to Cape Sable at the farthest end of the state.

Purv's earlier words to Jube about takin' me home to the "hammock" didn't mean a thing of course, 'cept their place was more'n likely somewheres back up in the woods. They was more high hammocks an' low hammocks than you could shake a stick at, all the way from the St. Marys River to the Florida Keys.

After mullin' things over a mite longer whilst I tucked in my shirt and started makin' tracks again, I couldn't think of nothin' else that was said what would be any special use to me. Lila's remark about her uncle Ravenant's "rules," an' the fact they'd somethin' to do with not takin' nobody along what had friends or kin anywhere about, was enough to stir up a feller's curiosity. But without a heap more knowledge than what I'd got at the moment, I couldn't begin to make head nor tails of it.

'Peared like the best thing right now was to not waste no more time worryin' about all them questions I didn't have answers to, but to start lookin' for ways to solve the problems which was closer at hand. Like what I meant to do when and if I managed to catch up to Lila an' Purv an' big Jube.

I could see from the way they was travelin' south, keepin' up a steady pace without pushin' their mounts no more'n they had to, that they wasn't too concerned about bein' followed. Which didn't surprise me, considerin' they figured I was dead and there weren't no witnesses to explain how it happened.

Oh, maybe there'd of been a embarrassin' question or two asked if they'd been real close at hand when the body was found. But it was mighty doubtful anybody'd believe a woman as young an' pretty and lady-lookin' as that Lila could of had somethin' to do with it. Womenfolks was right highly thought of hereabouts, and killin' strangers in cold blood weren't hardly no part of people's expectations of 'em.

Which sort of got me to ponderin' even more serious on what I'd do if I come across them three all to onct like I'd had in mind. Plannin' ahead ain't one of my long suits. I always been more the type to just cinch up my belt and walk in a-swingin'. But they was a couple good reasons now for doin' a tad more calculatin' than was generally my custom.

First o' course, was the fact that they'd got a couple pistols, a shotgun, and my Winchester repeater, along with maybe some other hardware I might not of took inventory of in the earlier excitement. And I hadn't got a solitary thing but the clothes on my back and my two bare hands. Which hadn't done me a awful lot of good earlier, against just Jube by his lonesome.

So under the circumstances, it might be a deal more healthy if I was to set eyes on them three before they seen me, instead of the other way around. And right then I realized that the way I'd been stompin' up the road like a ole bull through a thicket, without a bit more sense or caution than that dumb critter, was liable to get me kilt before I could do even the first thing towards gettin' any of my goods back.

I'd spent enough time out west in Indian country to know better from the git-go. But I'd been so all-fired mad about the trouble an' the hurts I'd got, which done a sight more damage to my pride than my body if I was to be truthful about it, that for a couple hours I'd sort of forgot to take time off from my stewin' to do any thinking.

Well, it weren't too late to make a change, fortunately.

I stepped over to the side of the road and took in a deep breath, lettin' myself settle down a mite and have a good long listen, whilst I studied the territory ahead and behind me. I reckoned my need to catch up to them three wasn't so pressin' that I couldn't manage to start tryin' to use my noggin in the process. And maybe even come up with some kind of a plan for what I meant to do once I did run into 'em.

They was thick woods all around where I'd stopped, with hills and ravines what kept the road from goin' straight even a hundred yards before it disappeared round a curve or up a rise or into some li'l draw. Could be it was that layout which sort of jogged my brain back to workin' in the first place. 'Cause if I was lookin' for a spot to ambush some unwary traveler, I sure couldn't do no better than this right here.

But after several cautious minutes, I was pretty sure there weren't nothing close by except a couple mockingbirds and some katydids back off in the trees. When I finally begun moving again, I done it a heap more quiet and watchful than before, with my ears pricked and my eyes tradin' off between the road up ahead, the ground at my feet, and the woods on both sides.

It were a sight harder followin' sign here than it had been earlier, too. Dead leaves an' pine needles lay thick over the road 'most everwhere I looked. Still, them three horses an' a mule couldn't help but leave some marks of their passin'. And a good hard rain the night before had made the sand more inclined to hold its shape whenever I got a chance to see it. But it weren't until I come into this open place at the crest of a ridge some two, three miles further on that I had any idea how far ahead them riders was, or what they was up to.

There was a fork in the road here, with the left branch headin' southeast towards Newnansville and then on to Gainesville some fifteen mile beyond. I'd traveled that way a couple months before, whilst I was huntin' work or some other means of puttin' change in my pockets.

The second road led more south, and I'd heard it caught up with a old stage route from Newnansville to the railroad at Arredonda, and then past it to the town of Micanopy.

It was mid-afternoon now, and there'd been enough traffic since daybreak so that it took me some several minutes to sort through all the tracks at that crossroads and locate the ones I'd been followin'. Turned out when I did, they wasn't headed for Newnansville a-tall. They'd took the right-hand fork towards Micanopy, and near as I could tell they was maybe two, three hours ahead of me by this time.

I happened to notice in passin' that the gent an' lady in the surrey had went the other way, and it almost made me sorry to see they had. I'd been half thinkin' about meetin' up with them folks someplace along the road, just long enough to explain to 'em that I wasn't no drunkard, and maybe offer a opinion or two about what I thought of travelers who'd leave a man layin' hurt on the ground, and go makin' spiteful comments about him to boot.

But what I'd got to say to them two weren't near as important as the business I'd got with Lila and her *compadres*.

So I pointed my feet to the south just soon as I'd got finished makin' certain of their trail.

A two-, three-hour lead weren't hardly nothin' over a long day's trek like this. Their mounts would be needin' to stop and rest a heap more than I would, and to graze too, sooner or later. That's why a man afoot in tolerable good condition can run down just about any horse in time. You could ask the Apaches about that, or some of their Mex Injun neighbors who never did bother learnin' to ride.

'Course I knew I wasn't makin' anything like the kind of speed a Indian might. I hadn't much practice travelin' on shank's mare lately, and I weren't accustomed to it. Besides, I didn't know no Injun alive who'd be fool enough to wear ridin' boots whilst he were a-hoofin' it. Though I meant to keep mine on, I'd got to admit they was something of a hindrance.

But I figured I'd catch up to them three before mornin', regardless. They'd be wantin' to make camp for the night somewheres, soon or late. And without no particular worries about what was on their back trail, I expected they might do it early, leavin' theirselves plenty of time to fix a meal and settle in comfortable before it got too dark to see good.

Me, I hadn't no plans for doin' any of those things until I'd got my outfit and my Ole Roan horse back. An' that there was enough of a thought to keep me hikin' right steady an' purposeful through the afternoon, blisters or no blisters.

When I was maybe two, three hours further along that south fork, still not seeing much in the way of folks except a occasional farmer with his mule way off in a field, I begun to hear this peculiar clatterin' and clankin' noise comin' up the road behind me. It was kind of faint at first, but kept gettin' louder an' louder by the minute. Nearest thing I could liken it to was some kind of a altercation between two bull gators in a li'l ole kitchen shack piled high to the rafters with pots an' pans.

I was out amongst some open rolling fields by this time, without no proper cover for a mile or better in any direction. There wasn't no question of hidin', even if I'd a notion that clankin', creakin' she-bang were something needed hidin' from. And I'd a pretty fair idea it weren't. Nothin' what made that kind of a racket was goin' to ever get close enough to do nobody harm, without their havin' plenty of warnin' and time to take measures to protect theirselves first.

But I was growin' almighty curious to find out what it was. So I kept slowin' my steps and peekin' back over my shoulder, until finally I just stopped altogether and waited alongside the road whilst that unruly contraption come over the top of the rise behind me.

3

IT WERE A MULE-DRAWED WAGON, the like of which I hadn't never seen in all my borned days. The bottom part appeared to be somethin' like one of them Conestoga cargo carriers what folks out west took to callin' prairie schooners. Except it was made out of cypress, and smeared with black tar everplace around the cracks. Up above, instead of a canvas cover, was what looked to be one of them box-top medicine show rigs I'd come acrost a time or two here an' yonder. The fact it was painted all over in bright reds an' greens an' yellows sort of helped that last impression along.

But then the owner or somebody had added a assortment of special touches what just made a fellow pause and scratch his head.

First, the back wheels was a deal bigger'n you'd expect on a rig like that, real wide at the rims and almost tall as a man was high. It made a kind of sense I reckon, for travelin' through these Florida swamps and the deep sand hereabouts. But it give the outfit a kind of a funny, lopsided look, like maybe the wagon body had got itself drenched in a rain so it shrunk up between them outsized wheels.

The varnished roof had this fancy trim what stuck out several inches all around, cut with ever manner of twists an' curlicues like you'd see on some big house in the city. And hangin' from each loop an' cranny of that there carvin' was the mixed-up-est assortment of fryin' pans, coffee pots, lanterns, kettles, tin plates, cups, bottles and other gew-gaws that anybody ever seen. They rattled an' crashed and banged together ever time them two black mules took a step, causin' a big part of the noise I'd been hearin' for the past half hour without guessin' what it was.

On either side of the driver's seat was a couple wood cabinets, and the stuff inside there seemed to be makin' noise too, along with who knew what-all might be in the wagon proper. And then to top it off, when this rig pulled up alongside me to give the mules a blow from climbin' that last hill, I seen some other little doors in the body, and this window what appeared to have a mechanical music box behind it. I could make out pipes, drums, chimes, and even a ole steel-stringed banjo through the dusty glass, each part shakin' and chinkin' and bangin' together to beat the band.

I mean anybody would of had to smile. And though I'd turned halfway round to keep the driver from seein' the grin comin' acrost my face, I couldn't help but take just one more little peek back over my shoulder to make sure I'd really seen what I seen.

And that's when I lost it en-tire.

I was bent over at the waist, a-whoopin' and a-guffaw-in', throwin' my arms up in the air and slappin' my knees, till the tears run down my cheeks and my sore ribs clutched up so's I couldn't hardly breathe. Afterwards I just hunkered down beside the road for a bit, clutchin' at my sides and grinnin' between gasps, while the driver climbed down from his perch and ambled over to have a look at me.

"Something troubling you, friend?" His voice was kind of mild and gentle when he asked the question, but I could tell right off that he weren't finding near as much amusement in the situation as I was. I sat back on my heels and pushed my hat off my forehead to study him better.

He was kind of a short, heavy-set gent, dressed in what appeared to be a right fine store-bought suit, but with the coat off now and the vest unbuttoned on account of the heat. When he lifted up his black stove-pipe hat to dab at the sweat with a calico kerchief, I could see he was bald was a hen's egg underneath, and burnt dark by the sun from crown to neck. His eyes was a real pale blue. And the way they had of peerin' at you from out of that brown creased face was enough to make a feller take kind of serious whatever interest they showed in him.

There weren't no way I could guess his age. The bald head and crows-feet round the eyes seemed to be tellin' me one thing, whilst them muscles I could see bulgin' out from his shirt sleeves, and the way he stood sort of cat-like an' limber but rock-solid at the same time, was sayin' something else entire.

After a minute he put his hat back on and shoved the kerchief into his pocket. Then he moved a step closer.

"I asked," he repeated, even quieter than before, "if there is anything troubling you at the moment." His eyes narrowed into two thin slits. "Perhaps you find something about myself or my equipment . . . amusing?"

Well, it weren't no great feat to catch his meaning. No man cares for bein' laughed at, and I'd of never done it this time if I'd had a mite of warning. But the whole outlandish she-bang come up on me so sudden, with it just nearly the funniest picture I'd put eyes to in a month of Sundays . . .

Still it wasn't nothing I felt inclined to fight over. I'd had me a long tryin' day already, and this here didn't seem hardly worth the effort.

Might of been different if I was a couple years younger. Back then I'd fought any man at the drop of a hat. And drop it myself whenever I couldn't find somebody else to do it. But lately I'd been realizin' there was plenty enough trouble to go around, without nobody havin' to put hisself out special lookin' for more.

So right then it appeared like the smartest thing to do was just eat a little crow, and let bygones be bygones. I give it my best shot, but maybe I hadn't got enough practice at that eatin' crow part yet. 'Cause it turned out my best weren't quite good enough.

I stood up from the ground and tugged at my hat brim, tryin' real hard to wipe the grin off my face as I did it. Then I said, serious as I could manage, "Now don't you go gettin' your feathers all ruffled, mister. I didn't mean nothin' disrespectful. It's only that, well, I'm kind of new to these parts. And I reckon I just ain't never had no occasion before to see somethin' like . . ." I felt the grin creepin' back, 'spite of all I could do to stop it. ". . . like that . . ."

Well, I turned around and reached out a hand to point towards his rig. And first thing you knew I'd took another good look at it and come down with the giggles so hard I couldn't finish what I was sayin'.

That was all Mr. Top-hat needed to make him shuck his temper for fair. And I suppose maybe I wouldn't of blamed him much if I'd seed it from his point of view. But what he done next roused up my own dander to where I plumb forgot about his feelin's, and changed my thoughts about fightin' too, in pretty near half a toad-frog's hop.

'Peared like one second I was bent down chucklin' over that bright-colored rig with its fantastical assortment of kitchen fixin's, and the next I'd been tripped up an' throwed sprawling so my chin was plowin' a furrow for the second time in one day. I rolled over an' come off the ground fast, meanin' to tear little Baldy's meat house down just quick as I could get my fists set to take a sizable swing at him. But he'd already turned and started off the other way, carryin' my hat in one hand and speakin' to his lead mule as if he'd plumb forgot I was there.

"Here's a little something I found to keep the sun out of your eyes, Cassius. It's not much, but the man who was wearing it looked a lot more foolish than you will in it. And he was more ill-mannered too. Now just wait until I cut a pair of holes for your ears . . ."

I got a hand on his shoulder whilst he was reachin' into his wagon for scissors, meanin' to spin him round and toss him out in the road the way he done me. Only it didn't work out just exactly like I'd figured.

That li'l bandy-legged gent was slippery as a moccasin and twict as quick. He ducked under my arm and took holt of it with both hands, then twisted round and hiked me over his shoulder faster'n you could say Jack Robinson. I hit the ground with a yelp and a grunt what took ever whisper of air clean out of me.

I was gettin' awful close to losin' my temper by this time. Bein' whupped by big Jube this mornin', and then by a little bald-headed runt half his size an' twict his age in the afternoon, weren't helpin' my normal cheerful disposition much a-tall.

But I reckon them bumps an' falls knocked a little sense into my noggin too. 'Cause this time I laid still and played possum after I lit, diggin' my fingers into the sand on the side away from Baldy whilst I was at it. Sure enough, after a minute his curiosity got the best of him, and he come over to where I was layin' to have a closer look.

I let fly with the sand in his eyes, twistin' round in almost the same instant to bring my other fist off the ground with everthing I'd got behind her. It caught Baldy square in the chops and knocked him spinnin', so he fetched up hard against the side of his wagon a dozen feet away. Whilst he was leaning there rubber-legged, shakin' his head amidst the clatterin' and clankin' of all them pots and pans, I climbed back on my feet an' bull-charged in, landin' a couple solid rights and lefts to the body soon as I was close enough to do some damage.

They staggered him, but he was tough as old saddle leather and plenty game. After he'd managed to sidestep away from a kidney-punch, he come back underneath with a head-butt what brought twinklin' lights to my eyes and made me drop my guard for almost half a second. Which give him all the time he needed to wrap them powerful arms around my body an' trip me up.

The two of us went tumblin' tail over teakettle through the dirt an' sandspurs by the side of the road for what seemed a good five minutes or more, with him squeezin' the air out from between my sore ribs whilst I gnawed on a ear and tried to get my fingers loose to where I could poke 'em in his eyes.

Each was tryin' to get some advantage over the other without havin' no success a-tall to speak of. I'd the edge in size, but ole Baldy was strong as a ox underneath them store-bought clothes. And it appeared like he'd done his share of no-holds rasslin' here an' there on top of it. Far as pure-out meanness went, I reckon we was pretty evenly matched.

Finally we just laid there, wrapped up in a death grip with the sweat pourin' off both of us, a-huffin' and a-gruntin' like a couple ole boar hogs rootin' through a cow pen. Prob'ly didn't look nor smell too much different from them sorry critters neither about that time.

Baldy peered up from where I'd got him pinned underneath me, and his blue eyes seemed to crinkle just a little round the edges. Then he give my ribs one more good squeeze that like to made me holler out with pain in spite of myself.

"What about it, youngster?" he wheezed, grittin' his teeth against the sharp twist I'd give his ear in reply. "You had enough yet? Or am I going to have to whip you some more?" He was grinnin' when he said it, so I knew he figured we'd done fought to a draw.

"I ain't too sure about the whippin'," I answered, gaspin' for breath my ownself between the words, "or leastways who's got the worser of it so far. But I got to confess that rig of yours don't appear half so funny as it did awhile back. Maybe if we was to let each other up I could take me another look, and re-consider my thinkin'."

"Fair enough." Baldy loosed his grip and we rolled apart. The two of us just laid there for several minutes, starin' up at the sky and tryin' to get our breathing back to normal. Then

I pushed myself off the ground, swallowin' a groan whilst I did it, and when I'd got to my feet I reached out a hand to help Baldy up as well.

He looked at me real suspicious before he took it. But I was only bein' helpful. They'd been enough fightin' and roughhouse today to last me at least another week. I weren't of no mind to take up where I'd left off with this gent. Not over no outlandish tin pot an' medicine-show rig, anyhow.

I stepped next to the wagon and leaned against one of them big wheels, restin' myself and looking her over at the same time. Baldy walked over to pick up his hat and the celluloid collar what come loose during the fracas, before startin' in to dust hisself off.

"I reckon," I said after a minute, tryin' to make my voice sound sincere and admirin', "that when the sun hits her just right she do have a kind of a fetchin' look about her. I mean, all that pretty bright paint with them shiny u-tensils an' everthing . . ."

"Pretty!" Baldy spat on the ground, then strode to the front of the wagon where he fetched a canteen from under the seat and uncorked it. He took hisself a long, deep swig.

"Pretty hasn't got a thing to do with it! In fact . . ." He wiped a hand across his lips and passed the canteen to me. "I believe this may be one of the ugliest contraptions ever put on this earth by God or man!"

I'd hoisted the canteen up, expecting to have myself a good-sized swallow of clear pure spring water. Only it wasn't water inside there, nor anything even close. When that raw bayhead hit my gullet I commenced to gag an' whoop like a man fit to die. I finally managed to choke about half of it down, whilst the rest burned a path up an' out my nose like a red-hot poker.

Baldy appeared not to notice. But when I bent over an' put my hands on my knees to catch a breath, I could see through the tears that he was lookin' mighty pleased as he turned around to start fiddling with one of them near-side trace chains.

". . . It so happens that what you see here," he went on without lookin' up, "was never intended to be a thing of beauty. But one of complete and utmost utility." When he'd finished with the traces he stooped to fetch my hat from where he'd dropped it earlier, walkin' back and handin' it over while still not exactly meetin' my eyes.

He kept on past me till he was able to take somethin' from a rack at the side of the wagon. And when he turned around, danged if didn't have in his hand this fancy wooden cane what he used to point out the features of his outfit as he explained about 'em — lookin' ever bit the medicine show hawker I'd already suspicioned he was.

"These oversized wheels are especially designed for travel through the swamps and sand trails of the Florida wilderness." Baldy was talkin' now in a manner what give me the idea he'd already made this speech a time or two before. "Their weight also helps to lower the center of gravity when crossing deep streams. The vehicle's bottom is caulked and water-tight, so that it becomes a very serviceable raft when occasion demands."

He tapped his cane against the body of the wagon. "The interior contains my living quarters, including a small but comfortable bed and wood-burning stove, as well as a laboratory for the manufacture of Professor Maximilian's Wondrous Serpentine Elixir, one of my principal stocks-in-trade."

The little gent's voice was gainin' strength as he warmed to his subject, and he seemed to grow a mite taller an' straighter too. Me, I just pushed my hat back on my head and let him spout. I figured he was bound to run out of steam sooner or later — more likely sooner, once he found out I hadn't even got what it'd take to buy a piece of penny candy off'n him, much less no "Wondrous Elixir."

Anyhow, he was kind of entertainin'.

"But I discovered long ago," Baldy went on — or Perfessor Maximilian as I reckoned he called hisself — "that a merchant who offers only a single product, no matter how beneficial it may be for the public at large, is like a fiddler who can play nothing but 'Turkey in the Straw.' The demand for his services wears thin after a very short time.

"—So I have expanded my inventory with household appliances and other useful items that are difficult to obtain on the frontier, until what you see before you now is a veritable itinerant emporium!" He reached up to run the tip of his cane amongst the rows of hangin' doo-dads, making 'em fairly sing.

"Cast iron skillets and cook-pots, tin-ware, lanterns, washboards, ladles, brooms . . ." When he come to one of them cabinets next the driver's box he flung open the doors and kept on without hardly drawin' a breath. ". . . bolts of fine calico, needles, pins, scissors, coffee, sugar, salt, assorted canned goods, —and one of the finest selections of patent nostrums and *objets de toilet* to be found this side of Savannah!"

I'd a mind to ask a question of my own about then. But when I opened my mouth to pose it the bald-headed Perfessor weren't lookin' in my direction. And he didn't seem near ready to start windin' down his spiel just yet.

"The Good Book advises that no man hide his light

under a bushel. And I take that to mean that if you've got something folks ought to know about, you'd better get their attention. The sounds you heard as my outfit approached are no accident, for they proclaim my coming to every citizen in the vicinity. And when I have halted to begin setting up shop, I continue attracting patrons through the mechanical artistry of this self-contained Orchestrion."

He took out a odd-lookin' key from his pocket and put it in a hole in the side of the wagon, turnin' it round a few times before steppin' back to let me catch a glimpse of what was happenin'.

All them levers an' hammers behind that glass window had started turnin' and thunkin', along with a little bellows I hadn't seen before. And there come out of that contraption the dangdest tootin' and squeekin' and caterwaulin' you ever heard in all your borned days. My ears hadn't fetched up against nothin' like that sinct them couple nights I spent a year or so back, up to this sportin' house in Denver.

I done my best to act impressed and admirin', bitin' down hard on the inside of my cheek flesh to keep from gettin' tickled and havin' to go two, three more falls with this rasslin' perfessor. But when the music finally run out I seen he was laughin' and grinnin' hisself to beat the band. So I figured it'd be okay to smile back just a little bit on my own.

"Pretty slick, huh?" Baldy put the key away and shoved his high hat over at a sassy angle before comin' to stand spraddle-legged in front of me. "You goin' to keep all that hooch in the canteen to yourself, or can a fellow get a little of his own back?"

4

I'D PLUMB FORGOT ABOUT THAT CANTEEN of firewater I was holdin'. But when I realized what Baldy meant, I took time out for another healthy snort before passin' it back — wonderin' as I did what happened to all that fancy perfessor talk I'd heard him spoutin' only a minute earlier.

He took the canteen and downed a good-sized wallop his ownself, before slappin' the cork back in place and turnin' to close up the cabinets at the side of his wagon. Whilst he was doin' that I recollected the thing I'd meant to ask him about when first he opened 'em up.

"I don't suppose you got any kind of a tol'able shootin' iron inside there? One you'd be willin' to part with?"

Perfessor Baldy looked at me kind of thoughtful-like over his shoulder. "I might," he answered after a second. "If the price was right."

I smiled at him. "Why don't you just go ahead an' show me what you got? Then afterwards maybe we can talk price."

He eased hisself a hair closer to the front of the wagon before turnin' to meet my eyes.

"I didn't just ride into this country on a load of turnips, friend. Either you've got what it takes to purchase a firearm from me or you don't. And if it should happen that you're as flat busted as you look to be, there's no way in the world I'm going to put any kind of weapon in your hands right now, loaded or unloaded."

His arm snaked up into the driver's box and come out a instant later with a wicked-lookin' little sawed-off shotgun about a foot and a half long. Them two 12-gauge barrels swung down to fix theirselves square on my belly.

"So if you've a mind to trade in guns," Baldy went on mildly, "I'll just be obliged to ask to see the color of your money first."

I took a step backwards and kind of shrugged, hookin' my thumbs into my galluses real slow and easy. "All right," I said, testin' out another grin what Baldy didn't return. "I reckon you got me."

Since there didn't appear to be a whole lot of use in lyin' from that point on, I decided I might's well tell him the honest truth.

"It's a fact I ain't got two thin dimes to rub together at the moment. And I guess the thought did sort of cross my mind to pop you upside the head whilst we was examining shootin' irons, just so's I could have me the borry of one till I got a chanct to pay you."

Them blue eyes was lookin' at me mighty unfriendly now. But I'd a idea Baldy weren't the kind to shoot a man in cold blood. So I figured I'd keep on explainin' things till he had some time to cool off.

"I'd of been good for it," I said truthfully. "Tate Barkley ain't never yet took on no obligations what he didn't re-pay the minute he was able. Only I couldn't think of no other way just now to get holt of the gun I needed to take back what's mine."

I went on then and told him everthing I could remember, about the bushwhackin' that morning, how I'd got myself whipped and had my outfit stole by Purv an' Lila an' big Jube, how they all acted like they knowed me although I'd never set eyes on 'em till that minute, and how I'd been followin' their trail on foot ever sinct.

The squat little Perfessor stood leanin' against his wagon listenin', his eyes narrowed down to slits with nothin' on his face what even give a hint as to whether he believed a word I was sayin'. I noticed that shotgun under his arm never lowered a fraction though, from beginning to end.

"You can call me a liar if you like," I finished up, "and I reckon maybe you've earned the right to be doubtful. But ever word I've spoke is the God's truth."

Baldy kept squintin' hard at me for several more long seconds. Then he lifted up his sawed-off shotgun and put it back in the wagon, underneath the seat.

"That's quite a story," he said, climbin' up on the box without entirely takin' his eyes off me. "I expect it's got to be true. There aren't many who'd be clever enough to make something like that up out of whole cloth. And in your case . . ." He shook his head and reached to gather the reins. Me, I just watched him.

"Well, come on." Baldy's voice sounded impatient all of a sudden. "Climb aboard and let's get going. I assume you'd rather ride than walk. —And since we seem to be headed in the same direction . . ." He glanced at me. "I've in mind to reach Micanopy before noon tomorrow."

I didn't wait to be asked twice. That big old wagon with only the two mules pullin' her weren't a whole heap faster than my shank's mare had been. But it was sure a sight easier on my corns, and I was grateful for the offer.

❖   ❖   ❖

We drove along pretty steady through what was left of the afternoon, stoppin' only now an' again to give the animals a blow, and me a opportunity to climb down and study the ground for sign. Not that that last seemed so awful important after we'd been on the road awhile together. 'Peared like Baldy had his own way of followin' a trail onct he took the notion. And I had to admire the offhand casual way he went about doin' it.

He was a right well-knowed character all through these parts it seemed, having pushed that outlandish rig here an' yon between Jacksonville and Tampa for some several months now. And there weren't a single one of them local folks he couldn't spare five, ten minutes for, to pass the time of day whenever they was close enough for conversation.

They'd be chawin' the fat, sharin' views on the weather or some new trinket Baldy was offerin' for sale, or somethin' else, when all of a sudden he'd snap his fingers and push his high hat back off'n his forehead with a remark like: "You know, I almost forgot. I sold one of these stock pots (or lightnin' rods or potato mashers or whatever) to some folks just this morning, and when I went to get my cash box so I could count out their change, they'd ridden off without even waiting for it. I don't suppose you've seen them? Man and a young woman in the company of a large Negro, leading an extra

45

horse? Seems to me they said they meant to be traveling this way."

I never seen Baldy make change out of anything but his pockets, and I reckon nobody else had neither. He prob'ly didn't even own no cash box. But folks was so willin' to help them poor short-changed travelers get their couple cents back, that they'd rack their brains and call their husbands out'n the fields or their wives an' young-uns out'n the house, just tryin' to put together some little piece of information what might help us locate Lila and her companions.

Upshot of it was, time the shadows was gettin' long and we'd passed by this place called the Haile Plantation on the way to Arredonda, we was mighty certain them three was still trailin' south ahead of us, even though with the fadin' light and the churned-up sand of the road thereabouts it was near impossible to pick up their tracks. 'Peared like they hadn't gained so awful much distance on us in the meanwhile, neither.

I'd been ridin' alongside Perfessor Baldy for a good three, four hours by then, and I'd got to know a heap more about the little gent than I'd ever expected to know — where he come from and what-all he'd done and the places he'd seen. He was a natural-born talker, and any time there weren't no farmers or travelers close enough for him to do his jawin' with, it seemed like he'd just got to turn it loose on whoever was handiest. Which happened to be me.

He'd been born an' raised away up north in some settlement called Wells River in the state of Vermont. When I 'lowed as how I hadn't never heard of it, he didn't act surprised. Said they was a-plenty of native-borned Yankees who never heard of it neither.

Bein' the youngest of ten on this li'l rocky farm what couldn't ever seem to grow food enough for nine, he started out to drift at a pretty young age. Wound up in New York City after a time, doin' whatever it took to get by, which meant livin' and workin' in some pretty rough places. That's when Baldy discovered he'd got a talent for rasslin'.

After a couple free-for-alls where there weren't no more at stake than his own pride an' survival, he was spotted by these big-city gamblers. It was them who put up the money and set him to rasslin' professional. With the bettin' generally heavy against him because of his youth an' size an' all, pretty soon he was makin' a right fair livin'.

I reckon I looked kind of funny at Baldy whilst he was explaining all this, but he just shrugged an' grinned. Said something about how it was a long time ago, back before the war.

He'd signed up for the fightin' when the call come, same as I did. Only we was on opposite sides. After comparin' notes, we figured we might even of traded shots a time or two that last day at Gettysburg. There weren't no hard feelin's about it though. What's past is past, and I reckon we both just counted ourselves plumb lucky to of managed to live through it.

Afterwards he'd kind of got the wanderin' bug, like a lot of us what lost our youth in that ruckus, and he spent the next five, six years tourin' the country with travelin' shows and such-like, offerin' to rassle all comers for prizes and side bets.

"But at last I started to get smart," Baldy said as he guided the mules acrost this li'l crick somewheres west of Gainesville. "I was losing a bit of quickness as I got older, and it seemed like the local boys they'd put up to match me kept growing bigger and faster all the time. I was still winning more often than I lost. But when I did get whipped I'd nothing to show for it but bruises and sprains and a long hard ride to the next settlement. Hell, I even lost money — whatever I'd sprung loose to lay out on side bets.

"One day I just took a long look in the mirror and said to myself, 'Monk my lad, there's got to be some easier way of making a living than this!' . . ."

"Monk?"

It come to me then that I still hadn't heard my travelin' companion mention his name. I'd been thinkin' of him as "Baldy" right along, but without ever sayin' it to his face. I reckon if I'd had occasion to call him anything, it would of been "Perfessor," or maybe "Mr. Maximilian." It sure's the dickens wouldn't of been "Monk," nor nothin' even close.

I could tell he'd a idea what I was thinkin', and that he weren't generally in the habit of sharin' that "Monk" handle with ever perfect stranger he met along the road. It just slipped out accidental-like when he weren't payin' too close attention.

He glanced at me real quick an' funny when I repeated it. Then it was a couple seconds longer before he went on to explain:

"It's a nickname from my wrestling days. Based on my size I suppose, together with somebody's idea of how I move in the ring."

After that he didn't say nothin' a-tall for a good four, five minutes. Longest I could remember him holdin' his peace since we'd started out ridin' together.

Me, I couldn't leave good enough alone.

"Monk Maximilian?" I asked, havin' to turn my face away to hide the grin I felt spreadin' out between my ears. I'd already seen how peevish this little gent could get whenever he thought somebody might be laughin' at him. And here I was, just a frog's whisker from doin' it all over again.

Only this time I had a surprise. 'Cause when ole Baldy-Monk had got through castin' a sharp look in my direction, he started to get tickled his ownself. Finally he just let out with a great big guffaw and slapped his knee with his free hand.

"All right, Barkley," he said, shakin' his head and grinning fit to kill. "I guess the game is up." He chuckled some more, and had to take a deep breath before continuing:

"Martinus Drucker's the label my ma and pa pinned on me. It's an honorable name — Grandpa Drucker came to this country after serving as a sergeant in the Napoleonic wars. But different places have different customs, and what a man's called can have a lot to do with the way local folks act toward him.

"In New York I started out wrestling under the name of Maxey Dugan, then later as Monk Dugan. In Toronto I was Maxime DuBecq. When I moved south after the war I called myself Marsh Dixon in one place, and Milt Davis the next. One time down in Matamoros, I even won a couple of matches as Manuelito Delgado!

"In fact," Baldy went on, lettin' his grin fade for a instant, "I guess almost the only time I've used my real name since leaving home at thirteen, is when I signed on the rolls of the Seventy-First New York. Maybe that's because I didn't want the good Lord to have so much trouble recognizing me in case things didn't work out and I turned up at the Pearly Gates."

"So what you're sayin' is, this here Perfessor Maximilian handle . . ."

". . . is as phony as all the rest. Or as real, depending on how you look at it. I'd rather you didn't go telling that to all the rub—, locals we meet along the way though. Ask yourself: Would you buy a bottle of curative elixir from somebody who called himself just plain Monk Drucker?"

Well, the honest truth of it was I wouldn't buy none of that snake oil tonic from the Pharaoh of Egypt hisself if I met him floatin' down the Nile with his thousand wives an' concubines, each a-beggin' me to have a swaller. I've tasted them homemade cure-alls time to time, offered to me by well-meanin' folks who absolute swore by 'em. But close as I could tell nary one had the healin' power of two-day-old bayhead whiskey. And without none of the smooth flavor that rotgut offered when it slid past your gullet neither.

I weren't of no mind to hurt Baldy's feelin's, though, now we was finally startin' to get along. So I just nodded and allowed as how I reckoned he had a point.

We come into the little settlement of Arredonda along about dark, and I'd the idea maybe Perfessor Monk would be wantin' to stop there and make camp for the night.

Me, I'd already decided what I was goin' to do if that happened. Which was bid him a thankful farewell and start right on in to hoofin' it again. I'd no plans a-tall to let Lila an' them other two scoundrels get any further ahead of me than they already was, and I'd a idea I might manage to come up on their camp somewheres durin' the night. Then we'd have us a little settlin' of accounts.

But as it turned out my new-found travelin' compadre weren't of a mind to call it a day his ownself just yet. He told me he'd done a fair piece of gettin' around during the dark hours hereabouts, and he reckoned he knew the trails an' roads through these Florida woods 'bout good as anybody 'cept maybe a Injun or a moonshiner. Figured the more distance he could put behind hisself now, the less he'd have to cover in the mornin' before settin' up shop in Micanopy.

Leastways that's what he told me. I was startin' to get the idea Monk Drucker had begun to take more'n just a passin' interest in this outlaw chase of mine, though I couldn't imagine why he'd want to do it.

But when he come back from knockin' at the door of a cabin near the railroad tracks to ask after Lila and her friends one more time, he sort of grinned an' winked at me. Then he went to rummagin' through one of them cabinets behind the seat of his wagon, and handed me out a brand-new Smith an' Wesson pistol in a shiny leather holster.

I glanced at him mighty curious when he done that, but I didn't ask no questions. I just took it and begun checkin' her over in the light from this coal-oil lantern Monk had hangin' up front above the driver's seat.

She was a beauty, all right: .45 caliber with polished walnut handles, nice feel an' balance. And a whole heap lighter than my ole Colt Dragoon. It was all I could do to keep from tryin' her out right there on the spot. But I didn't figure it'd be a good idea to go alarmin' the populace thataway, callin' special attention to myself an' all. So I just hefted her a couple times, tried the action, and then climbed down from the wagon to strap her on.

Monk couldn't hold it in any longer. "Well," he asked, leanin' forward on his toes, still grinnin'. "What d'ya think?"

I kept my peace whilst I tied the rawhide thongs about

my leg. Then I spun on my heel and tried a couple, three fast draws from the hip before lookin' back over my shoulder at him.

"If she shoots as pretty as she handles," I answered, "I reckon she'll do the job just fine."

When I started to climb back up in the wagon I noticed Monk didn't move to join me right away. And when he finally did, he was lookin' at me awful peculiar.

"Y'know, Tate," he said. We'd both been usin' first names for awhile now. "I've run across a gunfighter or two in my travels, out in Texas and elsewhere. Most of them weren't especially quick, just a little more ready to shoot than your average man. But among those few who did manage to get their guns into play in a hurry, I've never seen anybody do it faster than you did just now."

He paused to take up the reins and cluck to his mules. After we'd started rollin', he went on more thoughtful-like: "I hadn't realized until now that I was in the company of a professional."

I looked at him from underneath my hat-brim.

"Well," I replied, "that there 'professional' is a interesting word. Most folks would take it to mean the way a gent chooses to earn his livin'. But if it's your idea I'm some kind of a warrior for hire, I got to inform you you're flat dead wrong." I fell silent, keepin' my eyes on the swaying rumps of the mules out in front of us.

"I've drawn fightin' wages a time or two," I admitted finally, "whenever the cause seemed right and I needed the work. But mostly I just ride for the brand. If a man hires Tate Barkley he hires all of me, and that means anything I'm able to do middlin' good. Happens usin' a gun is one of those.

Along with breakin' horses, whippin' steers out'n the brush, followin' a trail, ridin' night herd, or you name it."

Monk Drucker nodded and didn't reply for a couple seconds. Then he glanced at me out of the corners of his eyes and observed, "You'd better douse that lantern. It can be seen for several miles out here in the woods. If that trio's made camp somewhere up ahead I'd rather we saw their light first, instead of the other way around."

5

WE WAS HEADIN' SOUTH now along this narrow sand road, with big old live oaks an' hickories on both sides, hung over by wild grape and Spanish moss. The frogs an' other night critters was singin' so loud the creak an' rattle of Monk's wagon was just one more noise amongst the rest. Still loud enough that a listenin' man could pick it out, but not near so noticeable as earlier in the day.

It was real dark all around us, what with them thick woods and the moon not yet high enough to where we could see it. The sky overhead was clear an' full of stars, though. So that white sand showed up pretty good for keepin' us pointed right. And the mules seemed to have a idea of where we was besides. Like as not they'd traveled this way a time or two before.

A hour or so after leavin' Arredonda we begun comin' acrost some open country in amongst the stands of hardwood an' low hammock land. Monk allowed as how we'd ought to be skirtin' the west edge of Alachua Lake about then. And after the road curved to the left a mite, he told me we was startin' to pass through a narrow stretch of ground with that piece of water on our left and Levy Lake to our right.

There was mostly low, sandy hills hereabouts, with open patches where cattle grazed in between the groves of live oak an' thick growed-up woods. Ever now an' again we seen a pole corral or a dark cabin, but without no way to tell from a distance whether folks was livin' there or the place had been abandoned long years before.

It was maybe nine or ten o'clock by then, and the moon was climbin' higher. Once in a while we'd come out from the trees or top a little rise, and be able to see almost a mile of open country before us.

The second or third time we done that, Monk Drucker whispered to his mules and all of a sudden drawed back on the reins. I followed his pointin' finger to a little stand of live oaks away off on our right, where the ground rose up before slopin' off towards what I figured must be the lake, although we couldn't see it from where we was. If you squinted up your eyes and looked real close, you could just make out this faint orange an' yellow glow next to the trunk of one of the furthest trees.

Neither one of us said nothin' for a minute. Then Monk turned his head towards me and whispered, "Well? What do you think?" When I didn't answer right away, he went on. "There's no cabin up there. And it appears to be a man-made light of some kind. Maybe it's the camp of those three we've been following."

"Maybe." I kept my voice low whilst I studied them trees in the distance. "Or maybe not. Could be just some local feller doin' a little night fishin'."

I hesitated before addin', "Or cookin' shine. In which case he'd prob'ly appreciate not bein' interrupted."

"Well, there's only one way I know to find out." Seemed like Monk was startin' to get a mite impatient with me. "Are we going to have a look-see, or not?"

"We?"

I glanced at him, and the little bald-headed gent shrugged.

"In for a penny, in for a pound I always say. We've traveled far enough together that I guess we might think of ourselves as partners now. And I've got a special dislike for thieves in any case. Having the chance to administer a little justice would give me a feeling of personal pleasure."

Monk took his shotgun from underneath the seat and made a move like he meant to climb down. Then he stopped and looked back over his shoulder. "That is, unless you'd rather tackle this job all by yourself?"

"Hell," I said, still keepin' my voice quiet as I threw a leg over and started easin' myself to the ground. "Come on along and welcome, if you're of the mind. It ain't no part of my nature to keep any man from his pleasures."

Tell the truth, I was glad to have somebody along for company at the moment. Leastways a man what been up the river and over the mountain like they say, and who could handle hisself the way this Monk appeared to do.

'T weren't that I didn't reckon I could of took on them three by myself if the need was there. But I figured it didn't hurt my chances any to have this gent with his sawed-off shotgun watchin' over my backside as I made my way up to them owlhoots' camp. I'd already learnt what brand of cold, hard customers they could be, with that Lila prob'ly the hardest an' coldest of 'em all.

It wouldn't of surprised me a bit if she'd arranged to keep one of 'em on watch through the night, purely as a matter of caution. Even though far as I could tell she'd no way of guessin' that I or anybody else was on their back trail.

When Monk got done tyin' his mules to a scrub cedar, we moved off a little ways into the shadow of some pines and had us a low-voiced council of war. That infernal rig of his didn't travel near quiet enough for me to feel confident about us reachin' this place without somebody takin' notice of our approach, even if they had to wake up from a sound sleep in order to do it.

It was a good half mile to where that light was showin', and the woods all round behind us ought to keep anybody from seein' the wagon's outline against the sky. But if they was payin' attention to sounds in the night, they'd sure as shootin' know something was out here, without maybe guessin' exactly what it was. What we needed was some kind of a scheme to sneak up closer and have a look, while not stumblin' into some welcoming committee that was all primed an' loaded to meet us.

The idea I'd got in mind was to make my way on down the road afoot for a good fair distance, then face about and Injun up on the camp — or whatever it happened to be — from beyond in the opposite direction. If it turned out they was expectin' visitors, that was the last place they'd think of to look for 'em, and it might give me a chance to get the jump on the entire party.

In the meantime I suggested to Monk that he follow along this here tree-line so's to get hisself as near as possible to that light on this side without bein' noticed. He could make up his own mind then about whether it was safe to sneak any closer acrost the open space between 'em. In any case he was to come on the run from wherever he was, just soon's he heard me start to make my play.

Monk seemed agreeable enough, and from his manner I'd a idea he was the kind of gent who could handle a job like that without gettin' flustered. And without takin' no foolish chances what could turn out with either or both of us bein' shot full of holes.

When I'd checked the action on that Smith an' Wesson again, I slid a shell out of the cartridge belt to load the empty chamber under the hammer before droppin' her back in the holster. As a general rule, havin' that one less shot is a heap safer than havin' some kind of a accident from a buckin' bronc or a unplanned tumble on the ground. But I weren't carryin' no extra weapons with me this time, and I seen a altercation or two when all six shots from a six-shooter didn't hardly appear to be enough.

Monk Drucker touched the brim of his high-hat in salute before we separated. And I started back down towards the road with a partin' wave.

It was high grass all around hereabouts, 'cept where the road served to part it a mite. And since the cool of the evening had set in, that grass was wet with dew. I didn't much appreciate gettin' my clothes all damp, and covered with stickers to boot, from snakin' through that thick growed-up prairie — sometimes on my hands an' knees and now an' again on my belly. But I favored the notion of a bullet between my shoulder blades a whole heap less, so I done what was needful. Took my time at it too, so's to make as little sound an' show of my passin' as possible.

It must of been the better part of a hour before I reached the woods on the other side of that stand of live oaks where we'd seen the light. And then it took a while longer to ease myself up through the trees an' brush towards a place where I could have a tol'able view of the surroundings.

I had to hope my new-found partner weren't startin' to get too impatient by now. Although there wasn't much help for it if he was. I was a right cautious man when it come to any game where my hide was part of the stakes, and I meant to stay that way. From all appearances, Monk Drucker was a gent who could understand that kind of thinkin'.

When I'd finally got myself up to maybe thirty, forty yards off from what was left of the campfire, I could see pretty good that that was exactly what it was. Only a couple red coals was showin' now, with ever onct in awhile a little yellow lick of flame from some scrap of bark or pitch what hadn't burned itself out entire yet.

I eased myself over to where I could hunker down behind a couple low-growin' bushes at the edge of the woods, and took my time studyin' the layout. That new Smith an' Wesson six-shooter'd done found its way into my fist by then, comin' easy to my hand like it was already some part of me.

I could barely make out several dark shapes on the ground near the fire what might of been bedrolls. But from where I was watchin' they could just as easy been the twisted-up roots of them big ole live oak trees. After I'd shifted my gaze back an' forth a time or two, lookin' for any movement what might appear at the corners of my eyes, I was reasonable certain there weren't nothin' nor nobody stirring about that camp at the moment.

So either the folks who'd built the fire was powerful sound sleepers. Or maybe they wasn't just exactly where I expected them to be.

Along about then it struck me that I hadn't come acrost no sign of horses nor livestock neither. Could be that meant the campers was just some strangers travelin' on foot, which was a more common thing hereabouts than out in them western lands I'd lived in till recently. But it might mean too, that I'd ought to take a little better look around before jumpin' to conclusions.

So after one more glance about the fire without seein' nothing I hadn't already seen, I eased myself further back into the shadows and got to my feet. If there wasn't no animals picketed out yonder in the grass, which seemed the likeliest spot unless somebody had concerns they might be noticed, it appeared the only other place to leave 'em would be right here in these woods where I was standin'.

I took a long, slow, careful look all around in ever direction, movin' nothing but my head and the hand what held the six-shooter. But underneath them thick branches everthing was so pitch black that I didn't expect I would of caught sight of a elephant if the critter was standin' a dozen feet in front of me.

Then I tried listenin' for the little sounds a horse or a mule will make, stompin' a foot or croppin' grass, or swishin' its tail at a insect. But a breeze had come up off the lakes about then, and with all them leaves a-rustlin' I couldn't be certain of anything partic'lar around me, unless it happened to be mighty close by. I tried to wait her out, but when she just kept on a-whisperin' and a-blowin' real steady for long minutes on end, I finally told myself "The hell with it," and started in to move.

I was still bein' watchful as a cat, takin' one step at a time and gettin' each foot set before pickin' up the other so as not to make no more noise than necessary. Kept my ears pricked for anything the least bit out of the ordinary too, the entire while I was moving.

Suddenly I heard what sounded like a low nicker a couple yards away, and I froze in my tracks. There was somethin' familiar about that horse-whisper, and when it come to me a second time I'd no doubt a-tall who it was had made it.

You can choose to believe that or not, I don't give a damn. 'Cause it's the honest truth. That ole roan horse and me had covered a sight of territory together, prob'ly spendin' more days and nights in each other's company than a lot of husbands an' wives. I reckon I knew his voice ever bit as good as he knew mine by then.

When I'd whispered a couple words to try an' keep him calm, I stepped up closer until I could lay a hand on his neck in the dark. Generally Ole Roan weren't much of a one for showin' his feelin's. But this time I guess he was so plumb glad to see me that he didn't care who knowed it. He was dancin' and tossin' his head somethin' fit to kill, and it near 'bout cost me a finger before I could get his hackamore loose from that picket rope it was tied to.

I was mighty pleased at the re-union my ownself, so it like to pained me to the quick when I had to grab holt of his nostrils an' pinch down hard to keep him from makin' any more ruckus than he already was. Still I figured we'd best be on our way without further to-do, 'cause it wouldn't be much longer until all Hell busted loose. The other horses was stirrin' about restless-like from hearin' me and the roan, and I could make out Jube's mule a-warmin' hisself up to sing 'most any second in the background.

I still didn't have no idea where Lila and her compadres

was situated at the moment, so it appeared my best plan was to just light a shuck with the roan, and worry about gettin' the rest of my outfit back some other time. If they mounted up to give chase, I'd a mind to lead 'em east towards Micanopy, and away from Monk's wagon.

For starters I managed to drag the roan a short distance off from the picket line and turn him, before grabbin' a handful of mane and settin' myself to swing up onto his bare back. Then as I was reachin' down to holster my pistol, I heard these two sharp clicks no more'n a dozen feet behind me.

I threw myself backwards and hit the ground rolling, just as Purv's shotgun split the air with a mighty blast a couple feet above my head. The second charge of buckshot chunked into a tree alongside my shoulder whilst I dropped down into a dry creek bed and skittered on my knees an' elbows for another dozen yards before comin' up a-smokin'.

I let fly twice at the sound of Purv's voice whilst he was callin' out to his friends. And it give me a feelin' of satisfaction to hear him yelp an' cuss when he realized why a gent with a unloaded shotgun would be a mite smarter to hold his peace.

They was some scrabblin' around in the woods between Purv an' the horses, so I changed position and tossed a couple more shots over thataway to remind big Jube and Lila not to get too careless about when and how they decided to make their appearance. Didn't hit nothin' this time, far as I could tell. But it weren't because I wasn't tryin'.

I reckon maybe it crossed my mind for a half a second there about how one of them I was shootin' at was a woman. But I didn't let it fret me. Generally I ain't one to make war on women, nor treat 'em bad in any other way. But this here

Lila had brought the war on me, ordering my killin' earlier in the day an' all. And she was totin' iron the same as a man.

If she didn't want more trouble she knew how to avoid it. And if she still meant to come a-huntin' it, the least I could do was make sure she didn't go away disappointed.

I'd dropped down on one knee after them last couple shots. Now I started easin' myself back to where I'd left Ole Roan. I didn't have no plans to lose track of that critter again, regardless of how this fight come out. Not after all I'd been through today chasin' after him.

When I seen a pistol flash and heard a bullet whisper through the brush right close to the spot I'd been kneelin', I didn't bother shootin' back this time, but just kept on moving. That would be Lila I reckoned, somewheres off on my left. Leastways from the sound I was pretty sure it was her .38.

A couple minutes later I was climbin' out of that dry wash not far from the place where Purv first tried to ventilate my hide. It was still black as the inside of a tar barrel under them trees, so I was bein' mighty careful about how an' where I put my feet. Trippin' and falling over one of them vines or roots hereabouts would of been embarrassin' enough. But it wouldn't be nothin' compared to the feeling I'd have whenever the whole neighborhood opened up shootin' at the sound from it.

Ole Purv'd had him plenty of time to slip a couple fresh shells into his shotgun by now. There was a chance I'd got some lead into him earlier. But if it weren't enough to keep him from hollerin', it prob'ly weren't enough to keep him from pullin' no triggers neither.

An' then there was big ole Jube.

I hadn't seen hide nor hair of that feller since first arrivin' at this place. But it was a safe enough bet he was some-wheres about. And I'd of sure give a pretty to know where it was.

Thinkin' about all them dangerous folks around me what I couldn't see had kind of slowed my steps, until I was standin' stock still at the moment, tryin' to puzzle out what I'd ought to do next. The odds didn't appear near so favorable now as they had when I first made powwow with Monk on t'other side of the clearing, plannin' to take everbody what was camped here by surprise instead of the other way around.

I'd more'n half a notion to take my Ole Roan horse and just light on out. If I could lay hands on the critter in the dark that is, without findin' one of them other three first.

Speakin' of Monk, I was gettin' right curious to know where that li'l high-hatted gent had got hisself to. I could sure use a tad of help about now. But after considerin' the sit-uation I realized he prob'ly wouldn't be able to offer much, even if he was close enough by to pitch stones at. In this dark he'd be as likely to fill me full of lead as one of my enemies, when and if the shootin' got started again.

Since I couldn't think of nothin' else to do, I was right on the verge of takin' a powerful gamble and callin' out to Ole Roan — when I felt this nudge in my back what like to made me jump clean out of my skin.

It took everthing I had to swaller a yelp about then. I jumped forward and spun round in a crouch, earin' back the hammer of my six-shooter and comin' just half a inch from lettin' the lead fly before I realized what it was had give me that push.

It was Ole Roan. I guess he decided not to leave the findin' in the dark to no weak-sensed critter like me, but just went ahead and took matters into his own hands. I grinned a mite to myself when I realized what had happened, and bent down to gather up his reins.

Which I reckon plumb saved my life. 'Cause a instant later they was two big booms that I recognized as comin' from my old Dragoon Colt, aimin' right square at the spot where I'd been standin' when I turned and clicked back that hammer. I hit the dirt and sort of clenched up my shoulder muscles without thinking about it, waitin' for Purv's shotgun blast what I expected to come pretty close on the heels of them two pistol shots.

But when I did hear a shotgun speak, it was a good forty yards away in the direction of the clearing. A second later I could make out Monk's voice shoutin' over the echoes.

6 🖐

"THROW DOWN YOUR GUNS and come out here in the open with your hands where we can see 'em! We got the whole lot of y'all surrounded, and we'd just soon set back here tossin' lead into them woods all evenin' if you ain't a mind to show yourselves. I'll give you just thirty seconds to do like I say. And then we start shootin'!"

Well, I'd had the occasion to meet up with a sheriff an' his posse once or twice in my travels, and I got to admit that Monk had the talk down pretty tolerable. Hell, he almost had me convinced.

I stayed put, huggin' the ground where I was layin', and pretty soon I heard Monk call out, "Twenty seconds!" There was some low-voiced cussin' from Lila, followed by a couple words I couldn't quite catch. Then I heard some scrabblin' round in the brush to my left an' front. A instant later Monk lifted up his voice to holler, "Fifteen seconds!"

By the time he'd got down to "Ten seconds!" it appeared Lila an' them was all together next to their livestock. And at "Five seconds!" I could make out the sound of three sets of hoofbeats tearin' off through the woods in the opposite direction. I knew Monk heard 'em too, 'cause about then he let loose with the second barrel of his shotgun to hurry 'em on their way.

I laid there for a good three, four minutes longer, till them hoofbeats begun to get theirselves lost amongst the trees an' the darkness, before finally climbin' up on my knees. After another couple seconds I called out sort of cautious-like: "Monk?"

"Right over here, Tate." They was a pop an' a click of metal as he snapped his fresh-reloaded shotgun back together and pushed off the safety. Then his voice begun to come closer. "Did they all ride out?"

"Ever mother's son of 'em. And the daughter too."

"Whoosh!" I could just make out the dark form of the little perfessor with his top-hat at the near edge of the clearing. "The Lord of mercy is watching over us tonight," he said with feeling. "I didn't have an inkling what I'd do if they called my bluff."

"I got the idea maybe them folks has had 'em a run in or two with the law before now," I answered. "When you hollered out an' said you had a posse along, it 'peared to sort of discombobulate their thinkin'."

I stood and gathered up the roan's reins, then stepped out into a little patch of moonlight some twenty, thirty feet from where Monk was waitin' with his sawed-off shotgun.

"Besides which," I went on, closin' the distance between us, "it's a right peculiar feelin' in amongst them woods, with it so inky black you can't hardly see a hand before your face. I just nearly got a teensy bit spooked my ownself."

"So?" Monk slipped the safety back on his shotgun and grinned. "I wouldn't have thought you were the type."

"Well, I ain't partic'lar superstitious," I answered, "if that's what you mean. Never put no stock in h'aints an' such as that." I give the roan's neck a rub before ground hitchin' him and breakin' open the Smith an' Wesson to re-load the empty chambers from my belt.

"But I am a 'type' what puts some better'n average value on this ole sorry beat-up hide of mine. So any time they's three murderin' bushwhackers out in the dark a-tryin' to shoot holes in it, you're just liable to find me more'n ordinary concerned."

"Well," Monk observed calmly, "they're gone for now at least. And from what you've told me I doubt if they'll be back. You weren't the man they were looking for, and all they've lost out of this whole business was a spare horse that didn't belong to them in the first place."

"Uh-huh." I snapped the pistol back together and dropped it into its holster. "Could be you're right," I agreed, scowling. "But they's still a item or two of mine they made off with what I've got a notion to have words with 'em about. I wouldn't say our account was entirely even up just yet."

Monk looked at me sort of curious for a second there in the moonlight. Then he shrugged.

"Your funeral. But it might be a good idea to wait and spend the night here first, then have a closer look around come morning. As big a hurry as those three were in when they rode out, you can never tell what else they may have left behind."

I had to admit that made a kind of sense. And now the excitement from the chase and the shootin' was startin' to wear off, I could feel the hurts an' weariness from everthing else what happened today seepin' into ever bone of my body.

A good six, seven hours of sleep looked mighty appealing right then, 'specially since we'd done managed to ruin Lila and her pals' own rest for the night. Besides which, with Ole Roan underneath me tomorrow, I hadn't too many worries about catchin' up to 'em somewheres further down the road.

I glanced at Monk and nodded. "Okay," I said. "We'll spread our blankets here in this clearin', then see what we can see come daylight."

After he'd gone to fetch his mules an' wagon, I found a piece of bark and moved the coals from the fire to another open patch of ground a few yards away. I figured Monk would prob'ly sleep inside that contraption of his accordin' to his custom, but I hadn't no intention of joinin' him, even if I happened to be invited. I never did favor the notion of bein' closed in by four walls like that, where I couldn't hardly hear nothin' outside to tell me of unwanted visitors. And anyhow, Ole Roan an' me had a sort of a understanding. He was right accustomed to standin' sentry for me through the night.

When Monk had moved his rig up close to the live oak stand and unhitched his animals, I borrowed a couple blankets and made my bed on that warm earth where the fire used to be.

Almost as soon as I'd laid my head down with the Smith an' Wesson in its holster a comfortable distance from my fingertips, I was sound asleep. I didn't know nothin' else until the sun was peekin' through the trees and I could smell fresh-boiled coffee comin' from that little wood stove inside Monk's wagon.

Monk was already outside and stirrin' about. When he seen my eyes come open, he went to pick something up from next to one of them live oaks, luggin' it over and droppin' it at my side with a dusty thump.

It was a big ole western saddle with a Texas tree, of which there prob'ly wasn't two dozen like it in the whole state of Florida. I didn't have no trouble a-tall recognizing this one as mine.

When I'd rolled out of my blankets to take a closer look, I could see the long whip I'd been usin' earlier durin' that cow-hunt was still coiled on the right side. And the scabbard for my Winchester was there on the left, with the rifle nested inside it just pretty as you please. That was a sure enough stroke of pure-dee luck, of the sort I hadn't hardly ever got the chanct to get accustomed to.

Monk stood there grinnin' with his fists on his hips whilst I took the rifle out and begun checkin' her over. Apart from a thin layer of trail dust, I couldn't see nothin' different from the way I'd left her the day before. I jacked out the cartridges before wipin' her off, and all sixteen was there. So I was pretty near certain she hadn't been fired.

My new *compadre* made another trip into the trees whilst I was busy reloadin'. When he come back he was carryin' my two leather saddle bags draped over one arm.

"Empty," he said as he laid 'em at my feet. "But at least you've got this much of your outfit back." He took a couple steps towards the wagon. "Coffee?"

"I reckon." I slipped the Winchester back in its boot and picked up the saddle bags, runnin' my fingers around inside 'em just onct to make sure Monk hadn't accidentally missed somethin', like maybe a coin or a few grains of tobacco. He hadn't.

By the time he come out of the wagon with two steamin' mugs, I'd done stamped into my boots and finished rollin' up the blankets. I bent down to pick up the gunbelt with the Smith an' Wesson pistol from on top of 'em, holdin' it in my left hand whilst I took a mug with my right.

"Expect you'll be wantin' this back now," I said, maybe soundin' just a mite regretful, "seein' as how I at least got holt of my Winchester again. I'm mighty grateful for the borry of it."

Monk took a sip of coffee without seemin' to hear. Then he turned and walked off a few steps to where he could look acrost that field of high grass we was camped in. The fog from the lakes around us had begun to lift a tad, so it hung over our heads now like some low, feathery ceiling with trees makin' a wall half a mile in the distance. It was about as quiet then as a Florida mornin's ever liable to get, what with the night critters already gone to ground and the day critters not quite ready to shuck off sleep yet and start their rounds.

"Where will you be going now, Tate?" The li'l perfessor's question took me by surprise, comin' out of the blue like it did and not havin' a awful lot to do with anything we'd been talkin' about. I swallowed some coffee and shivered while it burned its way down to a warm place in my middle. Then I took a step towards him and shrugged.

"Keep on followin' after them three I reckon." I stopped to swallow some more coffee. "Still don't appear to me the account's exactly even up just yet, in spite of all our good fortune gettin' Ole Roan back with my saddle an' all." I frowned. "They's still the little matter of some fifty dollars cash money they took off'n me, plus a couple weeks' supplies. And I reckon that whuppin' from big Jube grates in my craw a mite too."

I finished my coffee and rubbed the back of my hand against the couple days' growth of beard on my neck and the bruises underneath what that huge black feller had done left me to remember him by. "Wouldn't mind seein' another opportunity to pay him an' the rest of 'em back for some more of yesterday's aggravation if the chanct come along."

Monk took a swallow of coffee. "You're a vengeful man, Tate." His voice was mild, and he kept his back to me so I couldn't see his face. "One of these days you'll buy into more trouble than you can afford."

"So I been told," I answered, "once or twict. But it seems to me that any man what lets folks steal from him and whup up on him, and do him ever which-way they please without never gettin' his back up over it, ain't much of a man. And he don't exactly keep hisself free from trouble neither once its knowed they can do him thataway. If it turns out I got to quit this world afore my time, at least I expect I'll go out with my head held high, and a couple, three enemies at my feet for company."

Monk didn't appear to have no answer for that. And after a minute I stepped up beside him. "You goin' to take this here six-shooter, or not?"

He turned his head and looked at me. "Keep it. Pay me for it when you can. The price will be fourteen dollars."

I didn't wait for him to offer twict. I just bent an' started buckling the gunbelt around me. "Thanks," I said. "I reckon you know by now I'm good for it. But I'm obliged to you all the same."

"Save it. Just try to stay alive long enough to bring me the money." Monk reached in his coat pocket and took out a little notebook, what he put into my hand. "You might as well have that, too. I found it on the ground this morning, close to where that man with the shotgun was wounded."

I guess maybe I looked kind of funny at him when he handed it over, 'cause he smiled an' shrugged. Then he went on to answer my question before I could ask it:

"Blood on the leaves, two spent shells close by. Not very hard to figure out. I suspect he lost the book when he reached into his pocket for fresh shells."

"Uh-huh." I lowered my eyes to study the notebook, wonderin' to myself just what other talents this travelin' perfessor might have that you wouldn't expect of some citified gent in a store-bought suit and a top hat. Besides no-holds rasslin' and trailin' outlaws and readin' sign on the ground, that is.

What I held in my hand was a tally book like nearly ever cow-hunter in Florida or anywheres else was liable to carry with him, somethin' to tote up cattle in, write down brands an' earmarks, make notes about water an' range conditions, and so on. Bein' as Purv an' them was from a part of the country I hadn't never traveled through, most of it didn't tell me a thing I was able to recognize as useful. But when I'd thumbed through it to the last couple pages with writin' on 'em, I finally seen this one note what had a name with it, and even more important, a place.

What it said was:

AUG 28 —
527 hd
Maj Waltr Kineston
Ft Dade

Now, that was 'bout as plain as anybody could hope for who'd ever worked cattle. There'd been a delivery of five hundred an' twenty-seven head on the twenty-eighth of August, at a place called Fort Dade, either to or from this Major Kineston. I showed the note to Monk and he nodded.

"Today's the last of September," he said, "so that would have been just about a month ago. Probably not too long before they rode north in search of that other man named Barkley."

"Uh-huh." I frowned. "Can't recall ever hearin' nothing about this Fort Dade before. You reckon it's such a big place that that major would of been buyin' all them beeves for the army?"

Monk grinned an' shook his head. "Not likely. There hasn't been any military there for almost twenty years. It's the name of a town now. Grew up near an army post during the last Seminole war, and I guess the name just stuck." He shrugged.

"If I had to speculate, I'd say that's probably true of this Major Kineston too. An honorary rank left over from serving on one side or the other during the recent unpleasantness."

That stood to reason. A lot of officers had kept their rank as a form of address after the war was over, and I reckon they was entitled to it. Me, I never got no higher than sergeant, and I made that two, three times after gettin' busted back down for one thing or another.

Monk headed towards his wagon, sayin' something about fixin' a bite of breakfast before settin' out on the road for Micanopy. After a minute I followed after him, still mullin' over that tally book with the note inside.

It was likely somebody at Fort Dade would recollect a recent cattle drive an' sale of that size, even if both parties to it was total strangers. And prob'ly at least one or t'other was a knowed man thereabouts. If it turned out that was this Major Kineston, I'd a mind to have me a li'l talk with him before the week got much older. And if it was this gent Ravenant or his hired help who was the local ones, I might find me somethin' else to do with 'em besides just talkin'.

Monk was gatherin' bark and fallen wood for a fire when I come up beside him.

"How far you reckon that Fort Dade town is from here?" I asked, stoopin' to give him a hand. 'Peared like he'd decided to do the rest of his cookin' outside today, it bein' a pleasant mornin' and all.

"Pretty close to a hundred miles." Monk fetched a match from his coat pocket. "Maybe a little under." I nodded and plucked a blade of grass to put between my teeth whilst he lit the fire and fanned it with his hat.

"You know the way there good enough to give me directions?" I went on, after he'd sat back on his heels to admire his work an' dust off his hands. "Or at least put me in the neighborhood so's I can ask after it from the locals?"

"Nothing easier." The little gent turned to face me as the flames curled up amongst the hissin' and poppin' of the smaller twigs. "It's almost due south, right smack on the old military road from Ocala to Tampa. Just stay on this trail to Micanopy, then bear right and keep on going. You'll come to Fort Dade about thirty miles the other side of Sumterville. You can't miss it."

"Much obliged." I rose to my feet and walked out to where my roan horse was picketed in the grass. Then after a couple whispered words and a quick rub behind the ears, I led him back to camp. I was feelin' mighty pleased to have my ole four-legged pardner back with me again. But I reckon it would of embarrassed both of us to let it show too much in front of others.

Monk was standin' by the fire with his hands in his pockets when I bent down to take up the saddle.

"You're riding out now, before breakfast?"

"A hundred mile's a fair piece of territory," I said. "Likely take me a couple, three days to cover it, even ridin' steady. The sooner I make my start, the sooner I'll get to where I'm goin'." I threw my saddle up on the roan and reached underneath for the cinch.

"I guess that's so." Monk shrugged. "But you don't even know for certain where the thieves were headed when they left here."

"Got me a pretty good idea where they started out from now. And sometimes this here huntin' men is kin to huntin' turkeys. Onct you find their roostin' place, alls you got to do just settle in an' wait. They'll be along." I grinned. "Saves a heap of wasted effort."

The li'l perfessor was silent a second or two. Then he took his hands from his pockets and held one out to me. "It's been a pleasure knowing you, Tate. I hope we can hook up again later on."

"If we don't meet somewheres along the road," I answered, takin' his hand, "I'll come lookin' for you. Like I said, I ain't a feller what forgets his debts."

Monk nodded and took a couple steps away towards the wagon, callin' back over his shoulder: "You might's well go ahead and keep those blankets. And I've a few other things here you might find useful."

He started rummaging through one of his cabinets whilst I finished up with the saddlin'. By the time I'd got done tying the saddlebags an' blankets on behind, he'd fetched back a canteen of water and maybe a dozen other items in a li'l croker sack.

"There's some coffee, tobacco, tinned food . . ." The li'l gent handed me the canteen and reached up to put the sack in my near saddlebag. He looked at me with kind of a half grin on his face. ". . . and two extra boxes of ammunition, one for each weapon."

"I'm obliged," I said, "one more time. I mean to pay for ever bit of this too, soon as I get the chanct."

"I expect another couple dollars ought to cover it." Monk's smile got broader. "Call it a special discount for a friend."

When we'd shook hands again and I'd mounted up, I turned the roan's head away from the wagon towards the road. A instant before I was set to dust out of there, Monk called to me from beside the fire where he'd hunkered down to start cookin' his breakfast:

"There's one thing you might keep in mind, Tate." I looked over my shoulder at him, but he wasn't meetin' my eyes.

"I've stalked the wild turkey myself on a few occasions. But I can't recall a single time when any of those birds was armed and shooting back!"

7 🌿

THAT WAS A THING TO CONSIDER, all right. But I didn't let it fret me much as I give Ole Roan his head and we lined out through the fields an' trees of that low rolling country north of Micanopy. I'd stalked and been stalked by a whole passel of unsavory characters now an' again, armed ever which-way you could imagine. So far I'd managed to keep my hair and still be here to tell the tale. And I reckon I'd dealt out enough trouble of my own to satisfy most of them varmints whilst I was about it.

It felt too good at the moment just bein' up on the hurricane deck of my ole roan horse again, with the wind in my face and the bright morning dew all around us, to give much thought to any trouble what might come along further down the road. I could tell the roan was enjoyin' the morning's run as much as I was, so I let him get it out of his system real good before we settled in to tradin' off between a trot and a steady distance-eatin' walk for the rest of the journey.

We reached Micanopy before the townsfolk had done wiped the sleep out of their eyes good or begun stirrin' from their houses. And because I didn't have no partic'lar reason nor wish to tarry on this Monday mornin', I kept right on through the settlement without pause, turning south on the far side and followin' the west bank of another big lake where the road led towards Ocala.

By the time the fog was lifted up so's I could see the sun a-peekin' through the trees, we'd left that lake behind. I took my noonin' amongst rolling sand hills with thick stands of longleaf pine almost everwhere you looked.

I'd finally got up enough of a appetite by then to investigate the groceries Monk put inside my saddle-bag. They was four, five cans of tinned beef, which didn't have too much to recommend 'em for flavor except they wouldn't spoil in the Florida heat, with a couple big cans of Georgia peaches besides, and a mess of hardtack biscuits wrapped up in heavy paper. I made do with a can of peaches and a couple of them biscuits for the time bein', soakin' the last real good in water first so as not to break off a tooth when I went to bite into 'em.

I reckon that could sound like I wasn't proper apprecia tive of the provisions Monk bestowed on me at our partin'. But I was. A man what ain't got nothin' is right grateful for anything, 'specially when a feller shares freely from his stores with you what hadn't got no call to do it in the first place. The tinned beef an' hardtack would keep me from starvin' at least. And I figured to use some of them extra .44 shells for the Winchester before much more time had passed, to fill out my supplies with birds an' maybe a deer.

'Course there was beefs and hogs too, runnin' free all through these woods here close to the settlements. But it was a sure bet they was spoke for by somebody, for all their wild

LEE GRAMLING

manners an' appearance. Only a low-life thievin' scoundrel would consider shootin' one of them for his own use. And considerin' the usual frontier views on justice, a feller what might be kind of weary of livin' to boot.

I was grateful as could be for all of Monk's generosity. And at the moment that li'l bag of Bull Durham an' the packet of papers he'd thought to include with his foodstuffs pleased me about as much as anything. When I'd fetched 'em from the saddlebag and rolled myself a smoke, I laid back on the grass underneath a tall pine and for a while there was right close to bein' at peace with the world.

He was a funny kind of a gent, that Monk. A tough man, and a good one to have at your back in a fight. But likable enough in his Yankee sort of way. Generous to a fault, too. Or so it seemed on the face of it.

It ain't usually no part of my nature to be lookin' gift horses in the mouth. But all of a sudden I caught myself wonderin' about that last just a teensy bit.

I mean when you thought about it, here's this dyed-in-the-wool, borned in Vermont, Yankee merchant feller — a bona-fidey snake oil salesman an' probable charlatan to boot, what confesses to takin' on new names as easy as some folks slip into a fresh collar. But after meetin' this total stranger on the road and gettin' into a knock-down, drag-out fight with him, he winds up givin' the stranger a ride and risks his own hide in a shootin' scrape. Then he loans the stranger a top notch six-shooter with ammunition an' supplies, ever scrap of it on stone cold credit.

Well, I ain't had me too much reg'lar commerce with gents from New England. But I've run acrost one or two out west an' elsewhere. And this Monk just didn't exactly seem to fit the mold.

After a little bit I shrugged off my curiosity and went to mount up, plannin' to put another good long piece of distance behind me before the day reached its close. Like I'd said to Monk, I was a man what paid his debts. So I reckoned we'd meet up again sooner or later. In the meantime, it'd prob'ly do me a heap more good to set my thoughts toward what lay ahead instead of behind.

I made camp for the night in a grove of live oaks a few miles south of Ocala. After picketing Ole Roan close enough so that he could stand sentry for me against any night-prowlin' varmints of the four-legged or two-legged variety, I built a hatful of fire, boiled some coffee in the tin I'd saved from the peaches, and broke off a couple green sticks to roast them two Bob-White quail I'd managed to flush a hour or so before. Maybe it weren't the most liberal meal a man ever set hisself down to enjoy, but under the circumstances I found it plumb satisfyin'.

When I'd dumped some sand on the fire an' rolled up in Monk's blankets to fend off the skeeters, I had about as decent a night's sleep as any travelin' man like me ever expects to get.

By sunup the followin' morning we'd already left that place a hour or more behind, makin' our way acrost long stretches of hills an' open prairie with occasional stands of piney woods an' hardwood hammocks in between. It was pretty easy ridin' as Florida travel goes, and kind of pleasin' to the eye along with it.

Ever now an' again we'd come to a little settlement or a store along the road, and I'd stop to let Ole Roan have a drink if there was a water trough handy. Then I'd spend a few minutes jawin' with the locals in hopes of gettin' some kind of information about the country I was ridin' into.

Most the time there weren't a awful lot of use in it. Horses and ridin' stock was a unaccustomed luxury to your average dirt farmer hereabouts, so if a place was too far away to walk to by nightfall he just didn't bother goin' there. A lot of the younger ones hadn't never been more'n ten, fifteen miles from their homes sinct the day that they was borned.

I spent the second night on the banks of a little creek what a feller I met fishin' there told me run into this big lake to westward by the name of Panasoffkee. From the crossin' it weren't but only another mile or two into the town of Sumterville. But it was gettin' on to evening by then, and I couldn't think of anything partic'lar I needed from a town, even if I'd had some money to buy it.

So I traded that fisherman one of my cans of tinned beef for his cane pole an' line as he was gettin' ready to leave. Then I picked me a couple wild oranges from the trees that was everwhere around, found a comfortable spot by the creek a little distance from the road, and set myself down to fish for my supper.

Next mornin' I had a change of mind and decided to make a brief stop in Sumterville after all. I'd heard tell it was the seat of Sumter county once upon a time, and there might be somebody there who had a little better knowledge of the surroundin' territory than those I'd come acrost so far.

Sure enough, after askin' round a bit I managed to locate a storekeeper who had a map on his wall, and enough idle time on his hands that he was willin' to spend a hour or so of it answerin' questions and generally givin' me the lay-out of the country what was situated to the south of us.

'Peared this Fort Dade settlement lay just a little west an' north of the headwaters of two good-sized Florida rivers, the Hillsborough and the Withlacoochee. The Withla-coochee was the longer of the two, runnin' down the penin-sula in a big old bend for more'n a hundred miles from where it emptied into the Gulf south of Cedar Keys. The storekeep-er said it was a mighty crooked, twistin' river though, and he reckoned it'd be at least twict that long if you was to hitch a team of oxes to both ends and pull it out straight.

The Hillsborough was a good deal shorter, and had its outlet in Tampa Bay. Both rivers turned inland a little ways south of Fort Dade, and finally lost theirselves in a great big wilderness of wet prairie, palmetto flats and low hammocks, what stretched for a heap of miles to the east an' north.

It didn't sound so awful different as the storekeeper was describin' it, from that San Pedro Swamp up in Taylor an' LaFayette counties where I'd spent my growin' up years.

After I made it to the crossin' of the Little Withla coochee some fifteen miles south of Sumterville, it 'peared like I'd have swamp land to the east of me all the way until I reached Fort Dade. That was some wild, primitive country the storekeeper said, with hardly any settlements a-tall between there and Lake Tohopekaliga, a distance of more'n forty miles. Nobody ever had lived in it that he knowed about, except the Seminole Indians durin' their wars with the whites.

Them lands west of the military road on the other hand, between there and the Gulf, was beginnin' to fill up right smart with settlers now the War Between the States was over. Biggest reason seemed to be the number of ports an' inlets along the coast, together with the fact that travel by water always was a heap easier in this country than goin' overland. Been that way in Florida long as I or anybody else could remember.

I thanked the storekeeper for his information, and had another good long study of that map on the wall before finally takin' my leave of Sumterville. Since I didn't have no definite idea where I might have to go lookin' for Lila or her uncle Ravenant after I got to Fort Dade, it seemed like a worthwhile undertaking to try and memorize the lay of the land all round that place as best as I was able.

When me an' Ole Roan had finally took to the road again it was well along into the morning, and I took my noonin' at a little creek a mile or so south from the place where Major Francis Dade and his troops got theirselves massacreed by the Indians back in eighteen and thirty-five. That was a well-knowed event and a well-knowed spot amongst the folks what lived hereabouts, though it don't seem to of caused near the excitement around the country when it happened as ole yellow-hair Custer's run-in with the Cheyenne an' the Sioux a year or so back.

I made a meal of tinned beef an' hard tack there, purely out of necessity. But I promised to do a mite better by myself come suppertime. So when I'd crossed the Withlacoochee proper and come in amongst this high hammock country with all kinds of little creeks an' sloughs runnin' down towards the river, I stopped to make a early camp and try my hand at huntin'.

Luck was with me, and I caught a four-point buck comin' to water just as the day was fadin' into darkness. That night I feasted on venison steaks and Georgia peaches.

After dousing my fire and movin' a little ways off into the shadow of a big magnolia — purely a habit of caution from havin' spent a good part of my life in dangerous country — I rolled in my blankets to get a good night's sleep before facin' whatever the day ahead might bring.

Accordin' to my calculations, it weren't no more'n eight, ten miles now from where I was camped to the town of Fort Dade. A couple steady hours of ridin' ought to put me in there well before noon.

❖　　　　　　❖　　　　　　❖

Fort Dade was the biggest town I'd set eyes on since leavin' north Florida, which ain't to say it was exactly what some would call thrivin'. I counted maybe a half dozen horses tied up to hitch rails along the boardwalk what lined the sandy main street, with a occasional buckboard or spring wagon in between the false-fronted frame and log buildings. Even fewer folks was in sight, it bein' the middle of the week and the start of a hot day to boot.

I could feel the sweat beadin' up above my eyes and pastin' the shirt down on my back as I rode the length of the street kind of lookin' things over. And it hadn't even got to be ten o'clock in the mornin' yet.

As a general rule, the place to find out anything worth knowing in a town is the local saloon, where menfolks gather for talk an' company at least as much as they do for cards an' whiskey. I seen a couple such places as I rode past, and at least one of 'em appeared to be already open for business. It looked cool and dark inside there, past the bat wing doors at the entrance.

But at the moment I didn't even have the nickel it'd cost to buy me a small beer and standin' rights at the bar. Since there wouldn't be hardly no customers this early anyhow what a feller might talk up for information, I decided to visit some of the other places in town first to ask after this Major Kineston and the cattle deal between him an' Ravenant's people a month or so earlier.

When I'd got to the end of the street, which didn't take no real long stint of ridin', I turned Ole Roan in towards a hitchin' rail and climbed down from the leather. After tyin' him with a slip knot as was my custom, I used my hat to slap the worst of the trail dust off me. Then I started back down the boardwalk at a casual, lazy gait.

I reckon I was feelin' kind of salty and sassy now that I was nearin' the end of my hunt, with the comfortable feel of a tied-down pistol at my hip again and Ole Roan's steady legs at my back.

I hadn't gone but maybe half a block when this gent stepped out of a mercantile store a couple doors in front of me. He seen me an' favored me with a sort of a half-nod. Then he leaned back against the wall outside the store and started to fan hisself with a piece of cardboard he'd brought along from within. The fact he was in shirt-sleeves caught up by garters, wearin' a pair of wire-rim glasses and no hat to cover up his thinnin' sandy hair, give me a pretty good notion he was the feller what run the establishment. I come closer and stopped a couple feet in front of him.

"Howdy," I said, touchin' my hat-brim and smiling by way of a introduction. "Right warm day, ain't it."

"It'll do till something hotter comes along." The sandy-haired gent kept on fannin' hisself whilst he looked me up an' down, pausin' maybe half a second when he come to the tied down Smith an' Wesson at my hip. Finally he met my eyes with a curious squint. "Somethin' I can help you with?"

"Mebbe." I smiled again, pushin' my hat back off my forehead and restin' a shoulder against the roof-post in front of the store. "I'm lookin' for a tad of information."

"Information's a right cheap commodity," he allowed,

"'less'n it's about a feller's personal fishin' hole or a lady's age. I prob'ly got as much free information as anybody you're liable to meet hereabouts." The storekeeper stopped his fannin' long enough to give me a lopsided grin. "And ever bit worth nearly all it costs. What was it you had in mind to know?"

"You ever hear of a gent in these parts named Kineston? Major Walter Kineston?"

"Well, sure. Know him to see him an' speak to him, anyhow. Like most folks in town. He don't hardly live close by, though. Owns a big ranch and orange grove over west towards Hopeville. Comes into Fort Dade maybe four, five times a year, on business. A real well-heeled gent from all appearances." My new acquaintance studied me through his spectacles, maybe a mite more careful than before. I got the idea he was havin' a little trouble puttin' together my shaggy down-at-heel looks with what he knew of this Major Kineston. "You got dealin's with him?"

"Had in mind to talk to him, is all. About one of them business transactions I heard tell of."

The storekeeper shrugged. "I reckon you'd be able to find his place easy enough. Just take the road west to Hudson's Landing, maybe thirty-five mile away over on the Gulf coast. Then head south another five, ten miles till you come to Hopeville. Ask about the same as you're doin' now, and somebody's bound to point you right."

"Uh-huh." I wrinkled up my brow. It didn't take no mathematical genius to see we was talkin' another two, three long days in the saddle over to that major's place an' back. Just so's I could ask a couple questions what ole Sandy here or somebody else in Fort Dade might answer ever bit as good.

But then I got a notion maybe I hadn't ought to be too awful quick to let these locals know who it was I was really huntin'. Could be Lila an' Ravenant had friends hereabouts, somebody who'd pass the word along. And the whole trick to catchin' turkeys, or anything else, is to find their roostin' place before they got a chance to guess you're in the neighborhood.

I took off my hat and wiped the sweat from around the band with my fingers, lowerin' my eyes whilst I decided what to say to this storekeeper next. When I'd put it back on again, I give a sad shake of my head.

"That's a right far distance to travel," I said, "huntin' some kind of a job what might not pan out." I shrugged and stepped up closer out of the heat of the sun. "Feller back along the road told me this Major Kineston was a cattleman. He seen him runnin' a herd hereabouts a month or so past. And since cow-huntin's something I got a mite of experience with, I thought maybe . . ."

Then I pretended to have me a brand new idea. "Hey, how about that other gent? The one the major dealt in cattle with? He might be needin' some help his ownself."

I frowned like I was strainin' my thoughts to remember. "Can't call the name exactly, but it was somethin' like Davenant . . . Ravenall . . . You know who I mean?"

8

WELL, IF OLE SANDY'D STUDIED ME careful before, he plumb like to made a profession out of it this time. His eyes scrunched down into a couple slits, his lips puckered out like he was bitin' into a sour orange, and he just nearly forgot to fan hisself whilst he eyed me up an' down for what must of been a full minute or better.

At last he glanced off to his left an' right along the boardwalk and shifted his feet, answerin' in a voice what didn't sound near so casual as I figured he meant for it to:

"Ravenant. Heard tell of him, is all. They say he lives over east from here in that big swamp country this side Lake Tohopekaliga." The little merchant took off his spectacles and begun wipin' 'em kind of nervous-like on his shirt front. When he'd got 'em back on again they was settin' a mite crooked on his nose.

"Listen, mister . . ." he started to say after what seemed to me like a pretty long minute.

But I never did get to hear the rest of whatever he meant to tell me. 'Cause right then the bat wing doors of that saloon banged open a couple buildings away, and two broad-shouldered men in slouch hats and Boston ridin' boots come stridin' down the boardwalk towards us.

I hadn't never set eyes on either of 'em. But I knew the type. One had him a brand new Colt Peacemaker in a tied-down holster at his hip, and I could guess from his manner he weren't wearin' it that way only for show. The other carried a two-barreled steel shotgun in the crook of his arm, with a pocket model police pistol stuck down in his waistband just in case two loads of double-ought buck weren't enough to quite finish the job.

They was hard, cold men. And they had "hired warrior" written all over 'em.

I glanced at Sandy, and he'd gone to fannin' hisself mighty brisk with that cardboard of his. He didn't meet my eyes.

The way them two walked along elbow to elbow, lookin' straight ahead and actin' like they didn't even notice us, made it pretty clear they expected all us lesser mortals to hurry up and stand aside so they could pass. I seen Sandy peerin' kind of anxious toward the entrance of his store and I was sure he'd a mind to do exactly that. Only trouble of it was, I was standin' in his way.

And like I said earlier, I was feelin' kind of ornery an' full of ginger on this hot Wednesday morning.

Now I knowed all along that it didn't make no kind of sense to go seekin' trouble with total strangers when I could have all I wanted 'most any time now with folks I'd already met. But backin' up for troublemakers and bullies ain't ever been a thing I found partic'lar easy. And after what I'd had to put up with already this past week, I couldn't find no back-up in me this time no matter how hard I looked.

I didn't plan to start no all-out war, you understand. I just didn't mean to step off'n that boardwalk unless somebody showed me a mighty good reason why I should.

Them two gun artists was still comin' along, actin' like we was a couple flies on a sugar jar what they meant to brush aside whenever they got close enough to do it. Me, I turned to Sandy like they wasn't even there.

"You say that Ravenant feller has his place over east from here?" I asked.

Sandy glanced past my shoulder at the gunslingers. Then he looked at me and nodded. "That's what folks say. I wouldn't know nothin' certain about it my ownself."

I was standing in the middle of the boardwalk now, facin' the storekeeper who'd done backed up against that wall like he was tryin' to melt hisself through to the other side purely from wishin' upon it. My gun hand was hid from sight next to my body as I eased the thong off the hammer of my Smith an' Wesson.

"Seems like," I went on, "somebody up along the road told me that's some mighty wild, deserted country over yonder."

Sandy opened his mouth like he was goin' to answer, but then all of a sudden he closed it again. The sound of the two men's boots had stopped, and I knew they was just a couple feet away now, lookin' at us.

I turned towards 'em.

"Mornin'," I said, cheerful an' pleasant as could be. I reached up my left hand and touched my hat brim to 'em. Then I went back to speakin' to Sandy. "You was sayin'? . . ."

The storekeeper didn't answer, of course. His eyes was on them two hard cases behind me. And I knowed it was his conviction that I hadn't very many more minutes to live. The only question in his mind was whether he was goin' to have to join me, simply from exercisin' such powerful poor judgment as to stand there makin' conversation with strangers.

"Some folks sure do manage to take up a heap of space on this earth, don't they, John?"

I turned back an' seen it was the feller with the shotgun who was doin' the talking.

"I wouldn't of expected they was anybody in these parts," he went on, his voice real mild an' quiet, sort of half threatenin' and half humorous at the same time, "who cast such a big shadow that he needed all that space just for himself." It appeared maybe he was enjoyin' the situation just a little bit.

Me, I grinned at him.

"I reckon you're right as rain about that," I said, lettin' my eyes flick from him to his partner for the barest instant. "Ain't no man in the world needs more'n six foot by three foot by six foot of earth after everthing's said an' done."

We all stood there lookin' at each other then, for a long couple of minutes. I already knew what they was, and I could see from their eyes they was beginnin' to get the notion I weren't entirely no stranger to loud noises an' gunsmoke my ownself. Either that or I was just flat-out crazy.

Whichever of those was the case, it was better'n even money that if shootin' got started somebody here was goin' to wind up dead. And the trouble of it was, there weren't no way of predictin' how many or who it would turn out to be. I watched them two with a trace of amusement whilst they considered that. And then I seen 'em come to the conclusion I'd expected they would from the git-go.

Them boys was professionals. And no professional who's worth a hoot wants to risk his hide over a couple careless words that don't offer no hope of earnin' him a dollar. They wasn't exactly scared of me. But they wasn't gettin' paid to take chances tradin' lead with no big dumb stranger they hadn't met before neither.

After a minute the man called John, who wore the tied-down gun, shrugged his shoulders and spoke real casual to his companion: "You know, Pete, they's a drugstore over yonder acrost the street. And you've had that tooth what's been troublin' you for better'n a week now. Let's just take us a stroll over thataway and see can we find some kind of powders or somethin' to ease your pain."

John stepped off the boardwalk to start across the street, and after pausin' to favor me with a right unfriendly look, his companion with the shotgun followed him. I watched 'em go, and then I turned to the little bespectacled storekeeper next to me.

He'd located a kerchief in his pocket and was moppin' his brow with it somethin' fierce.

"Now, about that Ravenant feller we was discussin'," I said mildly. "Just whereabouts was it . . ."

But ole Sandy wasn't havin' no part of me no more. He just shook his head and hurried back through the door of his establishment, movin' like somebody'd done lit a fire underneath his tail. I called out a thanks to the darkness inside, but I didn't get no reply.

After glancin' up and down the street without seein'

anybody else in view at the moment, I hitched up my belt and allowed myself a little smile. It weren't like I'd won any great victory standin' up to them gun hands. But whenever things ain't been goin' your way for a while, just not losin' can sometimes feel like winnin'.

I started off walkin' up the boardwalk again, and my boots made a kind of a hollow, lonely sound in that hot mid-mornin' stillness. It was sort of a apt accompaniment to the thoughts what was rattlin' around inside my brain now.

I hadn't learned near as much from the little sandy-haired storekeeper as I'd wanted to. But at least it 'peared like Ravenant was a knowed man hereabouts, though he might not live close enough to be exactly a reg'lar visitor. And if what I took to be Sandy's nervous manner at the mention of his name meant anything, there could some kind of strong feelin's about Mr. Ravenant amongst the local populace too.

Either him or that swamp country where it was said he lived over to eastward. Maybe both.

I decided it wouldn't hurt to take a little different tack on my next try lookin' for information. There wasn't no sense stirrin' up any more curiosity about me amongst the local folk than what I already had. So I'd act like I just had me a notion to travel east now, which was the truth, and ask after the country like any stranger might, without lettin' on I'd ever heard about no folks what lived over there. Chances were I'd learn enough doin' that to set me on the right trail anyhow. And maybe a tad more if I found the right person to ask.

After I'd walked another block I figured I'd seen just the place.

The Fort Dade livery stable was easy to recognize, set back off the main street some thirty, forty yards on my right, with a split-rail corral at the rear under some trees, and big double doors in the front. The doors was standin' open now. And propped up against a post on the far side where the shadows was cool and there might be a little hint of a breeze, I seen a cane-bottom chair with its front legs off the ground. A white-bearded gent was settin' in it, dozing away the mornin'.

Ain't much goes on in a town what don't sooner or later come to be knowed by the feller who runs the local livery stable. Often as not he's the first one a new arrival meets an' talks to after days or weeks on the trail without no reg'lar conversation. And generally he's the last to see 'em leave too. In between times he's always there, a-settin' and a-watchin' throughout the live-long day. When he ain't too busy with his nappin', that is.

Just soon as I laid eyes on that stable building I'd got in mind to make a bee-line for it. Only I reckon maybe my head started turnin' thataway a instant before I could get my feet geared up to follow.

The next thing I knew I'd done bumped slap into a soft li'l bundle of honey-colored flesh an' homespun skirts, knockin' the lady plumb off the boardwalk and onto her backside in the loose sand of the street.

Well, I was more than a little embarrassed, as you might imagine. And when I stepped down real fast with a muttered apology and a hand stretched out to help her up, that gal's words didn't hardly make me feel no better about the situation a-tall.

"You big clumsy ox! Why'n't you look where you're goin'? You got blinders on or somethin'?"

"No, ma'am. I'm terrible sorry. It's just that I was . . ."

"Never mind." She got up without lettin' me help her, and stood there bent over whilst she went about brushin' the sand from her skirts. I figured it was prob'ly a good thing for both of us that there hadn't been no horses left their sign in that part of the street very recent.

She was a pretty little thing, with long gold-brown hair peekin' out from under her bonnet where it sat crooked on her head after the fall. And as she proceeded to dust an' slap at all them places what hit the ground, I could see she was a deal more woman than girl, though maybe not yet entirely out of her teens. In manners and speech she was what I'd have to call, well, right pert.

"Feller comes barrelin' down the street like you do, never lookin' one way or t'other to learn what's around him, ought to have a bell hung on his neck so's to give folks a warnin'. Why, if anybody was fool enough to put you up on a wagon behind a team, you'd be plumb dangerous!" She finished her dustin' and straightened up to glare at me with both hands on her hips.

And then all of a sudden this real strange look come over her face. I swear that gal's mouth dropped open for a good ten seconds without a word comin' out of it. She 'peared to be havin' a little bit of trouble catchin' her breath, too.

"Wh— What're _you_ doin' here?" she managed at last, speakin' in a kind of a rough whisper. "Have you gone an' lost your wits entirely? Don't you know that they're . . ." Then she fell silent and stared up into my eyes for a real long moment.

"Oh. You ain't . . ." She shook her head, almost like she was wakin' up from a dream. "I'm sorry. Reckon I took you for somebody different. For a minute there I could of swore . . ."

"Marty, you all right?" The voice come from behind me

on the boardwalk, and I turned around to see a young man steppin' out from the general store with a croker sack slung over each shoulder. Seemed like he looked at me mighty hard hisself, for just a second there.

"I'm fine, Cal. Me an' this stranger had us a little bit of a accident is all. No harm done."

"Well, we best be gettin' along then. Still got a good ways to travel today before we camp." The young man stepped off the boardwalk and swung his sacks into the bed of a spring wagon what stood waitin' around the corner of the building.

As he went to untie the two mules he give me another curious look, and his face was lit up by the mornin' sun underneath that broad-brimmed slouch hat he was wearin'. I realized of a sudden that I was seein' the face of a full-blooded Indian.

That was a mite peculiar, sure enough. I'd figured what few Seminoles was left was all holed up in the Everglades or the Big Cypress Swamp more'n a hundred miles to the south of here. I hadn't never even met one myself, though I'd been around plenty of other Indians durin' my travels in the West. It almost made me doubt my eyes to find one here, dressed in white man's clothes and travelin' with a white woman.

Not that it was any of my business, o'course. And nothin' I felt the need to be disturbed about neither. Most the Indians I'd knowed was ever bit as honorable as them of my own kind, and some was a good deal more so. It just struck me a tad odd, was all.

The gal named Marty had started off to join her companion at the buckboard. But before she'd took more'n a couple steps she stopped and turned back to me.

"Listen, Mister . . ."

"Tate," I answered, not even thinkin' as I gazed into them pert blue eyes to offer my entire name.

"Listen, Mister Tate, if I was you I'd travel mighty careful through this country hereabouts. 'Fact, I believe I would just ride out now, and not come back. You got a kind of look about you what . . ." She hesitated, then shrugged her slender shoulders. "Well, you might fetch up against more trouble here than you was a-huntin'."

T'wouldn't be the first time, I thought to myself. And I was more'n half a mind to open my mouth and tell her so. But with them last words she'd turned on her heel and walked up to the wagon, climbin' aboard without a backward glance. Her Injun partner clucked to the mules, and before a feller could blink his eyes twict, there wasn't nothin' left where they'd been except settlin' dust.

I headed off acrost that open patch of sand and pine needles between me an' the livery stable, thinkin' all kinds of curious thoughts and questions for what I didn't have no answers.

I'd a pretty good notion it was that same Barkley feller this Marty gal had begun to mistake me for, who was the one Purv an' Lila an' Jube had took me to be a couple days back. And it was makin' me almighty curious to learn who he was. Maybe just a mite jealous, too. Seein' how much handier that feller appeared to be than I ever was when it come to attractin' good-lookin' ladies.

In another minute I was standing inside the big open doors of the stable, lookin' down into the white-bearded hostler's sleepin' face. It were a face what 'peared old enough to of wore out two, three bodies: all seamed an' creased an' brown from the sun, with yellerish brown stains around the chin and mustache what I reckoned owed more to tobacco juice than age or outdoor livin'.

Just about the time I planted my feet in front of him, the old man opened his eyes and looked up into mine.

"Howdy," he said, not stirrin' in his chair but kind of lettin' his eyes rove down and up to take me all in. "Quarter a day fer boardin'. 'Nother two bits with corn and oats."

I hunkered down beside him and pushed my hat off my forehead. "Sounds fair, I reckon. Only I didn't exactly come here to see about boardin' no horse."

He studied me for a second or two longer.

"Ain't got no ridin' stock to hand right now. Best I could do's a buggy with a Tennessee trotter. Four dollars a day, or two dollars for half of it."

I whistled between my teeth. But the old man just shrugged his bony shoulders. "Onliest one for rent this side of Brooksville or Tampa. Folks either take it or go by shank's mare."

"I reckon I'll stick with what I got," I said. "Which is a rare fine animal, but even he ain't worth no four dollars a day. And right this minute I couldn't come up with the price for even ten minutes on that high-falutin' buggy of yours."

The hostler fished in his overalls for a plug of tobacco and his Barlow knife. "Didn't figure you could. You ain't no Yankee tourist. They're the only ones I know who's dumb enough or rich enough to spend four dollars for a ride in the country." He cut off a chew and snapped his knife closed before shovin' it back in his pocket. "And even they been knowed to cuss a mite whenever they hear my price."

He grinned at me. "But they go ahead an' pay it, more often than not."

9 🌾

"TRUTH OF IT IS," I SAID, "what I was hopin' for was a little bit of information about this country round here. I was reared up in Taylor County, two hundred miles to the north and almost nearly in the Florida panhandle. It's my first time travelin' so far down the peninsula, and this is all foreign territory to me."

The old man nodded and rocked his chair forward so's he could spit onto the dirt floor of the stable. "I reckon you come to the right place, then. Me an' my brother first brung our families into this country back in the spring of '42. Weren't no more'n two hundred white folks all the way from Crystal River to Tampa Bay in them days. Now I 'hear they's better'n twenty times that livin' here. It's got so crowded a man can't hardly find a decent fishin' hole without havin' to share it with two, three others."

"I heard that," I agreed. "I'm a travelin' man what likes a spot of elbow room his ownself time to time. Towns an' settlements never had much appeal for me."

I'd what I thought was a pretty good reason for sayin'

that at the time, which had to do with learnin' more about that wilderness country over east what I was partic'lar interested in. But when my new acquaintance cocked his head to one side and give me this funny squinty look, I realized I'd maybe left him with a impression I'd sooner not of give.

See, folks come into Florida for all kinds of reasons. Most of 'em is huntin' after somethin' — land, timber, a better climate, a new place to start a business. But they's always been the others too, the ones with somethin' or somebody huntin' them. And when a feller lets on like I just did, that he's a "travelin' man" with a hankerin' for empty spaces . . . Well, people is liable to jump to conclusions.

I'd a notion this ole hostler had just took it into his head that I was some kind of a desperate character on the dodge from the law. An' I'll admit more'n one person has told me I got the look.

But what's said was said, and I couldn't hardly take it back now without explainin' a heap more than I'd any mind to explain to this gent. So I decided I might's well let him think what he wanted for the time bein', and see if I couldn't turn it to my advantage. I didn't have no plans to spend any great part of my future here in Fort Dade noways.

"'Pears like," I said after only a little hint of a pause, "that most them settlements I heard tell of is north an' west of here. You know anything over east what might be worth a day or two's ride?"

Well, now, there was that look again. Not the squinty-eyed, suspicious one I'd just been noticin', but the same curious, twisted-up, almost fearful look what come acrost that storekeeper's face soon as the name Ravenant got mentioned.

The old hostler paused to spit a long stream of tobacco

juice halfway acrost the stable. Then he shook his head and spit again. When he finally looked up an' answered me, his words was clear enough. But his voice seemed a mite quieter than it had been earlier.

"Ain't anything over yonder I'd care to waste a day or more on, my ownself. Little settlement of Tuckerton's five, six mile east an' south of here. But after that they's just a whole lot of nothin'."

I'd a pretty good idea from how he said it that that "nothin'" meant "somethin'" in a right special way. And I was gettin' powerful curious to know what kind of somethin' it was made all these folks get their neck hairs up about it the way they seemed to do. Was it that feller Ravenant and his outfit what give 'em the willie-wumps so bad? Or was it somethin' else entire?

I'd perked up at the word 'nothin' like I figured any man on the dodge would of done. Now I put on a sly look as I went ahead with my questionin': "That means no settlements, I reckon. But what kind of country is it over yonder? Somebody said somethin' about this great big swamp stretchin' away there to the east."

"They did, did they?" The old man's eyes narrowed up a mite, and he took time out to spit another long stream of tobacco juice. "They happen to mention anything in passin' what a feller might find in that swamp?"

"Nope. But I reckon they 'lowed as how it weren't exactly the most favorable parcel of country for travelers."

"I expect that's the truth. Been so ever sinct I or anybody else can remember. Seminoles holed up in there durin' the Injun wars. Ain't none of our kind ever found much use in it afterwards. 'Cept . . ."

I was waitin' for him to finish his exceptin', but the next thing I knew he'd done changed the subject.

"I was in there bear huntin' a time or two, years an' years back when my brother was still alive. Ain't had no call to ride that way since. Nor no partic'lar desire to neither."

"Real uncivilized country, huh?" I allowed myself a little bit of a knowin' grin.

"Mostly 'tis. Swamp an' wet prairie, sloughs and low hammock all round an' about. Near impossible to make your way through it durin' the wet season. But then it ain't like that everwhere. They's hills an' high places where a feller might put up a cabin and get in a li'l crop. —If he didn't mind bein' plumb cut off from the rest of the world. Ain't no roads nor trails nowhere that's fittin' to drive a wagon over. And hardly no creeks deep enough for boat travel, neither."

He paused to study me up an' down for a long, careful minute. "'N of course there's the stories."

"Stories?" I looked at him real curious in spite of myself.

"Tales folks tell. 'Bout what's lurkin' in and around that swamp, and what happens to them as goes there. Most of it ain't nothin' but grade-A hogwash. Haints an' witchy-folks an' vandals an' such. Fables to affright young-uns with." The hostler shrugged.

"I never put no stock in that kind o' foolishness my ownself, sinct I was knee-high to a tadpole. Don't reckon you did neither. Feller hears it time to time, mostly from ignorant share-croppers an' dodderin' old ladies, what keeps their shutters latched an' never ventures out'n the house come sundown. Wouldn't think of mentionin' it to another growed man now. Only . . ."

I held my peace and waited, whilst he rubbed his face

an' tugged at his whiskers with long big-knuckled fingers. It appeared like I was finally goin' to hear somethin' about what went on in that swamp over to eastward.

"'Tain't nothin' a feller can rightly put his finger on," the old man said after a minute. "But it do seem they's been more'n a couple folks durin' the last four, five years what went ridin' off that direction and didn't come back."

I guess I might not of looked too surprised when he told me that, 'cause my companion give a kind of a half shrug an' went ahead to echo what was already in my mind:

"Oh, I know that don't sound so awful peculiar on the face of it, the frontier bein' what it is. One of 'em might got crosswise with a bear or a painter back up in the woods. 'Nother could of fell off his horse and broke a leg or a hip or somethin', and died before he could reach help. Others might of just decided to keep on travelin' in some different direction.

"But . . ." The hostler pushed his hat to one side so's he could scratch at his baldin' white head. ". . . the thing of it is, I can't 'call a single one what started over yonder that ever come back here to Fort Dade. And not all of 'em was drifters neither." He begun tickin' 'em off on his fingers, like he'd been keepin' count for some little while.

"First was that couple wagon loads of homesteaders three, four years back, which nobody thought much about at the time. And after them come maybe a half a dozen others, cow-hunters or settlers or what-have-you, before anybody started payin' it partic'lar notice. I reckon it weren't till that doctor's son from up to Asheville, North Carolina, disappeared last spring, along with his ridin' companion and a Negro helper, that the rumors really started flyin'." The old man frowned and shifted his quid to the opposite cheek.

"Not long after that this Yankee tourist from Boston rode out one bright sunny mornin', leaving behind a leather trunk and a valise at the boardin' house, chock full of fancy clothes and other gew-gaws — with five hundred dollars cash money besides. I know about that one personal, 'cause it was me who rented him the horse.

"Never did get it back. Me an' Miz Sheehan just finally took what we figured was owed us, and she locked up the rest for safe-keepin'. It's been pert' near five months now, and nobody come to claim it. She even wrote a letter to his people up in New England, but never got a answer." The hostler fell silent for a second or two before meetin' my eyes.

"Anyways," he said, "you can see why there might be a deal of talk and speculation goin' round, over what it is in that country seems to swallow folks up and not spit 'em out."

I nodded, thoughtful-like. This here was a heap more of a mystery than I'd any notion of discoverin' when I first rode into Fort Dade. And it raised some right serious questions for any man what had designs on travelin' into that swamp country to eastward — regardless of whether he believed it was spirits or something more natural had caused them folks to disappear.

But still there hadn't been no mention in all this long conversation of Ravenant or them people I come south a-huntin'. And now I'd got more of a cravin' than ever to know what their part in it might be, if any.

So I decided to try one last question, still takin' care not to let on what my real purpose was for askin'.

"That sounds like a mighty peculiar set of circumstances," I agreed, "sure enough. But what strikes me partic'lar curious when I hear you tell it, is the number of folks what seem to of got the urge to travel over yonder in the first place. I mean, if they ain't nothin' there except swamp an' fierce critters anyhow. You reckon they was all just out for the fishin' and the huntin'?"

The old hostler give me sharp look for maybe a half a second. Then he glanced away an' shrugged.

"Only more stories. Seems like they's this rancher has got hisself a place east of here, or maybe it's south an' east. Nobody knows for sure, and lately ain't anybody had much of a notion to go find out. But he's a mighty hard, tough man to all appearances, and that bunch what rides for him is rougher'n a cob for fair. They don't none of 'em come to town very regular, and mostly keep their own counsel when they do.

"As you might expect, that's caused some small amount of talk its ownself. They's folks who speculate he lives near or in that swamp, and knows more'n his share about the disappearances. And a few even claim that they heard tell he's some kind of a . . ." The hostler hesitated, then shook his head.

"Hell. Like I told you, there's all sorts of rumors circulatin' nowadays. And some of 'em is just plumb outlandish!"

The old man fell silent then, and for a long minute we just sat there without neither of us sayin' nothing.

I'd a feelin' our conversation was pretty close to bein' over. If the hostler knew much more than what he'd already said about this rancher — I was sure it had to be Ravenant — he weren't of no mind to tell it to me. For all his protestin' about not payin' no heed to "outlandish" stories, they was somethin' about this situation seemed to of put a button on his lips.

Finally, I stretched and stood up.

"That's all mighty interestin'," I said. I re-settled my gunbelt on my hips and reached up to give my hat a little tug. "But like you suggested, I ain't ever been much of a one to put stock in haints an' spooks an' such. Now that you got my curiosity up, I'm just powerful tempted to ride out and have a look for myself."

The hostler favored me with a sly smile between his whiskers. "I'd a notion you might. And it's fine by me, 'long as you don't ride off thinkin' you ain't been warned." He paused to spit out his quid and tilt his chair back against the wall.

"The way I figure it, you either come here to Fort Dade a-huntin' something, or you come here with somethin' huntin' you. If it's the first, you'll decide for yourself where you got to go seek it.

"But if it's the second, if you're on the dodge — and mind, I'm not sayin' you are or you ain't — then you ridin' off to the east now might wind up bein' a blessing for everbody. Them stories turn out to be false and you'll be in a place where a army of searchers could spend their natural lives and never come acrost your trail. If they's true, well I expect you'll just disappear off the face of the earth and never be heard from again." The old man leaned his head back and shifted his hat to cover his eyes.

"Either way, you won't be hangin' round Fort Dade and causin' us no more trouble than what we already got."

I wasn't sure how much I appreciated that last sentiment, but I understood it well enough. A man what wears a tied-down gun ain't ever too welcome in polite society, be he outlaw or lawman or just travelin' through. It appears some people figure a gun's a powerful attraction for trouble its ownself, whether the feller who wears it is huntin' trouble or not.

That always seemed a mite peculiar to me. I never noticed trouble havin' too much regard for anything a feller is totin'. It just comes along whenever it's ready, no matter what. Me, I'd rather be prepared to meet it halfway or maybe a little better when it does. And sometimes, like earlier today, a man who's set to dish it out as well as take it can nip a heap of trouble in the bud.

When I'd thanked the hostler for his information, I left the stable an' started amblin' back up the street to where I'd tied Ole Roan.

I'd a thing or two to think on now, an' that was a fact. Any how you looked at it they was a passel of mighty peculiar goin's-on in that country to eastward. Folks ridin' off from town and simply disappearin', stories of haints an' spooks an' such, local merchants and townsfolk actin' like they was scairt of their own shadows.

None of it made a awful lot of sense to me. Except somehow or another this feller Ravenant 'peared to have hisself a place staked out right slap in the middle of it.

Well, when you come down to it then, nothin' I'd heard so far made any difference to my future plans. If east was where I'd find Ravenant and his people, east was the direction I meant to ride. But I'd a notion it wouldn't hurt to do my travelin' extra careful now, with my Winchester acrost my saddle bow and my eyes wide open the entire time.

If I got crackin', I'd ought to be able to reach that settlement of Tuckerton the hostler spoke about a tad before noon. Maybe somebody there could give me a little clearer idea of where to go seekin' Ravenant's place afterwards.

I reckon I'd got myself so caught up with my thoughts

and my plannin' whilst I was walkin' back along the board-walk there, that I forgot to pay real close attention to anything else around me. That's how come I just nearly managed to knock two young women off into the street in a single day.

Only this latest was a one I'd had dealin's with earlier.

Lila 'peared at least as surprised as me when she first come high-steppin' out'n that mercantile store right smack into my arms. We stumbled against each other, did this sort of a quick turn-about together like we might of been dancin', and when we stepped apart I reached up to touch my hat an' mutter a hasty apology before I'd took a real good look at who it was I was facin'.

She was a sight faster on the uptake. I'll give her that.

After lettin' out with this little gasp of surprise, which might of meant anything a-tall to a unknowin' observer, Lila threw herself away from me and spread-eagled herself against the wall. Then she commenced to scream at the top of her lungs:

"Help! Help! Oh, God in heaven, help me! Save me!"

I glanced around, still not quite understandin' what it was she was up to or who she was actin' so afeared of. But when I didn't see nothin' behind me except the storekeeper at his doorway and a couple curious faces peekin' out from windows acrost the street, I got this sudden empty feelin' in the pit of my stomach.

Sure enough, when I turned back towards Lila, she was pointin' a shakin' finger right square at me.

"It's him! That's the man who attacked and tried . . . tried to take advantage of me on the road to Sumterville! — Oh, please, please somebody! Don't let him lay his filthy hands on me again!"

Well, it didn't take no natural-borned genius to see what direction the wind was blowin' now. For maybe half a split second I had this powerful urge to holler out that she was lyin' in her teeth, and that it was me who'd come out the worse for it the only time Lila an' me ever crossed paths before.

But I knew I'd be wastin' my breath. Nobody was goin' to believe no rough, shaggy, gun-totin' stranger over a fetchin' little woman with tears in her great big dark eyes.

More likely I was goin' to find myself spittin' out lead and swingin' from a tree branch before I even got a chanct to begin tellin' my version of the story.

I took another quick glance around an' noticed Sandy had disappeared inside his store to where he prob'ly kept some kind of a shootin' iron. And they was three, four other determined-lookin' men out in the street now, who'd already found their weapons and was walkin' our way.

When them two gun artists for hire stepped out of the buildin' acrost from us, I knew it was time and past time me an' Ole Roan started makin' some tracks.

10

It SURELY WEREN'T IN MY MIND to take on no entire town full of outraged citizens, even if I reckoned this was truly our fight. And these men wasn't doin' anything I wouldn't of done myself if I'd the notion they was some scoundrel here who'd treated a woman the way Lila made it sound like I had.

The hired guns was another story maybe. But if they decided to take a hand in this game they'd be only a little bitty part of the trouble I was already in. And I knew a good many of their kind didn't cotton to abusin' women no better'n your average law-abidin' citizen. Me, I didn't plan to stick around long enough to find out what they decided.

I didn't even bother drawin' my Smith an' Wesson, but just lit out runnin' as fast as I could. When I'd made it halfway to that rail at the end of the street where Ole Roan was tied, some gent stuck his head out of a upstairs window and let fly with a shotgun. He must of plumb forgot what he'd been usin' his piece for earlier though. 'Cause all that come out from the barrel was a fine spray of bird-shot.

It stung my legs an' backside enough to make me step a mite higher. But the distance between us was too far to cause any real damage, and in another second I'd reached my horse an' jerked loose the slip-knot what held him. I grabbed the saddle-horn and swung a leg over without even troublin' about the stirrup.

As I turned my mustang's head to get us started out of town, I looked back and seen a half dozen armed men hot-footin' it down the sandy street behind us. I seen something else too, in that half second or so I was lookin', what I expect all them others missed in their hurry to catch up to me.

The two gunslingers was still standin' on the boardwalk, not payin' no mind to the chase but watchin' Lila on t'other side of the street instead. And she was lookin' at them. I saw her give a little nod of her head, and the one with the shot-gun nodded in return. Then both them hard cases started up the boardwalk in the opposite direction towards where their horses was tied.

It appeared like they was some kind of a understandin' between those three. And like Tate Barkley had just earned hisself the professional interest of two professional killers.

Ole Roan knew the drill from here on out, it not bein' exactly the first time we'd ever took our leave from some-place on the spur of the moment. So alls I had to do was wrap my arms around his neck and hang on whilst he give a great leap and dusted out of that town with the whap of pistol bullets and the boom of a second shotgun blast at our backs to speed us along.

We was headin' south when we lit out, and I let the roan have his head for better'n a mile before I slowed him enough so's I could sit up in the saddle to have a look over my back trail an' study on the situation a mite.

I didn't have no idea whether them townsfolks would be organizin' a pursuit right away. But it seemed like a little better plan to assume they would than they wouldn't for the time bein'. That Lila had a mighty convincin' way about her onct she took it into her head to lie. And at least I could be reasonable sure from the little signal between her an' those two hired warriors, that I'd got them boys on my trail at this very second.

Leave it to her to have dealin's with hard cases like that, and mess up what till now had been a perfectly good Mexican stand-off.

Then they was Purv an' big Jube of course, what was prob'ly somewhere in the neighborhood if Lila was. I didn't recall seein' no sign of them or their mounts in Fort Dade. But I hadn't had no clue about Lila bein' there neither till I run smack into her. And after that there weren't a awful lot more time for lookin' around.

I surely didn't mean to be forgettin' them boys, though. Nor the little lady with the big eyes an' the .38 revolver neither. Once I got myself clear from this latest fix she'd put me in, I was goin' to be mighty thoughtful about how an' where we met up the next time. It was right troublesome to my pride to keep gettin' caught flat-footed by surprise like this. And I was a mind not to let it happen no more.

Me an' the roan galloped south at a pretty fair clip for another couple, three miles. It was a loose sand road and not partic'lar favorable for trackin'. But there hadn't been no turn-offs to speak of neither, so I knew I weren't goin' to shake nobody on my back-trail by keepin' on thisaway. Not unless I wanted to try an' outrun'em, which would mean leavin' the country entirely. And I hadn't no plans to do that just right yet.

We'd been in amongst what appeared to be a good-sized patch of forest for some little while now. So after another quick glance over my shoulder, I all of a sudden swung Ole Roan's head into the trees to the east, and we left the road behind.

We was forced to slow our pace a mite then, because of all the low-hangin' branches and roots and other places where the footin' weren't too certain. But I kept us movin' along real steady an' constant through them woods until I was convinced we'd come at least another mile from where we turned off the road. Then I pulled up underneath a big live oak to listen all around and let Ole Roan have hisself a bit of a blow.

Not that he needed it so awful bad this early in the chase. Bein' mustang-bred and used to travelin' rough country for days on end, this here was only a brisk mornin's jog as far as he was concerned. But a man like me what seems to draw trouble to him the way honey draws flies, just naturally gets in the habit of savin' his mount ever chanct he gets. I knew I might need all the bottom my roan horse had later on.

Besides which, I wanted a little break my ownself to figure out where we'd ought to go from here.

A better'n average tracker might of spotted that place we left the road back yonder the first time he come upon it. But with all the loose sand thereabouts it would of been a chancy thing. And afterwards a feller'd have his work cut out for him for sure, tryin' to follow our sign through them fallen leaves an' tussocks of grass what laid acrost the forest floor everwhere about. 'Specially since I'd been usin' all the tricks

I knew or could think of to backtrack an' mislead and mark false trails what didn't go noplace along the way.

I'd more'n a couple such tricks in my kit, considerin' I'd found myself in this here kind of a situation maybe once or twict before.

I ain't sayin' it couldn't be done. There ain't no trail in the world what can't be followed given time enough and skill enough on the part of the tracker. But I didn't figure I'd got to worry too much about somebody comin' along behind me in the next five, ten minutes anyhow. And maybe not for the better part of the day.

It was low rollin' sand hills where we was, with ever now an' again a little shallow ravine or a dry creek bed in between. The pines an' hardwoods was growin' so thick around that hill we was on so I couldn't see more'n thirty yards in any direction. I spent a good long while just settin' there on the roan and listening, but I didn't hear nothin' a-tall except some crickets and a occasional bird back off in the brush.

When I looked up I realized the sun was almost direct overhead, which meant it'd be another hour or two before I could get my bearings from it good enough to calculate direction. What with them dense woodlands and me not knowin' the country, that was somethin' to consider. Because I'd already made up my mind the way I meant to head from here was east.

If what the ole hostler had suggested about local attitudes was true, a trail leadin' east might discourage at least some of them folks from follerin' too long or too far. And it'd take me off into the kind of wild deserted country best suited for lyin' low in any case. Besides which, it was the direction

I'd a mind to be travelin' all along.

Still, it prob'ly wouldn't be such a good idea to stop and ask questions in that Tuckerton settlement now, like I'd planned to earlier. Word travels fast on the frontier, and what was likely bein' spread around concernin' me at the moment wasn't no way flatterin'.

Best thing would be to locate some well-hid place hereabouts and just hole up till nighttime. A man what don't do no movin' around don't leave no tracks to follow. And when it got dark I could slip on past whatever homesteads was there to eastward without givin' notice I'd been in the neighborhood a-tall.

I climbed down from the leather and shucked out my Winchester, figuring to do a little more slow an' careful scoutin' of these woods on foot. But since there weren't no way of guessin' what I'd run into when I did, and since I could find myself needin' to leave in a right powerful hurry for one reason or another, I took the roan's reins in my left hand an' let him follow along behind as I started easin' my way amongst the trees.

After a bit we come down off that ridge and climbed another one, movin' slow and watchful the entire time. I kept glancin' back at Ole Roan's head as we moved, knowin' he was more likely than me to suspect when other horses or folks was about, bein' raised up in the wild like he was.

When we'd got to the top of that second ridge we started comin' in amongst a fair-sized blow-down of trees, evidently left over from a storm of some kind once upon a time. The trunks was all dried out an' white with grass and vines growin' in amongst 'em, so it weren't anything that happened very recent. Them dead trunks and branches didn't make for very easy walkin' neither. But I noticed what appeared to be a more open place in the midst of 'em, maybe a hundred yards further on. So I decided to keep goin' that far at least, to see what I could see.

The clearing was right at the far edge of the blow-down, and pretty near the crest of that ridge as well. There was this big tall pile of dead trees an' brush beyond it where the ground begun to drop off, like some kind of a huge barricade throwed up by giants. When I craned my neck an' peered around it, I could make out little glimpses of hills an' open country in the distance. Seemed like if a feller was able to climb his way up to the top of that jumble of trunks an' limbs, he might have hisself a pretty fair view of whatever was around.

Even more to my liking after I done a tad more explorin', was this sort of a deep holler or dry creek bed what led down off the ridge in a different direction. It was all growed up thick with elm an' hawthorn an' such-like, covered over by branches and havin' its entrance partly hid by the roots of a great big overturned oak tree at one side of the clearing.

'Peared to me anybody who got hisself down in there good enough ought to be so well hid that a seeker'd have to be almost rubbin' elbows with him to know he wasn't a dozen miles away. Just the place I needed for Ole Roan an' me to spend the afternoon whilst we waited for dark to do our travelin'.

The first an' most important order of business though, was to have a long careful look over the countryside and make real certain there wasn't no little surprises awaitin' us. Like maybe some homesteader's cabin settin' right smack at the foot of this ridge.

So after I'd ground-hitched the roan close by to that big dead-fall and replaced my Winchester in its boot by the saddle, I stepped back to give a mite of consideration to a way to the top of it. Then I settled my gunbelt more comfortable about my hips and started in to climb.

It weren't but maybe fifteen, twenty feet up to the highest part, which ain't hardly nothin' for a feller who's spent a share of his life out in New Mexico and Arizona. But still it was treacherous goin', what with all that wood bein' dead an' brittle, and me tryin' hard not to make no extra noises I didn't have to. And whilst I was about it, keep from skylinin' myself or make any sudden movements what might call attention to theirselves from a distance.

When I'd finally got up high enough to where I could poke my head between two branches and have a look around, I come to the conclusion all my climbin' efforts was worth it after all. 'Fact, my vantage point on this here ridge was some better'n I'd had any cause to hope for.

There was maybe three, four miles of open rollin' grassland stretched out in front of me, with ever now an' then a little patch of woods or a live oak stand to break up the plainness of it. Nowhere I looked was any sign of cabins or cultivated fields. But linin' out acrost the very next hill, from left to right and prob'ly a mile off in the distance, was this narrow sandy trace I reckoned had to be the road between Fort Dade and Tuckerton.

Based on that map I'd studied up in Sumterville and everthing else I'd heard of this country afterwards, there weren't no other traveled routes here to the east of the military road. And no other settlements such a road would be leadin' to neither.

I meant to double-check my directions anyhow, soon as the sun was low enough to do it. But I was almost certain I was right. And that meant I'd just saved myself a heap of wasted time stumblin' round through these woods in the dark tryin' to figure out which way I needed to head from here.

As I looked down an' studied the hillside below where I was situated, I could pick out what seemed to be a fairly easy route amongst the trees an' out onto the open prairie too. From there it was straight as a arrow-shot to that road on the adjoinin' hill.

I reckon I might of chose to locate me a hidin' place a little further off the beaten track than this if I'd wanted perfection. But all things considered I weren't partic'lar worried. Anybody what started over here from the road to investigate would have a mile of open country to cover before they got near enough to concern me. And either me or the roan should hear 'em coming in plenty of time to take whatever measures was necessary.

After I'd climbed down from the dead-fall I took an' led Ole Roan into that dense growed-up holler on t'other side of the clearin', being careful not to leave no more sign than necessary behind amongst the grass and soft sand thereabouts. When I figured we'd come far enough, I fastened his reins to the limb of a scrub oak and took me another long, slow listen in ever direction. Once I was satisfied there still wasn't nothin' nor nobody close by that needed our attention, I loosed the roan's cinch a mite and sat down on a soft pile of dead leaves to take out the makin's.

When I'd rolled a smoke and fished out a match from my pocket to light it, I paused with the match between my fingers and listened again. There weren't no sounds a-tall in that hot Florida midday except a little bitty wind stirrin' the trees overhead, and some crickets what was finally beginnin' to get comfortable enough with me bein' here to start singin' again.

I struck the match on my trousers and leaned back to take a deep drag on my cigarette. This was a right peaceful place, what with the sunlight dancin' on the leaves nearby, and the stillness an' loneliness of the wilderness all around. For a minute or two there I almost started to feel at peace with the world my ownself.

Almost. Of course there was still the little matter of a town full of angry citizens what wanted my hide nailed to a barn for somethin' they thought I done but I didn't. And them two hired pistoleros on my back trail who couldn't care less about anything I'd done once Lila nodded her head and sicked 'em on me. And Lila an' Jube an' Purv theirselves, who give me that beatin' and robbin' up the country a couple days earlier.

None of them things afforded a man much cause to feel peaceable for long.

It ain't like me an' trouble has ever been exactly what you'd call strangers. 'Fact, when I put my mind to it I was hard-pressed to 'call many times in my life that I hadn't been facin' up to trouble of one description or another. Sometimes it almost made me mad to think on it. I mean after all, everbody ought to deserve some small measure of peace an' contentment in this life, hadn't they?

But then of a sudden it come to me to ask myself just how much of that trouble I'd got so used to facin' day by day was of my own choosin'.

Take for example bein' robbed by Lila and her *compadres*. I'd no way of helpin' that when it happened. But how about now? I'd got my horse and a part of my outfit back, and them bruises from Jube's beatin' was already close to bein' healed. If I took on another job somewheres I could make up the rest of what I'd lost in six or seven months, plus a couple extra months to pay back Monk what I owed him.

What more did I want?

I could ride out of this country today and never come back. 'T'weren't likely I'd need to concern myself much about Lila's accusations in the long run. People forget pretty quick when there ain't no proof to back such things up. And a woman like her was bound to reveal her lyin' nature some way or another in time.

I could climb into the saddle, take out a-runnin', and be shut of this entire business after a few days or a few hundred miles. Start all over again in some place that was more to my liking.

I *could* do that. I mean the choice was mine.

When I sat up to crush out my cigarette with the heel of a boot, I noticed Ole Roan lookin' at me with a peculiar expression in his eyes. Or so it seemed at the time.

"What it is, boy," I said, kind of quiet-like under my breath, "is that I been havin' me a thought or two about what it might cost a man to guarantee hisself a trouble-free life." I shook my head.

"But I reckon I ain't cut out for it. I just can't see how

I'd ever be able to find it in me to pay so high a price."

The roan snorted an' tossed his head, as if to say he figured all along I'd been wastin' my time even ponderin' upon it. Then he went back to pullin' Spanish moss off'n the limbs alongside him, whilst I stretched out on that bed of leaves to take a little nap.

11 🌢

For a minute or two as I laid there sweatin' in the afternoon heat with a couple blue-tail flies buzzin' between me and Ole Roan's legs, I couldn't recall what it was that had woke me up.

Out of habit my fingers closed around the action of the Winchester at my side, and then I raised my left hand real slow to move the hat away from my eyes. My ears pricked up at the noise of a horse and rig trottin' along somewhere in the distance. It didn't sound like it was very close, and it didn't appear to be comin' closer. Most prob'ly, somebody was travelin' that road out yonder on the prairie.

I got up quiet and went to tighten Ole Roan's cinch first, just to be on the safe side. Then, movin' stealthy and silent as a Injun, I climbed out'n that holler and made my way to the big pile of blowed-down trees a short distance off. When I'd pulled myself to the top of it, I could see real clear what it was I'd been hearin'.

And I got to admit I was more'n a little surprised.

I recognized that shiny black surrey with its high-steppin' gelding right off, though it'd been almost a week since I'd seen it, and I hadn't had a very long look when I did. But there couldn't be many such fancy rigs in the whole state of Florida, much less this far from them gentrified settlements of St. Augustine and the St. Johns River. None a-tall that I could imagine, where the owners bothered to tie red ribbons in their horse's mane an' tail for a week's journey in the country.

There weren't no trouble recognizin' the man that was drivin' it neither. It was that same gent in the broadcloth suit an' the straw hat what had called me a drunk whilst I was layin' in the north Florida dirt half dead from Jube's chokin'. And I could see he'd still got his female friend along for company, her with the big spiteful words and the high-falutin' manner.

They was headin' east, a-trottin' that gelding into a lather like they might be runnin' behind times tryin' to catch up to the Easter parade.

I couldn't find it in me to think many warm thoughts about them two, not after they'd left me hurt by the road like they done, without even stoppin' to find out what was the matter.

But I reckon I weren't still mad enough to do or say nothin' about it, even if there wasn't some pretty compellin' reasons for keepin' myself hid at the moment. They's just some folks who ain't been raised no better than to grow up thoughtless an' ignorant, and it don't seem to do no good a-tall for a ordinary feller like me to try and educate 'em.

Besides which, I figured if that dude was fool enough to take hisself and a woman into them lands over east from here, without no more idea of how to act in wild country than they 'peared to have, they was liable to fetch up on trouble a-plenty without no help from me.

I was curious to know what it was had brought 'em down here into the brakes of central Florida in the first place. But not so curious that I meant to lose any sleep about it. I'd already got more ornery and difficult folks to try an' keep track of than I wanted just now, without addin' two more to the list.

I watched the surrey disappear over a low hill to eastward. Then I took several more minutes givin' careful study to everthing around me. It was maybe three o'clock in the afternoon now, and I meant to wait till it was good an' dark before I did any traveling. But things can look powerful different by night than they do in the daytime, and I didn't mean to spend no extra effort gettin' myself turned around backwards or stumblin' into hidden ditches after I did start movin'.

When I was content I could recognize about ever tree and change of ground between here an' that roadway, I climbed down off the deadfall and made my way back to that holler where Ole Roan was tethered. After movin' him a mite and easin' up on his cinch, I took one more good careful listen all around. Then I laid myself down amongst the leaves to catch another forty, sixty winks until the day reached its close.

❖   ❖   ❖

The stars was out when I finally stood up from the ground and got set to travel. There wasn't no moon yet. But I'd slept light, kind of wakin' and dozin' and keepin' track of the time, so I knew it weren't but another hour or so till its risin'. Which was pretty much the way I'd had things figured to work theirselves out from the git-go.

The darker it was when I passed that Tuckerton settlement the safer I was goin' to feel. Even if the locals wasn't of a mind to keep after me this late, there was still them couple hired warriors Lila had put on my trail. If they was bein' paid to hunt me down, they was the type who'd stay with the job till they got it done. Add to 'em Lila and her pals Purv an' big Jube, and they was at least five folks in the neighborhood who wished me dead. Any or all of 'em might be waitin' somewhere along that road to Tuckerton. So I meant to slip on past there without drawin' no more attention to myself than I could manage, in the dark just shy of moonrise.

But afterwards I'd be travelin' east through unknown country. And I'd a mind to keep ridin' deeper into it until close on to daybreak. The moon with its light would be a powerful help then. Keep me from circlin' back on myself and gettin' lost, or bein' swallowed up by them swamps an' bogs I knew was all around here close to the headwaters of the Hillsborough and Withlacoochee rivers.

I led Ole Roan out from that holler into the clearing before mountin' up. Then we made our way at a walk to the foot of the hill and out across country till we cut the Tuckerton road.

Even after we was on it I still held the roan to a walk, so's not to make no more noise than necessary until or unless we was discovered. I was tryin' to avoid a chase. But if it come down to one I didn't have much doubt that we'd win it. Me an' that mustang has outrun more'n one gent what had a burr under his saddle and a notion he owned a fast horse.

It wasn't just the number of enemies against me that made runnin' my number one plan at the moment, though it surely was a consideration. There might be honest townsfolk out there too amongst them huntin' me. And I didn't mean to get in no shootin' scrape if I could help it, with people who'd done nothin' to me except believe the lies of a fetchin' young woman. —Lies I might of believed in myself if I hadn't had the opportunity to learn that gal's ways up close and personal a short time earlier.

They was pine trees linin' the road on both sides now. And ever so often I could make out what appeared to be a cleared field beyond 'em in the dark. It didn't come as no surprise when I finally seen the yellow glow from a shuttered cabin window some fifty yards ahead. I pulled up in the deeper shadows of the trees and laid a hand on Ole Roan's neck to sort of remind him to stay calm an' collected, whilst I took stock of the situation.

It was a fair guess that this road here led on through the settlement, and maybe past it a ways in the direction I wanted to go. That'd be right convenient to my travel plans. But it also meant I'd be in plain view of any settler who was curious enough to stick his head out'n the door at the sound of a strange rider. Or of anybody else what might be layin' in wait for this one partic'lar rider.

On the other hand, if I was to back up to try and find some different way around, skulkin' through the fields an' brakes of this unfamiliar country, I could spend most of the night skirtin' these cabins and still have no guarantee I wouldn't stumble into some farmer's chicken coop or cattle pen in the darkness.

A low noise from a dozen feet away made up my mind a heap sooner'n any amount of considerin' would of done. I glanced over between two trees and could just make out the hulkin' shape of this big bull mastiff, a-barin' his teeth and growlin' real ominous way back in his throat.

It appeared like that settler's homestead yonder and this stretch of ground here was both part of what he thought of as his personal territory. And he was lettin' me know in pretty definite terms that he didn't cotton to no late night trespassers.

I reckoned I'd ought to respect his wishes. That dog looked to be near two hundred pounds from the little I could see of him, and even if I'd a mind to try disputin' the issue with him — which I hadn't — he was gettin' hisself all primed to rouse up the entire neighborhood in just about one more minute.

The roan tossed his head and started side-steppin' like he was way ahead of me on this, and he wished I'd hurry up an' finish figurin' it out my ownself. I let him keep movin' into the middle of the road. Then I leaned forward and whispered in his ear, "All right, boy, let's start makin' some tracks!"

When I give him a little encouragin' kick in the ribs, which he didn't hardly need, we lit out at a gallop with that mastiff's deep-throated bark a-fillin' up the night behind us. By the time we was past the first cabin and I noticed a second one without no lights loomin' up near a bend in the road, they was dogs bayin' and yappin' from one end of that country to the other. I slapped Ole Roan acrost the rump with my hat and we proceeded to dust on through that settlement like the whole army of Satan was nippin' at our heels.

Funny thing about it though, was them dogs was the only ones anywhere that seemed to show even the slightest interest in us. We must of rode past four, five more cabins without nary sign of life from a single one. There wasn't no lights, the doors stayed closed, and the window shutters was bolted down tight as a drum on top of it. On a warm evenin' like this you'd of thought at least some folks might welcome a spot of air to ease their sleepin' under mosquito nets an' all.

I decided that hostler at Fort Dade hadn't been foolin' when he said folks this direction was a mite skittish about bein' out an' about after it come on to dark.

The road played out a mile or two further on. But by then the moon was up so me and Ole Roan could see without a whole lot of trouble. Once it become clear there wouldn't be nobody followin' close behind us, I slowed him to a walk in order to save him for the hours ahead.

There was a stretch of swamp an' thick hammock on t'other side of the settlement, and with nothin' but the moon an' the stars to guide us we couldn't help but take a wrong turn ever now an' again. It was prob'ly somethin' after midnight before we finally come out amongst broad patches of low prairie with little bogs and stands of cypress all round an' in between 'em.

That made the travelin' a heap easier, though I was some pleased the last couple months in Florida had been dry ones. Else I'd a idea these here flatlands would of been ankle-deep in water from one end to the other.

I'll admit that open country made me a tad edgy, too. With the moon high and bright like it had got to be, anybody who was lookin' would find it powerful easy to spot a man on horseback movin' across it. And I'd no way of guessin' what might be skulkin' back in amongst the dark shadows of them swamps an' woods that lay everwhere around.

I reckon I could of chose to skirt the edges of them cypress domes and wooded places more close-like, makin' my way round-about towards the east instead of goin' direct like I was. But there was a kind of a devil ridin' my shoulders, what kept after me to put this stretch of territory behind so's to get to what was on t'other side.

Not that I'd any real definite plans about where I meant to head from here. My first notion had been to lose myself deep enough in the wilderness so I didn't have to worry about no pursuit right away. Looked like maybe I'd already accomplished that, though it couldn't hurt to ride a bit further just to be on the safe side.

My second idea, which was only halfway formed, was to try and figure out where Ravenant's home place lay. If I could get myself between it and Lila an' her friends as they made their way back to it, then maybe I could set up a little ambush of my own. 'Course how I was goin' to do all that without no knowledge of the country and nobody to ask, was more'n I could picture right at the moment.

It could be the ole hostler's tales of strange doin's and travelers gettin' swallowed up without a trace added somethin' to the jumpy feelin' was comin' over me as we rode deeper into that dark an' lonely wilderness. For all I could tell me an' the roan was about as far from human company right now as a body's liable to get who ain't dropped off the face of the earth entirely.

But I'd done a fair part of my growin' up in a place not too different from this, in the San Pedro Swamp up to Taylor an' Lafayette counties. There'd been tales of haints an' spirits roamin' the night up yonder too when I was a young-un. Us folks who spent all our lives in the swamp never put much stock in 'em, though. Painters an' moccasins an' alligators an' desperate men a-hidin' from the law was plenty enough to keep a feller's guard up, without gettin' all excited over any critters that was more likely made out of fox fire an' swamp gas.

That was mighty rough country, of a kind that bred some rough an' ready citizens. I mind hearin' one feller say that whenever he walked through the Valley of the Shadow of Death he would fear no evil, 'cause he were the biggest, meanest he-coon in the Valley. Come to think on it, that feller could of been me.

When we'd been makin' our way through that low prairie for some several hours, the fog begun to rise up so thick out'n them cypress stands and marshes all around that you couldn't hardly locate the nose on your face usin' both hands and a coal-oil lantern. There didn't seem to be much point in continuin' under them circumstances, even if I'd been real certain what it was I was hopin' to set eyes on out here in the first place.

So when we come to this little higher parcel of ground with some pines an' palmettos here an' about, I called a halt and climbed down from the leather to make camp. Which is to say I picketed Ole Roan between two trees and dragged my saddle an' outfit off onto the ground. Then I spread my blankets where they fell and rolled myself up in 'em without hardly rememberin' to pull off my boots and unbuckle my gunbelt first.

I didn't even consider buildin' a fire or diggin' out no foodstuffs right then. Daylight weren't so far off that them things couldn't wait till it come, and what I wanted most was some rest an' shut-eye after a long night in the saddle. I didn't waste no time startin' in to get it.

❖   ❖   ❖

The sun was up, but the fog was still thick enough you could carve it with a knife when I woke to hear this low scrabblin' sound a couple yards behind me. My fingers found their way to the butt of my pistol without a thought, whilst I held the rest of me real quiet and steady, listenin' to them noises what appeared to be comin' from where I'd dropped my saddle an' saddle bags after pullin' 'em off Ole Roan.

My first idea was that some forest critter had come snoopin' round to see what it could forage from my goods. A possum or a coon was most likely. But it could be a bear, or somethin' else more dangerous. So I just laid still awhile and listened, rather than come barrelin' up out'n my blankets without no knowledge of what I'd be facin' afterwards.

I'd the notion it was a big animal, from the way it moved an' such-like. But it was bein' almighty quiet and stealthy too whilst it went to rummagin' through my supplies. That weren't exactly the custom of any bears I'd knowed; they was just clumsy critters by nature. And it weren't likely no painter neither. 'Cause most generally they favor their food warm and on the hoof.

Along with everthing else, I hadn't heard Ole Roan let out a peep sinct I first woke up. Assumin' that mustang hadn't worked hisself loose and gone galivantin' around the country, he'd of been plumb fierce an' uproarious some little while before he'd let any bear or painter get this near to him.

Which left only one other brand of animal as the likely suspect: the kind that travels on two legs instead of four.

I tightened my grip on the Smith an' Wesson, and my thumb was just startin' to ear back the hammer when I heard Ole Roan finally decide to snort and cut loose with a high-pitched whinny. By the time I'd shucked my blankets and got to my feet, alls I could see of my early morning visitor was this hulking broad-shouldered back disappearin' into the fog some thirty feet away.

"Hey!" I shouted, knowin' it wouldn't do my cause a bit of good in the world, "Come on back here and face the music like a man!"

Seemed they was somethin' familiar about that back, though I couldn't exactly put my finger on what it was. I was pretty sure it weren't nobody I'd made the acquaintance of in the past couple days.

I started after him, stockin' feet and all, and for maybe forty, fifty yards there we had us a right merry chase through them pine and palmetto flats. But then I stepped in a hole and got my toe caught underneath a palmetto root, tumblin' forward tail over teakettle and causin' myself no small amount of pain in the process.

I let my disappearin' intruder and the foggy woods around us have the benefit of ever cussword I ever knowed for the next two, three minutes, whilst I crouched on the wet grass an' nursed my throbbin' foot an' ankle. After feelin' round kind of gingerly I decided there wasn't nothing broke, but it was purely a wonder under the circumstances.

At last I crawled over to pick up my six-shooter from where I'd dropped it. Then I staggered to my feet and begun hobblin' back to where I'd left my saddle an' bedroll.

12

FINDIN' THAT PLACE AGAIN would of been a right worrisome task, what with the fog an' the trees an' all. Except Ole Roan seemed to of finally roused hisself enough to give out little encouragin' snorts an' nickers till I got back to where I'd left him. But still I wasn't feelin' none too charitable towards that mustang when I seen his ugly head loomin' up out of the mist.

"What in the blue blazes is the matter with you?" I asked, not botherin' to look him in the eye as I glanced over my outfit to find out what might be missin'. I seen my saddle and rifle was still there. But it appeared like both saddle bags had been emptied out on the grass and their contents picked clean.

"Least you could of done was give me some little hint of a warnin' whenever that low-life started pawin' through my goods," I went on, scowling as I knelt down and realized there wasn't a scrap of food left amongst the en-tire lot, "even if you was too dumb or too lazy to give notice the first time you caught scent of him. I mean, it ain't like I never left you to stand sentry before when I went to sleep in the woods."

Which were a sizable understatement, considerin' I'd hardly ever spent a night out with the roan that I didn't count on him to warn me of humans or other critters comin' close to our camp. It ain't exactly like you got to train no range-bred mustang to get spooked whenever he smells a strange smell or hears a strange noise. 'Fact, it's a sight more the other way around.

And this was the first time ever, in all the years me an' Ole Roan been traveling together, that I could recollect him fallin' down on the job. That was a powerful curious thing, and one I found more than a little troublin'. Was he startin' to get old an' weak in his senses? Or had we just spent so much time around towns an' people lately that strangers did-n't fret him the way they always done in the past?

I sat back on my heels an' looked at him then, hopin' without much reason for it to find some kind of a answer in his manner. But it was his turn to ignore me now, just to show he didn't appreciate the way I'd been talkin' and actin' towards him since I got back to camp. He'd swung around on his picket rope and went to croppin' grass, so all I could see was his backside and his twitchin' tail.

I begun gatherin' up what little was left on the ground, stowin' it back in my saddle bags and hopin' to at least come acrost a little pinch of coffee to start the day with. But I did-n't have no luck in that department. 'Bout all that big-boned scalawag had left behind was the spare cartridges Monk give me, of .44 and .45 caliber.

Now, that there was kind of interestin' when you thought about it. No man what was short on supplies and had him a gun them shells would fit was likely to pass 'em up entirely the way this feller done. Most gents with a shootin' iron wouldn't find theirselves so hard up for food in the first place, there bein' plenty on the hoof this far back in the Florida woods, even for a fair-to-middlin' pistol shot.

What's more, your average armed man who stoops to robbin' folks while they sleep ain't generally so all-fired thoughtful as to just light a shuck whenever the feller they're stealin' from comes awake and hollers at 'em.

So I figured I could guess two things about that no-count at any rate: One, he didn't have no gun, or leastways no gun that he could use. And two, he'd been one powerful hungry traveler. —Else it might of occurred to him to slip my Winchester out'n its boot first, before he went to grubbin' through my saddle bags for edibles.

I rolled my blankets and saddled the roan, not having nothin' to cook now and no other partic'lar reason to tarry here. Nor any way of guessin' when I might have to entertain more visitors what was some better heeled than this last one. Then I dug into my pockets for the little bit of cigarette makin's I'd kept about my person, and I built myself a smoke.

The fog was startin' to lift, and once I'd got myself set to travel I figured it wouldn't hurt to wait till it was high enough so I could study my surroundings a mite before movin' on. The biggest reason was to take a good look at where I was and what else was nearby, since I'd had no chance to do that when I come on this place the night before. But I'd a mind to give the ground hereabouts a quick once-over too whilst I was at it, just to see what kind of sign that thievin' feller might of left behind him.

There prob'ly wasn't much chance of locatin' him, if these swamps an' brakes was as thick everwhere as they 'peared to be from where I sat. But I figured it was worth at least another half hour of lookin' before I rode on my way. I was gettin' plumb tired of bein' stole from, even if this time it was just some food I hadn't paid for, by a man what maybe needed it worse than me.

If he'd asked, like any honest gent who was down on his luck, I'd of been pleased enough to share. But he didn't. And I wasn't.

There was something else in my mind too, as I smoked an' waited for the fog to climb higher. Leavin' aside his reasons for bein' in my camp, this here was the first and only human person I'd caught sight of since departin' the settlements. It might be that he had some knowledge of this country, includin' where Mr. Ravenant had his home place. If he could help me there, he'd be worth ever ounce of food he could tote an' then some.

By the time I finished my cigarette the mist was up to maybe shoulder high, and it was beginnin' to burn off enough so I could make out the fuzzy yellow bulls-eye of the sun amongst the trees. I took up my Winchester and begun walkin' in wider an' wider circles around my camp, treadin' careful and studyin' the ground for sign.

The earth was mostly soft clay hereabouts, covered over with several kinds of patchy grass. Since my visitor was a good-sized feller the same as me, his feet left right deep impressions here an' there, like my own did after I went to chasin' him.

It appeared he'd come up on me from the north, stoppin' a dozen yards away to look over the set-up. Might be he stumbled onto the place by accident, or maybe he'd got some idea where we was from the little sounds the roan made whilst I was asleep. There surely weren't no way he could of knowed about our camp from a distance, what with the fog an' the dark an' all.

After squattin' on his heels amongst the palmettos for a time, he up an' made a bee-line for Ole Roan, walkin' real slow an' careful on his tip-toes. That was to calm and quiet the mustang of course, though it was a wonder to me he was able to do it. I'd managèd it myself now an' again with other horses. It was a skill I'd cultivated since boyhood. But there wasn't many besides Injuns who had the knack, and even if this feller was a Injun — which he weren't from the glimpse I'd had of him — I'd still been surprised in this partic'lar instance. Because Ole Roan just ain't hardly ever cottoned to nobody but me.

After my intruder'd started busyin' hisself with my supplies and I'd jumped up to scare him, both our sets of tracks headed off to the east. I followed 'em to the place where I tripped, and managed to keep up with his trail for another twenty, thirty yards beyond. But then he come up on some higher, sandier ground with thick tussocks of bunch grass where he could step to hide his footprints, and that's where I lost him.

I reckon I might of trailed him further if I'd started sooner, before the grass had a chance to begin straightening itself up after his passin'. But it's like the feller says: If ifs an' buts was candy an' nuts, then we'd all have a merry Christmas.

I learned one thing anyhow, which I hadn't knowed before I begun to seek out his sign: This gent out here in the swamp all by his lonesome wasn't just short on food. He didn't have no shoes to cover his feet with neither.

Well, prob'ly not anyways. He might of took 'em off to help with his sneakin', but I was inclined to doubt it. It ain't altogether smart nor comfortable to go shoeless in the backwoods of Florida, what with saw palmetto an' stinging nettle an' sandspurs an' poison ivy, and a dozen other nasty things a feller could step in — most of which I seen growin' within a stone's throw of my camp. Not to mention snakes. Or palmetto roots, what I'd had me some first-hand experience with.

Some done it of course, though not always by choice. And most who did growed up goin' barefoot from the time they was infants. I'd got to see one or two clear prints where this feller put a foot down on soft earth, and his toes wasn't near splayed out the way folks' is when they spend their entire lives without shoes.

An' besides that . . .

I went back and knelt down to take a closer look at them couple of footprints I remembered. Sure enough, there was traces of fresh-clotted blood amongst the sand an' damp grass. Which made it pretty certain this feller had been used to wearin' shoes or boots, but he'd been doin' without 'em so long now that his feet was in a world of hurt.

I planned to keep him in mind from here on out, and to check my surroundings time to time for him or his sign. But the little bit of food he'd took from me didn't earn him near the attention I figured I still owed Lila and her *compadres*. The fog was almost lifted now, and it was high time I did some serious scoutin' for either them or that Ravenant place.

I walked back to Ole Roan and shoved my Winchester in its boot. Then I stepped up into the leather and made a long careful study in every direction.

To the west was that low, wet prairie I'd been makin' my way acrost the night before. To the south was more of the same. North an' east of us was dense hammock, all growed up thick with cypress an' bay an' water oak, plus a few pines and low-lyin' stands of palmetto scattered about the edges where the sun was able to reach 'em.

No place in all that broad country was there any sign of a cow pen or a cabin or a cultivated field. Nor anything else that might offer a clue to human presence.

The trees to the north appeared like they started thinnin' out after a little bit, and I could see the tops of more pines in the distance. That suggested a little higher rise of ground over yonder, and the travelin' might be a tad easier there than eastward. Since I'd a clear view west an' south for two miles or better from where I was sittin', and since nothin' much thataway encouraged a second look, I decided I might's well head north for starters, and see what I could see.

One direction was 'bout as good as another until I cut some sign of riders or found some tiny trace of civilization.

Sure enough, after a little less than a mile that hammock opened up to prairie again, with a handful of pines an' palm trees scattered here an' there until it finally run into what appeared to be solid woods another couple miles distant. We forded the little winding creek we was following, and I pointed the roan towards a place at the far tree-line where the ground sloped up a few feet and I figured to be able to look out over a fair piece of country.

I was keepin' one eye on the ground as I rode, watchin' for the tracks of horses or anything else what might of left its mark in the soft earth hereabouts. Maybe even that barefoot feller who'd snuck into my camp this morning. It was only pure-dee luck that I happened to glance up to get my bearings about the time a pair of riders crossed this little open place in the woods an' disappeared back amongst the trees a minute later.

They was travelin' east with their backs toward me, so I was pretty near certain they hadn't noticed I was there. But I was a mind to keep it that way for the time bein'. So I swung Ole Roan's head north and lifted him into a lope, gettin' us off that prairie and into the forest on t'other side in a couple shakes of a hound dog's tail.

Soon as we was no longer out in the open I slowed to a walk and started east, guidin' the roan toward the place where I'd seen them gents at a easy pace which wasn't intended to catch up to 'em so much as just trail 'em along. I'd a notion to try and learn who they was and what they was doin' here before I give 'em any call to guess they wasn't the only ones in the neighborhood.

I'd shucked my Winchester when I first laid eyes on 'em. Now I rode light in the saddle and watchful as a cat, with my toes restin' in the stirrups and my rifle across my saddle bow.

I hadn't got any real definite ideas about who these riders was. But there weren't nobody in this swamp that was any friend to me. They might be Ravenant's men, or a posse of townsfolk, or them two gunmen who was seekin' my hide. Or maybe just some hunters or men on the dodge who'd as soon be left alone. Could be they'd something to do with all them travelers that kept turnin' up missing in this neck of the woods, or could be they didn't know the first thing about it.

Me, I didn't plan on taking any chances.

After maybe fifteen, twenty minutes of cautious ridin',

I come to this clearing at the edge of the trees not far from where I'd sighted the men. I pulled up in the shadows of some pines an' scrub oaks on the near side, meanin' to study the country from Ole Roan's back for a bit before deciding whether to cross that patch of open ground or Injun around it through the woods.

There was flat, empty prairie everwhere I looked to the south, stretchin' out in a big half circle without no trees to speak of for maybe two, three miles. I couldn't see nothing a-tall movin' out yonder except a couple sandhill cranes skimmin' low in the distance. And apart from the soft rustling of leaves an' branches over my head whenever a hint of a breeze come up out of the west, that whole wide wilderness seemed uncommon quiet.

I let my eyes roam from right to left over them flatlands. Then I brung 'em back along the tree-line in front of me from far to near, still without seein' anything of partic'lar interest. For all I could tell from where me an' the roan was watchin', them riders I'd spotted might of never even existed. Finally I begun to pay more close attention to the edges of the clearing before us.

And that's when I seen the surrey.

All that shiny black enamel and leather weren't hard to pick out amongst the dull greens an' browns of the forest around 'em. But I hadn't been looking for nothin' in that direction until now, countin' on my ears instead of my eyes to tell me if there was anything close by what needed to concern me.

The rig was pulled back in between two low-growin' scrub oaks, with branches pushin' against the fringed top and a couple smaller ones reachin' inside acrost the leather seats. 'Peared to me somebody'd made a kind of a halfway stab at hidin' her there, prob'ly without expecting there'd be much chance any strangers would ever come lookin'. I couldn't see no sign of the red-ribboned gray what had been pullin' her, nor of the man and woman who'd been ridin' in her neither.

And believe me, I spent some long careful minutes studyin' that place, with my Winchester held level and my finger on the trigger.

It all seemed to be deserted now, and we appeared to be alone. After a bit I climbed down from the leather and took the reins in my left hand, leadin' Ole Roan around through the trees outside the clearing until we was maybe a dozen feet from where that rig was hidden.

I seen some flies hoverin' over the front seat as we come near, but I didn't pay it much mind. Then when I begun to step closer so's I could do some better investigatin', my mustang rolled his eyes an' snorted, shying away so fierce that I had to back him off a little distance and loop his reins around a tree branch instead. When I'd walked back to take a look inside the surrey, it weren't hard to see what it was had got him upset.

There was a pool of blood on the floor on the driver's side, over a foot around and still fresh enough so I figured it couldn't of been more than a couple hours old. And in the midst of that blood was two pale objects that I had to look twice at to be certain what they was.

I got a kind of a sick feelin' in the pit of my stomach when I finally recognized 'em. They was two human fingers, lopped off clean below the second joint like by somebody with a surgeon's scalpel or a mighty sharp knife.

And the smaller of them two fingers appeared to be a woman's!

I had to turn my head away for a minute there. And it

was all I could do to keep from losin' what little food I'd et the past couple days on that very spot.

It wasn't the blood on the wagon floor. I seen a heap more blood than that in my life, and a fair amount of it's been mine. I'd seen my share of severed arms an' legs an' what-have-you too, back durin' the war. It ain't ever no pleasant sight. But at least you could tell yourself it was needful then, to keep wounded men from bein' et up with the gangrene and to save their lives.

But this here . . . This weren't no medical necessity. To all appearances it was just plain an' deliberate mutilation. And to do it to a woman! Well, that's what made the bile rise up in my throat.

It made me grow a little hard an' cold around the eyes, too. I'd of give a pretty for five minutes — or five hours — with whoever it was that done it. 'T'would of pleased me considerable to show him two, three things I learned from the Apaches back yonder in Arizona.

After a minute I glanced back inside the surrey, just to be sure there weren't no doubt about what I'd seen. Then I walked all around it real slow, takin' in everthing about the rig and its surroundings before kneelin' by a scrub oak at the edge of the clearing to study the ground.

13

I COULD MAKE OUT THE WAGON TRACKS easy enough. Out there in the open where the earth was kind of soft an' damp, you could see 'em comin' along from the west for a good little ways. And there wasn't no other tracks with 'em when they turned off the prairie here.

It appeared like the driver pulled into the clearing and nosed his gelding up close to this scrub oak where I was kneelin', so's to tie up and give hisself and his companion a little bit of a break. They must of been travelin' along right steady based on what I seen of their tracks. Prob'ly since first light if not before, even with the fog an' everthing.

As I shifted my gaze to what was closer by, I could make out a couple sets of footprints in the loose sand next to the wheel marks, one set smaller than the other. And then I spotted the stub of a cigar on the grass a dozen feet away. Along with the signs of grazing and nibblin' made by the gelding as it was standin' hitched, that pretty much confirmed my suspicion them folks with the surrey had tarried here for a time, maybe as long as three quarters of a hour.

I took another cautious look over my shoulder towards them open flatlands an' the distant trees beyond, still without seein' no trace of the riders I'd noticed earlier. Then I got up and walked a little ways out into the clearing. It was sandy soil hereabouts with grass growin' over most of it, so readin' sign wasn't noway a definite science. But with what-all was in view from where I stood, the rest of the story weren't hard to puzzle out.

A bunch of horses an' riders had appeared from them thick woods to the north, and I expect they took that tenderfoot couple by total surprise. Prob'ly had the drop on 'em the instant they showed theirselves. Though from what I recalled of that Yankee and his ladyfriend, I didn't figure they'd of been able to offer much in the way of resistance in any case.

Some of the riders climbed down from their horses while the rest stayed mounted, and it seemed like they took them two prisoner without hardly a struggle. Afterwards they brung 'em both up to the footboard of the surrey, where somebody done the deed of loppin' off fingers.

There was blood on the ground where it happened, and more drops near that scrub oak where the gelding was hitched. After the surrey had been cut loose and pushed into the brush, the horse tracks led off through the woods to eastward, travelin' single file with the gelding amongst 'em. I figured the man or the woman or both had been ridin' it, since nobody was walkin' when they all left out.

What with the grass and that loose sand not holdin' the shape of a track, I couldn't be real sure about the number of riders, nor much else besides. I guessed they was four or five at least, and prob'ly not more'n six or eight on the upper end, judgin' from how much and how little the ground was tore up. Lookin' over their trail to eastward, it seemed like they'd a mind to keep on skirtin' the edge of this prairie, while stayin' mostly out of sight back in amongst the trees.

I'd a notion them men I'd spotted awhile back might be part of the bunch involved here, though I hadn't seen but a couple of 'em in that half minute's glance I'd got. They was headed the same direction anyhow, and ridin' single file to boot.

I reckoned I could follow behind 'em pretty easy, if I decided that's what I wanted to do. But it wouldn't hurt to spend a little more time investigatin' before I reached any definite conclusions. Much as I'd the urge to have words with any men who took to cuttin' off ladies' fingers for their morning's entertainment, they was still only one of me and a whole bunch of them. I'd prob'ly ought to consider on it a mite before I rode up to 'em just a-pawin' and a-snortin'.

I took me another slow and careful glance all around. Then I loosed the thong on my six-shooter and levered a cartridge into the chamber of my Winchester, before crossin' the clearing to where I'd seen the tracks of them riders come out from the woods.

They'd been in a sort of a line abreast there, with each horse makin' its own set of tracks. So while I was able to trail a couple of 'em back into the trees for maybe a dozen yards or so, it got almighty hard after that to sort out the hoofprints and trace 'em further in amongst the thick brush that was everwhere about. It weren't till I'd spent maybe twenty minutes scoutin' in wider an' wider half-circles outside the clearing, that I finally come across the route them men had took gettin' to this place. And without the sign left by their hors-

es I'd prob'ly of missed it even then. It was this narrow overgrowed path under several inches of standin' water, what led
northwest an' north back into the deep swamp.

When I'd marked it in my mind, I walked back to where
Ole Roan was keepin' hisself occupied pullin' Spanish moss
out'n the trees. And then I paused to do a mite of calculatin'.

Seemed like they was two different routes I could follow
at the moment, assumin' I chose to follow either one of 'em.
The first was trailin' behind them riders toward wherever it
was they was goin', and the second was back into the swamp
towards where they'd been.

I could be reasonable sure both led somewhere, and that
was somewhere more'n I was liable to get to if I kept wanderin' through this wilderness without no direction a-tall.
One or t'other might even take me to Ravenant or somebody
who knowed him. And I'd still in mind to locate his home
place if I could manage to do it. So the real question was,
which trail to take?

I'd glanced up at the sun while I was thinkin', mostly
out of habit. A man ridin' wild country gets accustomed to
doin' that. It's a way of tellin' the time as well as keepin' his
directions straight whilst he's about it. Not too different from
a railroad conductor who pulls out his watch ever now an'
again to have a peek at it.

When it struck me that it was still a couple hours shy of
noon, I knew right away which route made the most sense to
travel.

The place them riders was headin' for might be close by,
or it might not. They'd still got the better part of a day to finish their trip. But wherever it was they was comin' from
couldn't be no more'n a hour or two distant. Not unless them

boys was bigger fools than me to go galivantin' through that deep ole swamp in the fog an' the dark.

I reckoned it'd save considerable wear and tear on the Roan an' me if we was to have a look at that closer spot first. Maybe we'd find nothin' but a cold campfire in some clearing in the woods. But maybe it'd turn out to be somethin' more substantial, like that rancho where Mr. Ravenant an' Lila lived. And if that was the case, they'd ought to be a sight fewer folks there to offer us trouble than at most other times.

I gathered the roan's reins and mounted, turning his head to the northwest and walkin' him back into the swamp away from the clearing. We followed that narrow sandy trail for what must of been two miles or so, with it gettin' lower an' darker an' boggier almost ever step of the way.

Finally we come in amongst this tall stand of cypress an' swamp bay, with a slow-movin' black stream beyond it, windin' in and out snake-like amongst the trees. I guessed it was prob'ly the upper Withlacoochee River, from what I'd been able to learn of the country till now.

The trail I was followin' seemed to turn and head upstream twenty, thirty yards this side the water. And the reason for it was clear enough. Right there at the bank the cypress knees was so thick nobody on horseback could get up close without fear of riskin' his mount. But the river curved back on itself there, and they was this little spit of ground what a man might reach on foot and maybe have a fair view in several directions. I hauled back on the reins and studied the situation. Then I begun to dismount.

Whilst I was swingin' out of the saddle a sudden movement caught my eye. I seen this fat ole water moccasin easin' into the river from one of them cypress knees a few yards in front of me, which didn't hardly give me no comfortable feelin' about this place a-tall.

But he was goin' the other way and mindin' his own business, so I figured I might's well return the favor. I weren't partic'lar anxious to risk a shot just then in any case, not knowin' who else or what else might be in the vicinity with us.

After loopin' the reins around some low growin' branches I took my Winchester and made my way to the river, steppin' mighty careful and keepin' my eyes peeled above an' below for any more sign of that moccasin or his cousins. Seems like them critters is partial to cypress for some reason, though they ain't no slouch at climbin' most any kind of a tree when they set their minds upon it. I seen a-plenty of 'em hangin' from branches over the water as a boy. And if a feller don't look sharp where he poles his boat, they can be purely a caution.

I managed to work my way out onto that spit of land at last, where I could take a good long look both up and down the river. Downstream there wasn't nothin' to see but more river, with trees growin' solid along both banks and stretchin' their limbs out acrost it till they touched in the middle.

When I turned my head upstream it 'peared to be pretty much the same. But then as I got to studyin' them dark waters where they curved an' twisted back in amongst the shadows of the forest, I noticed what might of been a couple old rotted pilings barely pokin' their tops up from the river some hundred yards away. The more I stared at 'em, the more certain I was that they'd been part of some long-ago boat dock. And where a dock had been, there was likely a house or a cabin not too far off.

From the age an' condition of them pilings, the place was prob'ly long since abandoned. The Florida wilderness bein' what it is, t'wouldn't surprise me if there weren't even a stick left of any building what once stood by. Bugs an' worms an' wet rot would of seen to that, even if there hadn't been no fire. And fires was a common enough occurrence, from accidents as well as wars an' Injun troubles.

Still, it wouldn't do to take no foolish chances here in a country where I'd plenty of evidence they was more dangerous critters than water moccasins. The way that trail I'd been followin' appeared to turn upstream behind me, it prob'-ly led right past where that ole home place was. And I had-n't no ideas a-tall of ridin' up on it fat, dumb and sassy, without givin' consideration to keepin' my hair an' hide whole.

When I'd made it back to where Ole Roan was waitin', I spent a couple long minutes listenin' to the quiet woods all around us. Then I took holt of the reins and started followin' that forest path upstream, walkin' slow and careful with the roan trailin' behind.

It was dark and cool in amongst them big old cypress an' bay trees, with water oaks and swamp elm addin' their leaves to the dense thatch overhead. Grape an' buckthorn vines thick as a man's arm twisted down from the branches, sweepin' the ground and then startin' back up again to take hold on another limb. Long gray beards of Spanish moss hung over everthing. And underneath was thickets of possumhaw and devil's walkin' stick, what made a feller kind of cautious about accidentally steppin' too far off the path.

Sure enough, before long we come up on this kind of a open place all covered over with dead leaves between us an' the river. And right smack in the middle of it was a ramshackle old cabin, set up on cypress pilings maybe three, four feet above the ground. I halted the roan back amongst the trees and put a hand on his neck to caution him about keepin' his peace. Then I dropped down on my knees and inched up behind the thick leaves of a titi bush to have a better look.

That cabin was in mighty poor shape. They was boards missin' from the steps and the porch. One corner of the overhangin' roof was sagging precarious-like where a column had rotted through and just finally fell to the ground. And if they'd ever been anything like clay or moss pluggin' up the chinks between the log walls, it had worked itself loose a long time since, leavin' the inside open to the swamp air and all manner of varmints and flyin' critters. At first glance almost anybody what laid eyes on the place would of swore it was abandoned, and had been since Methuselah was a pup.

But as I squatted there lookin' at it, I begun to notice a faint smell of wood smoke, like from a fire what had been put out a short while before. When I'd took a couple more sniffs I was pretty sure I could make out other smells of human livin': bacon grease and the stale scent of old linens an' unwashed bodies, somethin' odd an' tangy what was a little like turpentine but I decided was prob'ly roots an' herbs somebody'd used in cookin'. . . .

There wasn't nothin' magical about me noticin' all them smells onct I'd got my thoughts set upon it, even though I was still a good forty, fifty feet away from the cabin. Human quarters got a real distinctive aroma about 'em after they been lived in awhile, and it ain't like nothin' else a body's liable to come acrost in the wilderness. I've heard that back durin' the Seminole wars the Indians was able to sniff out a white man's settlement from miles away whenever the wind was right.

So it appeared this old cabin here by the river weren't near so vacant an' lonely as seemed on the face of it, and I'd got the evidence of my nose to prove it.

'Course my first thought was of them riders I'd been backtrailin'. I reckoned this would be a likely enough place to make camp of a night, what with the ready-made shelter and plenty of room for the horses. Might be they used it fairly regular, whenever they happened to be travelin' this direction.

But somehow I wasn't convinced. A now an' again line cabin for a bunch of men didn't exactly seem to match up with the kind of smells I'd been smellin'. I couldn't explain it no clearer than that, but I knew it was so.

When you got right down to it, there was somethin' about this entire set-up I didn't much favor. Some kind of a feelin' what come over me as I knelt there in the shadows and studied that fallin' down cabin with the gloomy bald cypresses borderin' the dark river beyond; and the vines an' Spanish moss hangin' like shrouds everwhere about.

It surely weren't no place I'd choose to spend the night if I was able to avoid it. And though I couldn't say why, I'd a idea there wasn't many others would be anxious to spread their blankets in this partic'lar spot neither.

I still hadn't seen no actual signs of life, apart from what my nose was tellin' me. No kind of movement, nor smoke from the fallin'-down clay an' wattle chimney. Nor nothin' else that spoke of human doin's. And yet the longer I knelt there an' watched, the more uneasy I felt.

When I glanced back at Ole Roan it 'peared he was

havin' some of the same thoughts about this place that I was. His head and ears was up and his eyes was big. And his nostrils flared out like they'd caught wind of somethin' he didn't care for even a little bit.

"Hey, you out yonder in the bushes!"

I near-'bout jumped out of my skin when I heard that voice. It weren't my surprise at hearin' it so much as the way it echoed through them dark, gloomy woodlands — soundin' like something between the creakin' of a ole rusty gate and the cacklin' caw of a settin' hen.

"You goin' to squat out there by your lonesome the live-long day? Or do you mean to come a-callin' proper-like on a poor solitary ole woman?"

She laughed then. And I swear that screechin' bark of a laugh made all the hairs on the back of my neck stand straight up on end.

When I looked towards the cabin I could see this skinny figure standin' up on that rickety old porch, with her fists on her hips and her eyes squinted up, a-peerin' right square at the titi bush where I'd thought myself hidden.

"Well," she said, maybe lowerin' her high-pitched voice just a trifle, "what's it goin' to be? If you want to be neighborly and have a proper visit, then come up here to the porch an' set. If you're the mind to keep on skulkin' through them bushes like some kind of a wild Injun, go on and take the wide way around an' leave me be."

With that she plopped herself down on the steps and begun to fill up a homemade corncob pipe with leaf tobacco what she crumbled between bony fingers, still watchin' me time to time out of the corner of her eye.

When she'd lit the pipe an' puffed it to life, and I still

hadn't moved, she went to scratchin' at some real or imagined itch whilst observin' mildly, "I don't hardly bite a-tall son. —Ain't had no teeth to do it with this past twenty year!"

She begun to giggle right hearty at her little bit of humor, makin' this high-pitched wheezin' caw what like to give me the gallopin' fantods all over again. "Besides," she finished up after she'd got her breath back, "you can see I ain't totin' no wee-pons with me."

Well, that part was true anyhow. I didn't figure she could of managed to hide no shootin' iron about her person even if she'd wanted to. Her faded old dress appeared to of been made out of feed sacks, without no pockets and a deal too short to boot. It come to just below her knees as she was settin' there, showin' off a pair of spindly blue-veined legs with big men's brogans on both feet.

There weren't no reason in the world for me to be scared of a skinny old woman like this, and I reckon I knowed it from the start. But with the eerie feelin' in that clearing and all, it took another couple, three seconds to get done convincin' myself.

At last I shrugged and stood up from the ground. When I'd led Ole Roan a little closer and fastened his reins to a low-growin' bush, I begun to approach the cabin.

I stopped a dozen feet away with my Winchester still under my arm, and reached up to touch my hat by way of a greeting. The old woman nodded, and for several minutes we studied each other without neither of us sayin' anything.

14 ⚡

Now, it ain't no part of my nature to ever talk disrespectful of womenfolks. But I got to tell you that this here was the ugliest specimen of human female I've had the occasion to look upon in many a year.

Her leathery old head appeared to be a couple sizes too big for her scrawny body, with this droopin' hawk's-beak nose in the middle of it what was a size too large for that. She'd got one brown hairy mole on the tip of her nose, and a couple more on her pointy chin to keep 'em company, with enough wrinkles an' furrows all round and underneath them two watery red eyes to make a fair-sized plantation. Near as I could tell, her mop of stringy white hair hadn't knowed the acquaintance of soap or a comb sinct it first clouded up over Noah.

There weren't no tellin' what she thought of me. Her face didn't reveal nothin' by way of a expression. And I kept my opinions to myself too. Finally she took a draw on her pipe and spoke again:

"You ain't from around here." It sounded more like a

statement of fact than a question, but the swamp woman seemed to be waitin' for some kind of answer. So I pushed my hat back from my forehead an' met her eyes.

"Nope," I agreed.

"You ain't the type."

I kept on watchin' her, curious-like. "What kind of type is that?"

"Oh, types an' types." The old woman took a deep draw on her corncob, lettin' the smoke out slow between toothless gums. "I seen a heap of types this past sixty year. Shy types. Dry types. Spy types. Snipin' types. . . ." She paused, not exactly lookin' in my direction, but more beyond me and over my shoulder. ". . . Viper types. . . ." Then she begun to giggle, softly to herself and for no good reason in the world that I could imagine.

I let her get it out of her system, though her gigglin' like to give me the goose-bumps and the ice-cold sweats all the way from the soles of my boots to the crown of my head. It was pretty clear this ole woman weren't exactly right in her mind. And I was beginnin' to wish I'd never come close enough to strike up a conversation.

"Affrighted types," she went on after a minute. Her giggle stopped as sudden as it started. "'Specially lately. I seen hard men an' soft, men from the cities an' men from the country, some of 'em kindly and others meaner than a stepped-on snake." She paused with her head cocked to one side, studyin' me thoughtful-like.

"But all of 'em scared." Her voice got quieter than it was before. "Anybody could see it around their eyes. And with good, honest reason for it too!"

"And I ain't?" I was wonderin' to myself what she meant by that last remark.

"Scared? Not so's a body could tell." She pulled her pipe out of her mouth long enough to spit on the ground. "Which means you're either too hopeless stupid to be scared, and that I got a notion to doubt. Or you're some kind of a newcomer to these parts who just ain't got him enough learnin' yet to be scared."

"Learnin' about what?" It was a serious question. Assumin' she was right and I weren't too stupid to scare — which a few here an' there might argue — I'd already got me a pretty fair list of dangerous folks I at least figured to be cautious of in this country. Was there somethin' or somebody else?

The swamp woman didn't answer right away, actin' for a minute like maybe she hadn't heard me. She squinted up her eyes and glanced all around that gloomy clearing and the dark trees beyond, before finally bringin' her gaze back to me.

"I don't expect you'd believe me, even if I told you. Man like you ain't the kind to learn nothin' the easy way. You'll have to be showed." She shook her head and paused to take another draw on her pipe. "But after you been showed, it'll be too late. *He'll* of come an' put his mark upon you. Then your soul won't no longer be your own!"

"He?" I was watchin' the old woman's eyes right close now, though I still couldn't guess much about what was behind 'em. For another minute she sat there and seemed to consider. Then she set her pipe aside and looked skyward, beginnin' to rock herself slowly back an' forth whilst she was at it.

I ain't too certain what it was I'd been expectin' to hear next. But it surely weren't nothing like the words that finally come out from her lips after she'd busied herself with rockin' for another ten, fifteen seconds:

"The adopted son of Satan incarnate!" she screeched, liftin' up her arms and beginnin' to make what appeared to be a series of mystical passes and gestures in front of her face. "Him what can't die, and can't be killed, and ain't rightly livin' neither the same as you an' me!" She bent forward to spit on the ground again, then rubbed it in with the toe of a boot.

"Him and his ill-got handmaiden rule over this swamp with their legion of destroyin' angels, and there ain't no hope nor escape for any of us as fall into their hands! They will bind our souls to them forever!"

She kept on making them gestures an' passes, and for the first time it struck me that this here swamp woman was missin' the ring finger off'n her left hand — cut clean away above the first knuckle! When I recalled them other two severed fingers in the surrey, my entire body all of a sudden got cold as ice. Like some freezin' wind out'n the North Pole had just blowed acrost this hot Florida swamp.

The old crone kept up with her gesturin' for a bit. And then her arms folded about her body and her voice dropped nearly to a whisper as she stopped her rockin' and finished up with, "The final days are upon us. King Lucifer's army is on the march!"

Me, I couldn't hardly do nothin' but stare at her. I ain't never been no church-goin' man, though Ma did give it a try for a time when my brother Luke an' me was boys. I reckon I sat through enough of them Bible-thumpin' sermons about hellfire and the end of the world to at least have some notion what this woman was talkin' about.

But I couldn't persuade myself to put no stock in it. Not

here an' now, not in Florida in the U. S. of A. in the year eighteen hundred and seventy-seven. It just didn't make no kind of sense a-tall to my way of thinkin'.

If I was wrong, I guess it wouldn't be the first or the only mistake I'd have to answer to my Maker for when the time come for settlin' accounts. I figured He'd prob'ly be inclined to overlook a little one like this, in favor of some of the more colorful an' conspicuous affairs I been involved in.

It was clear enough that this old woman believed it, though. She was settin' on the porch steps with her eyes closed now, huggin' herself and rockin' gently side to side whilst I pondered her words. I'd a pretty good idea who she'd been referrin' to, of course. And if Ravenant was even half of what he appeared to have got these local folks believin', he must be one hell of a feller. Not that I figured it was exactly the same as bein' a feller from Hell like I'd just been told.

As for Lila, well she surely weren't no angel. But I'd had enough personal contact to testify that she wasn't no spirit neither. Ever bit of that gal was flesh an' blood, from her toes on up to her eyelashes. And right womanly flesh into the bargain.

I took in a deep breath and decided I might's well try one or two more questions, just to see what I could learn about Ravenant and his doin's whilst I had somebody to ask. Doubtful as this here source 'peared to be, I might still find out somethin' useful regardin' any earthly dangers I'd be facin'. And those what could fetch me a bullet in the gut and leave my soul a-wanderin' free was the ones that concerned me most at the moment.

When I'd stepped up closer to the cabin and hunkered down by the porch, where the old woman was still swayin' back and forth with her eyes shut, I cleared my throat and begun: "Ma'am," I said, in what I hoped was a respectful-soundin' voice, "I 'preciate all that you've done told me, though it don't sound too hopeful for either one of us if I've understood you aright. . . ."

I hesitated then, not able to tell if she was listenin' or not. Finally I made up my mind to just go on talkin' and see what happened.

"I reckon I'm still havin' a mite of trouble gettin' ever-thing straight in my thoughts, though. Like this son of Satan you mentioned. Has he got a name? Somethin' mortal folks call him by?"

Even though I suspicioned I knew who it was she'd been speakin' of, I'd a mind to make certain. Just in case there was some other crew of bad men in this wilderness I hadn't yet heard about.

My companion let out with this low-voiced keenin' noise. Then she lifted up a hand in a sign what I seen other swamp folks use to ward off the Evil Eye.

"Ravenant!" she whispered. "The un-dead, the devil's spawn! —And the name of his witch-woman consort is Lila!"

"Yes, ma'am," I answered. After a second I went on mildly, "And you say they got this gang of destroyin' angels workin' for 'em?" Soon as I'd said it I knowed that prob'ly weren't the best way to describe what she imagined was the devil's hosts. But it was how I looked at the situation, and my new acquaintance didn't seem to notice.

"Infernal riders!" she moaned, claspin' both arms about herself again and rockin' more violent than before. "Accursed, cruel, Hell-born fiends of darkness, what seek an' scourge this whole country over!" Her voice was liftin' into a kind of a sing-songy chant now.

"They rise up from the mists to seize the body and enslave the soul! Native an' stranger, wary and unwary, saintly an' sinful. It don't matter a whit! Take holt of each and bind 'em to eternal slavery. Slaves to work the devil's will!"

For a minute there again, I was at a teetotal loss for words. It wasn't like I didn't understand what she was tellin' me. That was plain as the nose on your face. Only I couldn't seem to get it to fit in with anything I knowed or believed of this world, or this swamp, or Ravenant an' them around him — assumin' they was the flesh an' blood humans I hadn't many doubts they was.

"If all that's so," I said finally, thinkin' it through as I spoke, "then how come you're still livin' here in this cabin by your lonesome, and doin' like you please? I mean, if everbody in the entire territory's got their souls took from 'em an' been turned into slaves, then why ain't it happened to you?"

I thought it was a pretty good question. Maybe one that could even bring this old woman back to the real world a little bit so she could see the foolishness of what she'd been sayin'. It 'peared like she felt the need to ponder on it anyhow. She stopped her rockin' and sat there for what seemed to me a right smart spell before openin' her mouth at last to speak.

But when she did open it, nothin' that come out of it made a bit more sense than anything I'd heard so far this mornin'.

"It serves *his* purpose to let me be for now, just as it serves mine to stay on here and abide. I ain't lived no sixty-odd years in this swamp without gainin' some knowledge of the dark arts my ownself. Of charms an' spells an' such-like. Reckon I mightn't be so easy and willin' a slave as all them others. . . ."

162

She kept her eyes closed and raised up her left hand — the one with the missin' finger — to hold it before her face. ". . . But you can see that he's put his mark upon me. When he calls, I got to come. And there ain't nothin' on this earth will keep me from it." She shrugged her bony shoulders.

"Till he does, I imagine I'm right exactly where he wants me to be. And that suits me fine as well!"

I sighed an' nodded my head, though I knowed she couldn't see me do it. "All right, Ma'am. Whatever you say."

Seemed like I wasn't about to get no kind of sense or useful information out of this old woman, no matter how hard I tried. I took a breath and stood up. Then when I was right on the verge of sayin' my good-byes and turnin' to leave, I recalled what it was had brought me here to this clearing in the first place. I decided it wouldn't cost nothin' to make one last stab at a question, something real specific an' particular I wanted to know.

"I was backtrailin' a half-dozen or so riders when I come here," I said. "'Pears like they must of all passed by this cabin not long after daybreak." The swamp woman turned her head towards me and opened her eyes. "You reckon you could give me some kind of a idea where they might of left out from? Or what lies further on down this here . . ."

I seen her chin lift up, and her expression changed from mild to fearful so quick that it almost made me take a step backwards. It was obvious she weren't no longer payin' the slightest attention to me.

"Too late!" she cried, "Too late!" Then she jumped up on her feet and throwed her arms in front of her face. "Too late! —The devil and his spawn are here!"

Me, I stood still like I was frozen to the spot. The flesh between my shoulder blades had got real itchy and crawlin' all of a sudden, and it was a feelin' I recognized from past experience. They was somebody standin' behind me. Somebody with a gun more'n likely. Pointed at my back and all set to blow me to Kingdom Come.

"Well, Naomi." The voice was silky smooth and low-pitched, like the rumblin' of a storm way off in the distance. "What it is that we have here now?"

For a minute I thought that ole woman up on the steps was goin' to be struck out-an'-out dumb with fright. She tried workin' her mouth but couldn't get no words to come. Then she swallowed a couple times, cleared her throat, an' tried again. Finally she managed this kind of a croakin' whisper what was so quiet I almost couldn't hear it my ownself, standin' just five or six feet away from her.

"Strang—, stranger in these parts," she said, wringin' her hands and lowerin' her eyes so's not to look at whoever it was behind me. "Come a-skulkin' up the trail from the south-west maybe half a hour ago." She paused, then took a step backwards up onto the porch, and turned her face away. "I ain't ever seed him before."

Me, I was mighty curious to have a peek at this man who'd give her the shiverin' dreads so bad, though I reckon I'd already guessed his name was Ravenant. Trouble of it was, I needed to be mighty careful right then so's not to make no sudden moves what might be misunderstood by any feller who'd got him a shootin' iron and a nervous trigger finger to go with it.

I figured the safest thing was just to ask.

"You mind if I turn around and introduce myself prop-er?" I said. "I ain't too comfortable socializin' with any folks I can't look at eyeball to eyeball."

The man with the deep voice chuckled a little under his breath. Then he said, "By all means. Just take care that you do your turning very slow and very easy. And don't be lifting up the muzzle of that rifle, not even a tiny bit. I can't help noticing that you are quite heavily armed for a casual traveler. As we are ourselves. A man can't be too careful this far from the settlements."

Well, if I'd any earlier doubts about whether Ravenant an' his people would turn out to be haints or humans, I hadn't no longer. Call it reckless speculation on my part, but I couldn't imagine no reason a-tall why spirits from Hell would be totin' guns along with 'em for protection. Not when they could of chose lightin' bolts or somethin' else a mite more spectacular to do their fightin' with.

When I'd turned around, makin' certain I followed Ravenant's directions to a tee, I seen that they was a half dozen men standin' in that clearing in a semicircle about me. All but one of 'em had a gun pointed in my direction. Most was pistols. But there was one Henry rifle, and one shotgun what I recognized just soon as I set eyes on its owner.

I nodded and grinned at Purv, before turnin' my attention to the man who wasn't holding no iron.

There wasn't any doubt in my mind this was Ravenant hisself. He was a tall, solid-built gent, who managed to appear even taller because of the prideful, commandin' way he had of carryin' hisself. It was easy enough to see that he'd the notion he was the ole bull of the woods hereabouts. And he didn't expect any others in the herd to have no questions about it.

He was dressed in black from crown to toe, with this narrow flat-brimmed hat and shiny Boston riding boots what come almost to his knees. On his chin he sported this little black patch of a beard, with the sides and his upper lip shaved off clean. He was wearin' what appeared to be two old Army Colts in holsters underneath his coat. And the fact he hadn't drawed one or both of 'em was his way of sayin' he didn't see no need to dirty his hands personal with the likes of me.

He was talkin' again. And he'd got a way of doin' that too, what made a feller tend to sit up an' pay attention.

"I don't know what Naomi here has told you," the man in black said, "but we don't see very many visitors in our part of the country, Mr. . . . ." His eyes squinted up and he stared at me, so's I wouldn't have no doubt that he meant to have a answer before he went any further.

"Barkley," I said mildly. "Tate Barkley's the name. I'm right pleased to make your acquaintance too, Mr. . . . ." I met his look straight on and waited for him to answer me.

That seemed to take him back a little bit, 'cause he glanced over at his companions before returnin' his eyes to me with a mite more careful look than before. I reckon maybe Purv hadn't got around to tellin' him yet that they was more'n one Barkley who traveled this Florida country.

I couldn't guess what it was he thought about it, and at the moment I didn't much care. I'd a notion the best thing they'd got planned for me was that I was goin' to lose a finger I hadn't much stomach for losin'. The worst, well . . .

15 🌿

"RAVENANT," THE BIG MAN SAID. "Jacques Marie Louis Ravenant, at one time of LaFourche Parish, Louisiana." He bowed from the waist whilst them half-dozen guns stayed trained on me and didn't budge a inch. "At your service, Mister . . . Barkley."

The way he said it had a kind of a funny sound to it, one I didn't hardly take to a-tall. But there weren't nothin' I'd got but time goin' for me right then. So I figured I might's well try and gain a bit more of it, maybe satisfyin' my curiosity a little whilst I was at it.

"'Pears mine's a right common name in these parts," I said, glancin' at Purv out of the corner of my eye. "Leastways common enough so they might be a couple of us Barkleys who managed to get mistook for one another."

Purv looked a little uncomfortable, but his boss-man didn't seem to pay it no mind. He just shrugged and hooked both thumbs inside his waist band, cockin' his head to one side and watchin' me with curious eyes.

"That other one was a troublesome man. A big man,

powerful and strong like yourself. But troublesome." Ravenant took a step closer, while still keepin' a safe distance between us. And believe me, I was watchin' mighty close for any kind of a opening him or them others might offer. "Are you a troublesome man, Mr. Tate Barkley?"

"They's been a couple here an' there has thought so." I managed a peek over towards where I'd tied Ole Roan while I was talkin'. He was still there, on t'other side of the clearing from them men. But it was a heap too far to make a run for it. "Most of them are dead though, so you won't hear 'em do much complaining." I swung my gaze back to Ravenant.

He smiled with his lips, but the eyes underneath his black hat was cold as ice. "Myself, I find such troublesome men annoying. I find that what is needed with them, is some small lesson of obedience." He made a gesture to the two *pistoleros* standing closest to him.

"Nicholas, Henri . . ."

Those two started toward me, the one named Henri reachin' back with his left hand to slip a big wicked-lookin' bowie knife out of its sheath as he came. I swallowed hard an' tensed up my muscles, havin' already made up my mind there wasn't none of 'em goin' to lay a hand on me whilst I could still draw breath.

But I wasn't expectin' to keep breathin' a whole lot longer, neither. 'Cause I could see that them others was all set to ballast me down with hot lead the instant I made my move.

All of a sudden I heard this sharp 'hoot-hoot' of a barn owl on t'other side of the cabin, followed right afterwards by the low, mournful, whistlin' wail of a whippoorwill's cry. It had been so quiet in that clearin' up till then that the sounds

168

took ever one of us by surprise. And for my part anyhow, the surprise was a mite greater because I knowed neither one of them birds was much accustomed to do its singin' in the middle of the day.

Now maybe them bird calls by theirselves wouldn't of made so much difference to what was about to happen. But the second they rung out that ole swamp woman up on the porch, who I reckon ever one of us had just almost forgot, started in to raisin' such a ruckus of high-pitched keenin' and caterwaulin' that it plumb set us off our timin' altogether.

I seen out of the corner of my eye that she'd fallen down on her knees and was liftin' up her arms to the heavens now, cryin' out for mercy from God an' the Devil at the self-same time. And like I suggested earlier, she'd got a right disconcertin' gooseflesh-shiverin' screech about her once she had herself wound up good.

It caught Henri's an' Nicholas' attention for a second, anyhow. And everbody else's until I dropped down into a crouch an' whipped up my Winchester, cuttin' loose with a spray of '44 lead what took their minds off that ole woman's hysterics pretty quick and abrupt.

Purv was staring at her with his jaw hangin' open when I put a slug through the third button over his belt buckle to remind him I was there. That boy still had a heap more to learn about gun-fightin'. But now he weren't never goin' to have a chance to learn it.

I turned on the man with the Henry rifle next, slammin' his shoulder back against a tree with my second shot and then puttin' another into his side, low down where it'd bother him some.

After that I made a dash for the woods, runnin' three,

four steps and hitting the ground in a low rollin' dive. By that time all kinds of lead was whisperin' through the bushes and kickin' up dirt around me. I rolled a few feet deeper into the shadows and come up shootin'.

One of the other gunmen was down, though I couldn't recall sendin' no lead his way. But there was still three more countin' Ravenant, who'd found him a bit of cover behind a rotted-out stump now, and was blastin' away with a Army Colt in each big fist.

I sprayed a couple more bullets in their direction, mostly to encourage 'em to hug the ground a mite closer. And then I made a try for the roan.

He was maybe thirty feet away from where I'd been crouchin', with his head lifted up and his eyes big an' round like he'd just soon be anyplace more peaceable than this here clearing. I'd a mind to agree with him, and if I could manage to reach that tie knot on his reins I figured to do what was needed to bring it about.

I skittered an' crawled over the distance between us, throwin' a shot behind me ever now an' again to keep Ravenant and his henchmen from takin' too good a aim. Then I reached up an' pulled the slip knot loose what held him, and Ole Roan an' me begun losin' ourselves amongst the trees on that far side of the cabin.

There weren't no trail where we was, and them cypress knees an' vines an' palmettos was as thick around us as green frogs after a rain. So rather'n mount up, I just kept holt of the reins whilst my horse broke trail to lead us deeper an' deeper into that grim-lookin' hammock.

I didn't hear nobody comin' after us right away, and I reckoned I could imagine why. I'd already put enough lead into a couple of them "destroyin' angels" so the rest knew I could hit what I was aimin' at. And here in these thick woods a feller could lay in ambush and pick off about any seeker what come near. Under the circumstances, I don't believe I'd of been so awful quick to follow along behind me my ownself.

I considered holin' up like that, and waitin' for them to come to me. But they was still three of 'em to my one, with no tellin' how many others in earshot of the cabin who might come runnin' at the sound of our ruckus. That offered too much chance they'd manage to find some way to get me boxed in, sooner or later.

So I kept us movin', pushing our way through the vines an' the tangle of young trees what hadn't had a chance to get drowned out by floods yet. And tryin' to keep myself and the roan as quiet as possible the whole time we was doin' it. I reckon we traveled maybe three hundred yards like that before we come up to the banks of the river again, where it curved back on itself one more time.

'Peared like my choices now was to either swim acrost with the roan, havin' no way of guessin' what I'd find on the other side, or turn right — which was south — and prob'ly run slap into that east-west trail I'd been followin' after it run past the cabin.

I didn't much care for either of them plans. But the river looked to be the lesser of evils. I knowed that trail was the one used by Ravenant an' his men. And not too far along it was the place they'd all left out from this mornin'. I put a hand on Ole Roan's neck, so's to start leadin' him towards the water.

We was havin' to watch our steps mighty careful here, what with the undergrowth an' the cypress knees an' all. And with me still keepin' a right vivid memory besides of that moccasin I'd seen earlier. It weren't no wonder we never caught sight of the wire until we'd run plumb up against it.

First I knowed about it was when I felt this sharp stingin' prick near the top of my leg. Havin' snakes on the mind didn't help a bit when that happened, and it took ever ounce of will I could muster to keep from hollerin' out loud at the top of my lungs. Even so, I jumped back about six feet and brung my Winchester up so quick that I let the roan's reins drop in the process.

I reckon my mustang was some surprised when he seen me do that. But it weren't nothin' compared to what happened to him next. He'd begun to sidestep away from me as I moved, and his flank brushed up against some bushes close to where I'd been standin'. All of a sudden he let out with this high-pitched whinny and reared up on two legs. In another second all I could see of him was his backside and his archin' tail as he lit out into the woods on the other side from the river.

I had one quick glimpse of this row of little spots of fresh blood on his side when he rushed past me into the trees.

For a minute I was torn between followin' behind him or stayin' on to investigate what was there in them bushes. But I knew the roan prob'ly wouldn't go too far into this strange country. And scared as I was to find out, I'd do best to learn what I could about whatever it was had bit the two of us.

'Course snakes and scorpions was the first couple things that entered my mind.

But it weren't nothin' like that after all. When I'd got up the nerve to have a close look, I could make out three strands of wire stretched tight between the trees there along the river bank. The lowest was a couple feet off the ground and the highest was about chest level, with the middle one just even with my thigh. And ever so many inches along the length of all three of 'em was these wicked-lookin' little metal twists with sharp pointed ends.

I knew what it was right off, having met up with a barbed wire salesman or two durin' my years in the West. They wasn't very popular fellers amongst ranchers an' cattle-men, and it surely weren't no great mystery now to see why. Tell the truth, I hadn't never witnessed the stuff bein' actual strung up for fencin' until this very minute.

And a Florida swamp was purely the last spot on earth I or anybody else would of thought to be lookin' for it. In the first place, this here was open range country the same as the West. The only fences any landowner could build legal-like was around his crops to keep cattle an' hogs out.

In the second place, what could possibly be the point of spendin' all that money and effort stringin' wire through some God-forsaken wilderness what was already doggone near impassable without it? And barbed wire to boot? It didn't make no kind of sense a-tall that I could see.

Unless this Ravenant had him somethin' going on that he didn't mean to take no chances of anybody ever havin' a look at. . . .

I shook my head and turned my back on the Withlacoochee with its barbed-wire fencin', meaning to follow and catch up to Ole Roan as quick as possible, before our enemies could have any longer time to discover where we was. It 'peared like our options for travel had just got their-selves reduced down to one. And if I'd any hope of makin' my escape thataway, time surely was a-wastin'.

I knowed the roan was upset, and I didn't blame him. I hadn't much appreciated gettin' a hole poked in my leg by that infernal wire my ownself. I just hoped he'd understand it weren't none of my doin', and after he'd had a chance to calm hisself down a mite he'd see that his best chance was to stick by the partner he come here to the ball with.

Anyhow, his trail through them bushes weren't so terrible hard to follow. He'd been a mighty determined stallion in his hurry to get away from whatever it was had stung him. And anything that couldn't move itself out of his path had just naturally got trampled into the ground.

Sure enough, after I'd walked maybe fifty, sixty yards I seen him standing underneath the low-hangin' limbs of a big old swamp oak, still breathin' kind of heavy and lookin' mighty accusin' at me.

I stopped where I was and spoke to him, keepin' my voice low and tryin' to sound as comforting as I could manage. Then I begun movin' closer, one cautious step at a time.

At first the roan shied an' backed off a little distance into the trees. But I kept talkin' soft an' easy to him, and pretty soon he stood still and just watched me come. I could tell he didn't have no real plans to be shut of me. Mostly I figured he just wanted a little sympathy an' understanding, same as you or me or anybody else who'd had theirselves a altercation with a barb-wire fence.

I'd put nearly ever ounce of attention I could muster on that stallion right then, 'cause the last thing in the world I wanted was to make some accidental move or sound what would spook him into leadin' me a long chase deeper into these woods. Any more runnin' he done today, I'd a mind to be up on his hurricane deck and travelin' with him.

So I reckon the first clue I had that the two of us wasn't alone, was when I glimpsed this sudden roundhouse swing comin' at my head out of the corner of one eye. It was the thick dead limb of a tree what was doin' the swingin'. And the feller at the other end of the limb was huge ole Jube.

I managed to twist around an' jerk my noggin out of the way just in time to keep it from bein' knocked clean off my shoulders and over acrost the river. At the same time I brought my right arm up without thinkin', so's to catch most of the force from the limb.

I mean I could feel that blow all the way up into my neck and back down to my toes. My entire arm went numb, and my Winchester slipped to the ground out of useless fingers.

There weren't no question of drawin' my pistol after that. The best I could hope for was to try and stay out of Jube's way until maybe I could get a little feelin' in my hand again.

He was rarin' back with the limb to have another go at me, so I spun on my heel and put a dozen yards of distance between us. I weren't feelin' no shame a-tall about runnin' away from the thrashin' he'd in mind for me. Even with both arms workin' proper, I'd just soon let him have this little piece of woods all to hisself if I could figure out how to manage it.

I glanced at the roan, who was standin' his ground for the time bein'. But Jube was between me an' him, and I hadn't no illusions a-tall about my chances of makin' a run for it while keepin' out of reach of a ten-foot limb with a seven-foot man attached to it. 'Specially not when I recalled how quick on his feet that black feller had been the first time we crossed horns.

I weren't about to go off an' leave Ole Roan by his lonesome though, even if they'd been some reasonable way to escape without him. Him an' me was pardners, and neither one of us had any other friends we could count on in this swamp country.

Jube took a couple steps in my direction, and I ducked underneath a branch so's to put it between me an' him. He stopped, and then it 'peared like all of a sudden he noticed me glancin' at the roan. I seen him take a quick peek over his shoulder at my mustang. And when he looked back at me they was this sly, squinty-eyed grin startin' to spread acrost his face.

Next thing I knew that big man had begun slewin' crabwise over towards where Ole Roan was standin' with his head up, not runnin' away but just kind of eyein' the two of us curious-like. When he was maybe eight feet away, Jube lifted that heavy branch over his head and spun around real quick, like he meant to slam it into the roan's neck with ever bit of strength he could muster.

And right then was when I begun to see red.

Lookin' back on it, I reckon it was kind of foolish for me to act the way I done next. Ole Roan wasn't no pilgrim, and he could of prob'ly managed to take care of hisself without help from me. Even a feller big an' quick as Jube would of had him more trouble than he was lookin' for if that mustang took a notion to light into him with teeth an' hoofs a-flyin'.

But I wasn't exactly thinkin' calm an' reasonable at that moment. I seen a man tryin' his natural best to kill a animal I'd growed kind of partial to over the years, and I just plunged in without givin' no deep consideration to the whys an' wherefores of it.

I let out with this big Rebel yell and charged through the brush, only rememberin' my hurt arm long enough to turn the other one towards Jube a second before I crashed into him underneath the rib cage.

He backed up a mite, and I reckon that was something of a accomplishment on my part, considerin' his size an' the fact it was more than I'd got him to do the entire time back there on that road north of Newnansville. But he didn't go down. And when he'd got over bein' surprised enough to let go his tree branch, he started layin' about him for fair with them great big fists an' elbows.

Oh, I managed to land a few my ownself, mostly to his midsection whilst I was clinched up tryin' to stay close. I think he might of even felt a couple of 'em.

But they was one of mine for ever two of his, and pretty soon I was feelin' mighty regretful that I'd started this ruckus in the first place.

Jube cut my cheek open with a right, and followed it up with a hammer blow to the kidney with his balled-up left. Then when I started slippin' to the ground, his big callused elbow caught me over the eye and opened up a gash all the way down to the bone. I tried to back away and get a hand on my gun, but by then the blood was pourin' down my face so bad I couldn't hardly see where he was to take a shot at him.

It's a sure-enough fact I never seen that last blow what hit me. It come out of nowhere just about the time my Smith an' Wesson was clearin' leather. My teeth rattled around in my mouth and my eyeballs banged together, and they was fireworks inside my skull what would of put a big city Fourth of July to shame.

My whole body went limp, and though it seemed like I heard some kind of shootin' way off in the distance, it might of only been them fireworks inside my head. In another second my world faded out amidst red-flecked lightning and heavy black thunderclouds.

16 ⟅

WHEN I COME TO I WAS LYIN' on a blanket stretched over hard boards of some kind. And it seemed like them boards was movin' ever so slightly, though several minutes had to pass before I could be real sure it was the boards movin' and not just the effect of them blows I'd took upside the head.

I felt a gentle hand touch my face, and then somethin' soft an' damp begun wipin' the blood away from around my cheeks an' eyes. When it got to that cut on my forehead it stung so fierce that I twitched an' moaned, and all of a sudden I was full awake.

"Settle down. You ain't as bad hurt as it feels like. Just bruises an' cuts mostly, though you surely ain't no dainty picture to look upon." I opened my eyes to find out who the speaker was, already knowin' from the sound of her voice it was a woman.

I was lyin' in the bottom of a shallow-draft boat, pushed back up into some bay or slough where the sun filtered down through a thick canopy of leaves an' branches overhead. And kneelin' there beside me, her face no more'n a foot away from mine, was this slim little vision of gold-brown hair an' light green eyes what I recognized right off from our short conversation in Fort Dade, after I'd got done knockin' her off the boardwalk into the dust.

"I reckon I ain't ever been that," I said, glancin' past to her Injun companion, who was standin' like a statue in the bow of the boat with a long-barreled rifle in his hands. He wasn't lookin' in our direction, but I'd a notion he was listenin' to ever word that was spoke.

"'Dainty' ain't the way most folks would describe me," I allowed, "even when I ain't had my face pounded to a pastry by some overgrowed fugitive from a circus side-show. . . . —Ow!"

"Hush." She'd got to the cut on my cheek now. When she didn't say no more, but just kept workin' away at my face with that wet cloth in her hand, I decided I might's well hold my peace and let her keep on with what she was doin'. She'd rigged up some kind of plasters with medicine on 'em to stick down over my cuts. I closed my eyes an' flinched a mite as she laid 'em on. But I didn't do no more complainin'.

"Thanks," I said finally. "I'm grateful for your care an' attention, Miss . . ." And that's when I realized I'd plumb forgot her name. I guess I still wasn't thinkin' as straight as I'd liked to of been, what with all the poundin' on my noggin ole Jube had set hisself to doin'.

"Martha Jane MacAllister," she answered without hardly skippin' a beat. "Marty, to my friends." She grinned, and it like to lit up that entire forest when she done it. "I reckon maybe you could qualify as one, since we 'pear to have some of the same collection of enemies."

"Thanks again, ma'am, —Marty." I favored her with a hint of a smile my ownself. "My name's Tate Barkley."

Well, she give me this funny look. And even the Injun in the front of the boat turned his head around to glance at me. Then the gal with the gold-brown hair pressed her lips together and nodded, like she'd solved a riddle what had been troublin' her for some little while.

"Of course," she said, almost to herself. "Wonder why I didn't think of that before?"

I must of stared at her right peculiar. 'Cause I couldn't fathom the tiniest part of what she was talkin' about. Marty sat back an' studied me for a minute, up an' down from head to toe. Then she gazed into my eyes and said in a voice so soft it was barely a whisper:

"You're Luke's brother, ain't you?"

Well, I'd a brother named Luke all right. Who I hadn't seen in more'n fifteen years and hadn't got but maybe two, three scrawled-out scraps of mail from in all that time. We'd both done a heap of travelin' durin' the war an' afterwards, and composin' letters, even on them rare occasions when we'd some idea of where to send 'em, weren't a task us Barkley boys much took to.

Now, how this young gal here knowed about me an' Luke was more than I could imagine. She couldn't been knee-high to a grasshopper when the two of us left Taylor county back in '62 an' '63. And we hadn't left no family alive behind us when we did. Last I heard, Luke was headed out Californee-way. And I'd just come back to Florida a year ago my ownself, after travelin' them high, dry lands between Texas and the Rockies for a decade without once runnin' acrost his trail.

I reckon Marty seen my puzzled look whilst I was noddin' "yes" to her question. But she'd no way of guessin' all the other thoughts that was rattlin' around inside my brain right then.

The next thing she said, after a little shake of her head, just went on to perplex me more:

"You surely do favor. If I didn't know for a fact they was a couple years between, I'd swear on a Bible the two of you was twins!"

"Uh, listen here, ma'am, —Marty." I took a deep breath to kind of sort out what it was I meant to say next. "I know I'm prob'ly still thinkin' kind of fuzzy from them knocks I took on the head. But you done left me beside the trail about a half a mile back." I managed to get a arm underneath me so's I could raise up and look in her eyes.

"My brother Luke an' me ain't seen hide nor hair of one another for a passel of years. Last I knew he weren't no closer to this Florida swamp than a three, four months' journey." I paused an' eased myself to a more comfortable position. "You mind tellin' me just where it was you happened to meet up with him? And how you know about the two of us?"

I guess it was her turn to be surprised, 'cause she kind of blinked and glanced towards her Injun friend in the bow of the boat. Then she looked back at me with a shrug of her slender shoulders.

"Why, up at Okahumkee Landing there by Leesburg. Three . . . no, four days ago now." I just stared at her with my mouth propped open. But she weren't near ready yet to pause in her explainin':

"He was in mighty sorry shape, what with the beatin's and everthing else had happened since he was took prisoner

182

by Ravenant. But he was a proud one. Wouldn't hardly accept no help from us a-tall 'cept a little food an' doctorin'. I reckon he might of took the borry of a horse about then too, only we didn't have one to loan him. Them mules of ours ain't saddle broke, an' besides which we needed 'em our own-selves to draw the wagon. . . ."

I lifted up my hand to slow her down a trifle. "Hold on, now. Let's just see if I got this straight so far. You say Luke was took prisoner by Ravenant?" Marty nodded, her face and eyes grim. "And so I reckon the reason he was up there by Leesburg was 'cause he'd managed to escape somehow or another?"

"Uh-huh." She nodded again. "Said he'd bided his time till his guards got to lookin' the other way. Then he knocked 'em both in the head with a tater hoe and took off through the woods."

Well, it's the kind of thing I'd of done, all right. And I guessed brother Luke was pretty much cut from the same cloth. "Okay," I said. "Now what about this Ravenant? Is he generally in the business of holdin' folks prisoner, or was Luke some kind of a special case?"

Marty's green eyes got awful hard and cold there for a second, and if she'd been the type I believe she would of spat. "From what Luke told Cal an' me, I'd say it's his business."

She eased herself up onto one of the thwarts from where she'd been kneelin' in the bottom of the boat, and glanced all around. Then she went on in a little lower voice than before:

"He's got maybe three, four hundred acres cleared back up in the swamp so far, where he raises corn, sweet potatoes an' sugar cane. Plus a lot more that ain't been cleared for cattle an' hogs. The cane an' extra corn he mostly turns to whiskey, so it'll be easier to tote and sell." She frowned deeper, then added, "The taters he uses to feed them poor slaves what work his fields!"

"Slaves?" I give her a questionin' look.

"I don't know what else you'd call 'em. 'Pears him and them bush-rangers who ride for him take holt of anybody they can who's fool enough to travel this country: white folks, black folks, it don't make no nevermind. Pen 'em up outdoors like cattle, beat 'em an' starve 'em till the fight's been took out of 'em, and then set 'em to workin'. Whenever one gets too weak or too sick to pull his load, he just ain't there the next mornin'. And the gators in the sloughs all look a little fatter."

I whistled low between my teeth. That would sure enough explain them disappearances the citizens at Fort Dade was so wrought up about. And most the stories about this here swamp and Ravenant along with 'em. If he wasn't the devil hisself like that half-crazed ole woman back at her cabin believed, he'd at least him got a pretty fair franchise on doin' the Old Boy's work in this section of the country.

"What about Luke?" I asked after a minute. "He happen to tell you how he managed to get tangled up with this Ravenant bunch in the first place?" The gal next to me shook her head. "Or what he's been doin' these past fifteen years and why he decided to come back to Florida?"

"No. He weren't much for talkin' about past history it seemed like. Prob'ly he'd got more pressin' matters in his head right then. Like how he meant to stay shut of them pursuers that he knowed would be doggin' his trail!"

She looked at me kind of sassy-like, and I met her gaze. "But somehow or another," I observed calmly, "he found the time to tell you all about him an' me, and our growin' up in Taylor county."

I think I seen her blush just a tad, underneath her tanned skin an' calico collar.

"Luke spent the night at our camp on Okahumkee Run," she said, "and I reckon we did talk a little, about this an' that."

"How about after you an' him parted company? Did he leave you with any idea of where he might be headed?

Marty lowered her eyes an' shrugged. "He didn't get the chance. Me an' Cal was talkin' about helpin' him make his way down-river to Jacksonville. But along about daybreak we had a visit from that *woman* and her two hired thugs . . ."

It was pretty clear she meant Lila, along with Jube an' Purv, who I realized now had been huntin' Luke when they come acrost me a few days earlier. It was also evident my new-found acquaintance weren't especial fond of Lila. If ever a body was able to make two cusswords out of "that" and "woman," she managed to do it.

"Luke heard 'em comin'," Marty went on, "and managed to slip off into the woods just a minute before they rode into our camp. 'Course we pretended we hadn't seen hide nor hair of him, and I reckon they believed it, at least for the time bein'."

She sighed and shook her head. "But it didn't make no difference in the long run. We talked to old Naomi last night, and she told us she seen Luke bein' dragged back to Ravenant's place all trussed up like a hog the very next day."

For a second the gal with the gold-brown hair looked like she was fixin' to cloud up an' cry. But she swallowed hard and held it in.

"First Evan and Harry, then your brother Luke . . . I swear it 'pears like ever man I ever knowed an' liked is goin' to wind up leavin' his bones in this mis'able swamp!"

"Who's Evan and Harry?" I asked, mostly because she'd mentioned 'em. Me, I was still tryin' to picture my brother Luke hog-tied an' helpless at Ravenant's mercy.

"Harry MacAllister's my brother, the only kin I got left in this world. And Evan Hardaway is — was — his best friend, from Asheville, North Carolina." I glanced at her then, and her eyes started gettin' kind of damp an' red as she went on to explain:

"They come down to Florida last April, for a couple weeks of huntin' and fishin'. I was off visitin' friends at the time, and nobody else give much thought to them not comin' home exactly when they said they would. Evan's pa's a doctor, a widower without no other kin, so money weren't a problem. And with Harry still readin' for the law, neither one had to be back at no special time.

"Only Harry an' me's been awful close since Ma an' Pa died; we raised each other, mostly. And we ain't been apart so long as a week that we didn't write at least one or two letters back an' forth. So when I got home to Bryson City an' didn't find but one piece of mail waitin' for me, posted at Fort Dade, I knowed somethin' was wrong."

"And that's why you come all the way down here, lookin' for him?"

"Not right off, though I reckon it was in my mind. First I tried gettin' in touch with Evan's pa. But it turned out he'd been ailin' pretty serious lately, and he hadn't heard nothin' from the boys either. With the old man not able to leave his bed and me havin' nobody else to look to for help, that's when I decided I'd got to make this trip. Harry always took care of me whenever I needed it, and now it was my turn to do it for him."

She glanced from me to her companion up in the front of the boat. The Indian was listening, silent and stony-faced, whilst still keepin' a sharp lookout on the woods all around.

"Cal here's been a good friend to both of us ever since we was young-uns," Marty said. "And him bein' a full-blood Cherokee, he's mighty knowin' of forest ways. So when he heard what I was plannin' and offered to come along, I was pleased to have him do it. What with preparations to make for the journey an' everthing, it was already September 'fore we finally set out. And we'd just made it as far as Okahumkee Landing when we run acrost your brother Luke."

"And he had news of your own brother an' Evan?" I asked, already guessin' what kind of news it prob'ly was.

Marty blinked and turned her head away so I couldn't see her face.

"Evan's dead," she said, her voice so quiet it was almost a whisper. "Some kind of a fever accordin' to Luke, what wore him down to nothin' and finally kilt him." She paused to wipe her eyes on the sleeve of her dress, still not lookin' in my direction.

"And now Harry's come down with the selfsame fever. He . . . He ain't expected to live."

The gal lowered her head into her hands, and I just let her have at it without sayin' nothing for a long couple of minutes. Finally she turned her red-rimmed eyes to me.

"You see what I mean?" Her voice was low an' husky. "Evan, and Harry, and now Luke too. Ever single one of 'em looks doomed to leave his bones in this Florida swamp!"

"Mebbe," I answered slowly. "An' then again, mebbe not. 'Least I ain't so powerful certain about Luke as you seem to be. Us Barkleys take a heap of killin' before anybody can salt us down."

And when I said it I had this picture in my mind, of a familiar-lookin' pair of broad shoulders disappearin' into the mist outside my camp 'long about sunup this morning.

After a minute I shifted myself into a sittin' position in the bottom of the boat, closin' my eyes and wincin' a little as I done it. I'd still got this mountain grizzly of a headache from that beatin' I'd took. But I expected I'd prob'ly live in spite of it.

"Come on," I said, reachin' out to lay a hand on Marty's arm. "You traveled all the way down here from North Carolina to help them boys, and it appears like one of 'em could still use the help. Now ain't no time to be speakin' hopeless an' give up the ghost. Now's the time to be makin' smoke and talkin' war talk."

She looked at me, and I knew she wanted to believe. Only she was havin' trouble right then finding anything reassurin' about the situation.

"But you saw 'em yourself," she said, "Ravenant an' the kind of men he's got. Luke told us they's more'n a dozen all told, ever one armed to the teeth and mean as a treed wildcat." She glanced at Cal an' shrugged, not meetin' my eyes. "How could the three of us do anything against all of those?"

I picked up my hat from beside me and settled it sort of gentle on my head. "What I seen," I replied, "is a bunch of hard-case 'angels from Hell' what turn out bein' able to bleed an' die just about as good as any other mortal men. And I seen somethin' else too this mornin', what leads me to believe Luke Barkley ain't so helpless an' out of this fight as you might of thought."

Then I explained about my crack-of-dawn visitor, and how I'd a notion from what I recalled of the incident and what I'd been told since, that it was Luke hisself what come light-footin' into my camp searchin' for victuals. "'Pears to me," I finished up, "he give 'em the slip again yesterday or last night, and this time he went south instead of north hopin' they'd do their lookin' in the opposite direction."

I frowned. "Prob'ly didn't fool nobody, 'least not if them riders I seen first was the ones huntin' him. But I don't reckon they've caught up to him yet neither, or else Ravenant would of mentioned it whilst he had me in his sights there at the cabin."

I paused to glance around that backwater where us an' the boat was hid. "Where are we now?" I asked. It was high time an' past time I got started tryin' to work my way back to where I'd last seen Luke, before them riders of Ravenant's managed to beat me to it.

"Down-river from the cabin. Half mile to a mile, maybe." It was Cal who spoke, for the first time since I'd come awake. "We slipped past the bend while they were tendin' their hurts and huntin' for you."

I looked up at him. "How'd I get here, anyway?"

"Drug you."

"We were watchin' from the river when you and that big Negro had your set-to," Marty explained. "When it appeared he was fixin' to bust your skull in, I singed his ear with a rifle shot and Cal jumped out of the boat an' brought you to it."

"I'm obliged," I said, "to both of you. That feller tried

killin' me with his bare hands once, and I believe he'd got it in his mind to finish the job this time." All of a sudden I had a thought. "Say, if you two was hidin' along the river there, you wouldn't happen to know nothin' about no daytime-singin' owls an' whippoorwills, would you?"

Cal, he just grinned.

"Well, that's twice I'm obliged to you. 'Cause I reckon if you hadn't stirred up that ole woman's caterwaulin', I'd of been salted down with lead before I ever got a chanct to meet up with Jube again."

17 🖐

ABOUT THEN I SPIED MY WINCHESTER layin' in the bottom of the boat alongside this big old-fashioned percussion rifle, and I upped it to three times obliged in my mind, for Cal's thoughtfulness in bringin' my weapon along with me.

But there was one more thing I wanted, and my luck had been so good this far I was almost scared to ask anything about it.

"I imagine it's prob'ly too much to hope for," I said after a second, "but did you happen to notice if my ole roan horse made it off into the woods without bein' caught up by them riders?"

Cal, he smiled again.

"Behind you in the forest, maybe five-, ten-minute walk."

"Huh?" I stared at him, not sure if he was funnin' me or what.

"He followed as I was totin' you to the river." The Injun shrugged. "Couldn't get him in the boat, so I swum him across. Shame to leave such an animal behind for men like those."

Well, I couldn't hardly believe it. Aside from a little bit of blood an' skin off my noggin — which most folks wouldn't consider no vital part of me anyhow — I'd still got everthing I rode in here with, and a couple fresh allies to boot. Now if I could manage to find an' hook up with brother Luke before Ravenant's troops run him to ground, and if he were anything a-tall like the rough-an'-tumble young-un I remembered, I'd a idea they was people in this swamp who was right on the verge of discoverin' what Hell really was.

I took holt of my Winchester and got to my feet, easin' the boat closer to land by pullin' on limbs. Marty, when she seen what I was about, pitched in to hold her steady whilst I stepped ashore.

"I got to hurry an' find Luke before anybody else does," I told her. "After that we'll see what can be done about helpin' your brother and them others." I glanced from the young lady to Cal, touchin' my hat by way of a salute. "My thanks to you for everthing. Reckon I'd ought to be back sometime tonight, or tomorrow at the latest. You got any idea where'd be a good place for us to meet?"

The Cherokee pushed his hat aside and scratched his head. "It ain't goin' to be so simple gettin' where you want to go from here. You saw what's south an' east: Ravenant's men and Ravenant's wire. This here river spreads out into broad swamp with lots of channels a short ways west, so the closest place to make a crossing is maybe six, seven miles downstream."

Cal paused, watchin' me. And I knew he knew I weren't much pleased by what he was sayin', 'cause it meant back-trackin' toward the settlements and a added delay in reachin' the spot where I'd laid eyes on Luke. But I hadn't no doubts this Injun knew what he was talkin' about. So I just nodded to show I understood.

"You look close 'round where your horse is tied," he went on, "and you'll find this little narrow trail headin' west. Follow it till you come in sight of the river again — like I said, six or seven miles — and make your crossin' there. Southeast from that place ought to take you back the way you traveled last night. When you find your brother . . ." I 'preciated his choice of words in not sayin' "if," though the worries were beginnin' to crop up in my own mind now. ". . . you come on back to that same river crossin'. I'll find you."

"Okay," I agreed. "Sounds like a better plan than any other I've had this past week an' a half, so I'll do her." I glanced at Marty, then back to Cal. "You folks'll be all right in the meantime?"

"We'll stay out of sight till dark, then make our way downstream by water. A boat don't make much noise, and it doesn't leave no tracks. I reckon we'll do fine."

I took a step up the bank in the direction Cal had pointed when he'd mentioned Ole Roan. Then I turned to share one last thought before leavin' 'em behind.

"If they's any need for a signal between us," I said, "you use that barn owl I heard at the cabin this mornin'. I'll answer back the bob-white quail." The Injun nodded, and I started off through the trees.

"Take care of yourself, Tate Barkley." That was Marty's voice, kind of quiet and concerned-soundin' as I walked away. I replied with a partin' wave.

❖   ❖   ❖

I made it a point to ride mighty watchful after we'd swum the Withlacoochee back to the southward side, keepin' in the shadows of the trees as much as possible and skirtin' the edges of them cypress sloughs instead of ridin' straight out acrost the open prairie like I'd done the night before. By the time Ole Roan an' me finally come up on that grassy rise where I'd slept and had my visit from Luke, the sun was below the tree tops and night was only a hair away from closin' down on us.

There was a wind comin' up from the west, and the rustlin' of it through the limbs an' palmetto fans made a eerie sound in that lonely place. I glanced at the sky and seen dark clouds scuddin' past, leadin' the way for a bunch of high rollin' thunderheads away off on the horizon. We'd have rain before mornin', more'n likely.

For a time I just sat up there on Ole Roan, studyin' the country and tryin' to figure out how to go about makin' contact with Luke. He hadn't no more reason to expect I was in this part of Florida than I'd the notion of seein' him here a few hours earlier. The fact we hadn't recognized each other this mornin' was a testament to that, along with the number of years what had passed in the meantime.

I smiled a little when I recollected that big hulkin' shape I'd barely got a glimpse of whilst I was chasin' him through the mists. Ole Luke had put on a few pounds around the shoulders an' arms since them younger days, with maybe a inch or two in height to go with 'em. And neither of us boys was exactly what you'd call frail or skinny from the git-go.

I found myself wonderin' what else he'd gained, in the way of knowledge an' experience, and heartache an' all them other things each of us collects along the road to becomin' a man.

Finally I shucked out my Winchester and climbed down from the leather, leadin' the roan back in amongst the trees to where I'd last seen Luke's tracks.

"Luke?" I called, not very loud and without much hope that he'd be close enough to hear me. "Luke, boy. This is your brother Tate."

There wasn't no answer. Just more of that steady whisperin' wind in the trees. It was pretty much what I expected. By now Luke could be miles from here if he was a mind to. And even if he was still in hollerin' distance — even if I'd a notion to throw caution to the winds an' raise my voice up to a full-blowed shout — he prob'ly still wouldn't of answered me. I wouldn't if I'd been in his place.

Far as he knowed, there wasn't nothing but enemies out here for several days' ride in ever direction.

Ravenant or his men could of learned my name somehow; after all, Marty knew it. And anybody who knew it could of hollered it without askin' my permission. That's a trick I imagined Ravenant would find appealin' to his nature. And way too many years had gone by to hope Luke might recognize my voice.

But what else could I do? How could I get the word out that I was here lookin' for him, in a way he'd believe an' pay heed to but without rousin' up the entire country and telling 'em where I was into the bargain.

Then all of a sudden I recalled something I hadn't thought of in a long, long while.

Whilst Luke an' me was growin' up back in the San Pedro Swamp, it was ever bit as thick an' pathless as this here country 'peared to be. And like kids most anyplace, we'd take it into our heads to go explorin' ever chanct we got. Sometimes we'd get so far off the beaten trail it would of took a pack of hounds a month of Sundays to run us to earth. Time to time we even managed to lose the way back to the homestead our ownselves.

Pappy, he didn't have no leisure time to spend huntin' through the brush for two wayward young-uns whenever he wanted us for a chore or somethin'. And havin' been a boy hisself, he knew he wouldn't get very far just tryin' to give orders for us not to leave the house. So from the time we was each knee-high to a toadstool and able to move under our own steam, he'd taught Luke an' me to heed this real special way he had of whistlin'.

It was high and shrill, skippin' up the scale and runnin' back down again in a sharp little melody what couldn't be mistook for no bird nor anything else a feller might hear in the wilderness. And it would carry a mighty long way, further than most men could shout.

Soon as we heard it, no matter where we was or what we was doin', Luke an' me knew we'd got to drop everthing and high-tail it towards that sound. Either that or face a whippin', which Pappy didn't mete out lightly or for too many offenses, but which he done a mighty thorough job of once he took the notion.

'Course we both taught ourselves to do that whistle too, just soon as we was able. And when we'd each added a note here an' there, or dropped one so's to make it our own, we used them personal whistles to call to one another in the woods the whole time we was growin' up.

That weren't a thing Luke would be likely to forget.

And though the sound might be heard by others, him an' me would be the only ones in the entire world who knowed what it meant.

It was sure worth a try anyhow, and I didn't have no other plans goin' for me at the moment. If it didn't work I'd at least know I'd got a pretty serious trackin' job ahead of me in the mornin'. 'Cause in that case Luke was either too far away to hear my whistle, or something had happened to keep him from answerin'.

The sky was near-'bout black now, with so many clouds overhead there wasn't even a single star could be seen. Which suited me fine, since Luke an' me wouldn't need no light to recognize our whistles.

I hitched myself up, stuck two fingers in my mouth, and let her fly. Ole Roan was startled by the sharpness of it, and I had to grab his nostrils real quick to hold him quiet so's I could listen. I strained my ears into the gathering darkness, but there wasn't anything a-tall I could make out except the wind amongst the trees.

Well, I told myself, in for a penny in for a pound, as ole Monk used to say. I whistled again, loud and shrill as I could manage. Then I held still like a statue and listened again.

After a long minute there was a answering sound, almost lost in the rustlin' of leaves close by and the distance between us. A couple seconds later it come again, from away off to the east. This time I recognized it right off as Luke's personal whistle!

I give him one more of my own, and heard him answer back. Then, grinnin' a mite to myself in the dark, I took Ole Roan's reins in my left hand and sat down with my back against a pine tree to wait. My cocked Winchester rested acrost my knees, with me grippin' the action in my right hand pistol-fashion, just in case.

It seemed like a mighty long wait, all alone there in the dark with nothin' but my thoughts for company, and the little noises my mustang made stirrin' about and croppin' grass time to time. I kept still, listening. And I held off speakin' to the roan, not even in a whisper.

With Ravenant's people all over this wilderness thick as fleas, there could of been one close enough to hear our whistles and come investigatin'. So I'd a powerful strong wish to hear anybody what was nearby before they heard me, be it Luke or Ravenant or the Devil hisself.

The minutes dragged on, and I was beginnin' to get edgy. I even wondered finally if I hadn't ought to forget my earlier idea and take a chance on one more whistle. But before I could make my mind up to do it, I heard Luke's own low-voiced signal maybe a hundred yards off in that palmetto scrub to east of me.

There weren't no question of waitin' for him to come closer now. He wouldn't of whistled a-tall unless he was havin' some doubts about which way to head next. I eased myself into a kneelin' position, keepin' the pine tree beside me for partial cover. And then I answered back with as low a whistle as I could manage and still be heard from where I figured him to be.

He was ever bit as cautious as I was. With mighty good reason, considerin' he was unarmed an' barefoot out yonder, havin' no way to defend hisself but his two bare hands. There weren't no response to my latest whistle, and I didn't hear nothin' else for several long minutes. I stayed where I was, waitin'.

"Tate, boy." The soft whisper seemed to come from a stand of palmettos a dozen yards to my right. "Is it really you?"

"It's me, Luke. And mighty pleased to hear your voice. You about ready to get shut of this . . ."

"Hist!" There was a faint rustlin' amongst the palmettos, and the next time Luke spoke he was some twenty feet further away on my left: "Look sharp, Tate. We ain't alone out here!"

Me, I was already hunkerin' closer to the tree trunk. My finger curved around the trigger of my Winchester without givin' it a thought. I could feel a coldness at the base of my neck as I strained to pick out stray noises from the darkness around us.

It had got uncommon quiet in these woods all of a sudden. The wind had died down to nothin', and even the crickets an' frogs what generally kept up a right lively dialogue during the early evenin' hours, seemed to be holdin' their breaths. I glanced around me, left, right, an' back again. But everywhere I looked was black as the inside of a tar barrel. I couldn't see or hear a thing.

Then without warnin', Ole Roan shied and jerked up his head. I'd still got his reins looped around my left hand, so when he done that it near lifted me off the ground and give me one hell of a start to boot. As I come to my feet an' turned in his direction, I seen this dark figure lunge out of the shadows towards me.

I didn't think or hesitate. I just seen him move and I moved my ownself. The butt of my Winchester swung up an' around, catchin' that feller square on the jaw and crunchin' bone in the process. He grunted and stumbled backwards, whilst I got the rifle turned rightways-to, jammed it in his belly, and squeezed the trigger. Seemed like that took the fight out of him, 'cause he slumped to the ground, moaning and whimperin' for mercy.

I dropped to one knee right afterwards, and it was a mighty good thing I did. A yellow-orange flash from a pistol split the air not more'n ten feet away, the bullet thunkin' into that pine tree and sprayin' shivers of bark all over me an' the roan as it spun into the distance. I levered a shell into the Winchester an' fired at the flash, but couldn't hear nothin' what suggested I scored a hit.

Whilst I was workin' the lever to get set for a third shot, Luke's voice called out above the echoes, "Hold up a minute, Tate! I got this one!" There was the sound of a couple heavy blows, laid on with force and feelin' behind 'em. Then a kind of a sighin' moan and one final blow, followed by silence.

"I don't think there's any others close by," Luke said quietly, soundin' a tad out of breath. He busied hisself about the man on the ground for a minute, then stepped nearer to me. I could see his big shape in silhouette, thrustin' a six-gun inside his waistband. "Them shots'll carry a far ways into the night, though. We best be makin' some tracks, and that right quick!"

I didn't need no second invitation, and neither did Ole Roan. I mounted and slipped a foot out of the stirrup, reachin' a hand back to help Luke up behind me. Then we lit out of that place like they was a fire underneath our tails.

It was dark as pitch, without no stars nor moon to guide us. But I'd a pretty good idea which way was west, and I figured my mustang prob'ly had a better one. So I let him have his head for a mile or three, without worryin' much about whether we was goin' back exactly the same way we come or not. The most important thing was to put some distance between us and where them noises an' gun flashes had took place.

Dark as it was, I didn't expect there'd be much chance of anybody followin' after. Nor guessin' where we was a-tall, unless we was just so plumb shorn of luck as to stumble acrost 'em accidental.

After a bit I slowed Ole Roan to a walk. Then a while later as we come into the deeper shadows of one of them cypress domes, I pulled up and me an' Luke swung to the ground to let him have a breather. That was one game animal, and he might of kept goin' all night if I'd had it in me to ask him. But even one of us Barkley boys was a sizable package. The two of us together was more'n I'd care to see any critter have to tote over much of a distance.

Besides that, I figured we'd come far enough now so we could spare a few minutes to try and get our bearings. And take a long, careful listen all over the country whilst we was at it.

We didn't hear or see nothing out of the ordinary. The crickets an' frogs in that swampy place was havin' theirselves a reg'lar frolic waitin' for the rain that we could smell comin' on the night air. I noticed the sky was growin' a little lighter to eastward now. But the risin' moon was still hid from view behind them thick clouds what lay everwhere about.

18 🌱

LUKE AN' ME HADN'T HARDLY SPOKE a dozen words to each other durin' that first hour's ride. I was right pleased to see him, and I reckon he felt the same about meetin' up with me. Beyond that, neither one of us saw much need for lengthy conversation whilst we was ridin' for our lives.

But now we was stopped and waitin' for Ole Roan to finish his blow, I hunkered down beside where Luke was restin' with his back against a tree, and ventured kind of quiet-like under my breath:

"You sure do cover a sight of country in your travels, little brother. Last I heard, you was on your way out to that far promised land of Californy."

"Uh-huh. I made it, too. Seen near ever foot, from San Francisco an' Silver City to the pueblo of Los Angeles an' the Mexican border." He paused to pluck a blade of grass and stick it between his teeth.

"I reckon you done a mite of travelin' your ownself,

Tate, now you happen to mention it. There's still a few out Arizona-way who recollect the name of Barkley pretty sharp. You made a right lastin' impression on one or two I met."

I glanced into the shadows where he was settin', but it was too dark to see his face.

"Trouble?" I asked.

"None I couldn't manage." Luke paused to take the grass stem out of his mouth. Then he shook his head and added wearily, "I'd got to come all the way home to Florida before fetchin' that kind of trouble." He fell silent, and it was a second or two before I spoke again myself:

"Looks like to me you done all right under the circumstances. There was some upset people ridin' the country even after that first time you made your run for it."

"Mebbe. But I wouldn't of had no reason to be upsettin' 'em a-tall if I'd kept my wits about me after I set foot off that steamer in Jacksonville."

Me, I held my peace, waitin' for him to explain. I knew Luke'd get around to it in his own way an' time.

"I was feelin' mighty flush when I took it in my head to cross the country back east to Florida," he said finally. "It's plumb amazin' the number of gents who'll pick up cards in a game without no more idea of the finer points of poker than a mule's got of cotillion dancing. And it's surely a sight easier to mine gold and silver out from a table full of miners than sweatin' over a pick an' single jack in the California hills .

"I'd got me a road stake and a playin' stake, with enough left over to live high on the hog for a time and do a mite of investin' besides. Thought I'd put part of it into land an' cattle hereabouts, and the rest into a riverboat or a hotel so's to live off the Yankee tourists." He shrugged and shook his head.

"I'd high an' mighty plans, all right. Only I reckon I was feelin' just a hair too sure of myself for my own good. When I met up with Lila there in Jacksonville . . ."

"Uh-huh," I interrupted him. "I had a notion her name would come up in the conversation sooner or later."

"You know her?" Luke sounded surprised. He looked at me and I nodded.

"Our paths has crossed a time or two."

"Well, then you can prob'ly imagine the rest of it. She's a awful fetchin' package there on the face of things. And it seemed like she took to me too, the minute our eyes met across that hotel lobby. We got to talkin', and I asked her to dinner, and afterwards one thing led to another. And the next day I found myself travelin' south to meet her uncle, who she said had some land an' livestock he might be willin' to offer for sale."

"But when you got here and was introduced to uncle Ravenant," I suggested, "you discovered he'd a couple other ideas in mind besides buyin' and sellin' cattle."

"You ain't whistlin' Dixie. First chance she had, Lila cuddled up and shucked me out of my shootin' irons, slick as a weasel. She already knew where I kept my hide-out from the night before. . . ."

I nearly opened my mouth to say somethin' preachy and big-brotherly about that. But it'd only be rubbin' salt in the wound. Besides which, Luke didn't stop talkin' long enough to give me the chanct:

"Next thing you knew, four, five of Ravenant's boys had jumped in and thrashed me within a inch of my life usin' sticks and coiled-up cow whips. I mean it plumb took the wind out of my sails for several days afterward. When they'd got through, they stripped off my boots an' everthing else I owned except my shirt and britches. Then they tossed me into this barb-wire cow pen with a bunch of other poor souls who'd already been taught the same kind of a lesson."

"Modern-day slaves," I finished up for him, "to work Ravenant's fields and help serve his moonshinin' operation."

Luke swung his head around to peer at me in the darkness. "That's right. But how come you know so much about it?"

"Well," I drawled, makin' him wait half a second for my answer, "it happens Lila ain't the only one of your ladyfriends I chanced to make the acquaintance of in these Florida backwoods."

"Marty—?"

"Uh-huh. Matter of fact, that's who we're on our way to join up with this very night. Her and that Cherokee companion of hers."

"Well, I'll be . . ."

All of a sudden a blindin' flash of lightning lit up the woods an' the prairie around us bright as day. And whatever it was that Luke was allowin' he'd be got drowned out by the huge clap of thunder what followed after, grumblin' and echoin' for some seconds off among the distant trees.

We both blinked an' rubbed our eyes. Then Luke got up from where he'd been settin' and remarked kind of irritable-like: "The sky's fixin' to open up any minute, fit to choke a frog. You reckon that mustang of yours is finally ready to make some tracks?"

"He'll do what's needful," I said, gettin' up my ownself and goin' to tighten Ole Roan's cinch. "But if both of us ride, he can't manage much better'n a walk over the long haul.

You go on an' mount up. I'll take the first turn travelin' shank's mare."

Luke was a mind to argue. But after I'd pointed out that besides the fact he was barefoot, he'd had a right tryin' ordeal and maybe weren't in such good shape yet to try whuppin' his older brother, he done like I said.

We set out at a lively pace, me leadin' the way from memory and what little I could see of the country during lightnin' flashes. And all the while I knew that we'd never make it to shelter before all three of us got soppin' wet.

Luke an' me kept our conversation goin' for a time, low-voiced and watchful for any trace of Ravenant or his men. In the process I learned somethin' about how they'd got their place layed out back up there in the swamp.

There was maybe a mile square of cleared fields, spread acrost low hills an' circled everwhere about by thick marsh and wet prairie. Beyond that was barb wire fencin' in two, three rows maybe half a mile apart, the outermost bein' the one me an' Ole Roan had our difficulties with upstream from Naomi's cabin.

The prisoners, or slaves, or whatever you wanted to call 'em, was kept in two double-fenced pens out in the open, with a couple palmetto lean-tos for shelter and armed guards always close by. They was discouraged from tryin' to escape by workin' 'em near to death, while keepin' 'em half-starved and beatin' 'em regular into the bargain. Luke said they was a couple dozen the last time he was there.

Ravenant's home place sat up on the highest of the hills, built solid out of logs like a fort or a block-house, and havin' a good clear field of view in ever direction. A log bunk-house was right next door.

Nobody appeared concerned about any visits from unwanted strangers, and with good reason it sounded like to me.

When I asked, Luke allowed that they was prob'ly fourteen, fifteen gun-hands, ever one mean as a gator with the tooth-ache and just as dangerous. And that weren't takin' into account them two hired killers I'd met on the street in Fort Dade.

Luke seemed kind of puzzled when I mentioned them, 'cause I didn't reckon they was the kind to get theirselves tied down to no day-to-day employment. They'd struck me as hunters, pure and simple. Men who'd do a job, pocket the money, and ride out lookin' for fresh territory.

"You say Lila pointed you out to 'em soon as she spotted you in Fort Dade?"

"Uh-huh. She 'peared right definite an' determined about it, too."

Luke was silent a minute. Then he said, "That don't make no kind of sense, Tate."

"What don't?" I glanced over my shoulder at him.

"Unless . . ." Luke hesitated again, thoughtful-like. "You suppose that was her idea, and not Ravenant's?"

"'Course it was her idea!" I turned my attention back to leadin' the roan through a patch of high brush. "That's one murderous little filly you got yourself tangled up with, baby brother!"

"I know it," he agreed, soundin' a mite sharp an' testy, "'least as good as you. But the last I seen she wasn't totin' no crystal ball along with her!"

"Huh?"

"How'd them killers know to meet her in Fort Dade,

unless somebody sent for 'em ahead of time? And if you was the reason, how'd she know to send for 'em? —When she hadn't even met you till a week ago, and didn't guess you was still alive an' breathin' till the day they arrived?"

Luke let what he was sayin' sink in. And there was another big flash of lightning with rollin' thunder before he went on:

"Nothin' personal, big brother, but I don't expect you was any part of that plan till Lila suddenly took it on herself to include you in. There was some other reason them men was sent for. Or some other target, I should say."

Big, cold drops of rain had begun whisperin' and spatterin' through the leaves. I took Ole Roan's reins and looped 'em round a bush whilst I helped Luke undo the bedroll and slicker what was tied behind my saddle.

"Who you reckon it'd be?" I asked, shakin' out my slicker and handin' it up to Luke. "You, maybe?"

"Might be, if I was still on the dodge at the time." He pushed the slicker away and reached for one of the blankets. "You wear that. It'll suit you better, bein' afoot and all. I'll make do with a blanket."

It hadn't escaped my notice that Luke didn't made no offer to trade off ridin' and walkin'. When I glanced up an' seen him shiver whilst he wrapped the blanket around his shoulders, fumblin' to clutch the ends together with his free hand, I knew he was a sight tireder than he'd been lettin' on. His chin dipped down almost to his chest, and it seemed like he nodded off for a second there, before raisin' up his head to show me a lopsided grin.

"If Ravenant hired them two to come after me," he said wearily, "he surely wasted his money. I ain't fittin' quarry for a tenderfoot possum hunter after a month of his beatin's and other hospitalities, plus sleepin' out in the swamp an' all . . ."

His voice sort of trailed off, and first thing I knew he was sound asleep in the saddle. I finished tyin' up Monk's second blanket inside its oilcloth cover. Then I undid the reins and started leadin' us north an' northwest again.

I'd got to admit it didn't make no sense to call in two professionals to chase a unarmed man through the swamp. But who else would they of been brought here to kill? Marty an' Cal? Not likely. Even if Ravenant knowed about 'em and guessed their purpose, he wouldn't of thought 'em worth all the trouble. So who else?

The heavens opened up for sure pretty soon afterwards, and it was all I could do to keep me an' the roan movin', and Luke in the saddle, without ponderin' no longer on questions I didn't have answers to.

That downpour lasted a good solid hour or better. Then it settled into a cold, steady rain what come an' went all the rest of the night till near-'bout daybreak. I mean I was sore tempted a time or two to just call a halt and try riggin' some kind of shelter to wait her out. But there wasn't no place anywhere this side the river it would be safe to make camp. 'Specially not with a nice warm fire like Luke an' me needed.

When it come first light it was still drizzlin' off an' on, and I found out I'd been travelin' considerable more roundabout than I'd had plans to do in the rain an' the dark. But there wasn't no help for it. So I said a couple choice cusswords to myself, and couple more encouragin' ones to the roan, who hadn't enjoyed his night's outing any better'n I had. And soon as I could get my bearings, we made a bee-line for that river crossing where Cal an' me said we'd meet.

When we got close I nudged Luke and he jerked up his head, 'bout as wide awake as I'd seen him since first it started rainin'. He'd been noddin' in and out all along, but mostly out. And I was right pleased to see he was enough of a horseman to keep hisself in the saddle whilst he was sleepin' so sound.

I whispered a word or two about what Cal an' me'd planned. Then I shucked out my Winchester from its saddle boot and cocked it underneath my slicker.

We could hear the faint ripplin' of water as we got close to the river, amidst the reg'lar honkin' of tree frogs and the pit-pat of rain drippin' from the trees. But nothin' else reached our ears for a long couple of minutes.

My fingers was beginnin' to tighten 'round the action of my Winchester before I finally heard the low, moanin' "hoot-hoot" of Cal's barn owl, from somewhere right near the water's edge. I lifted up my head to let out the whistlin' "bob-white" we'd agreed on. And when I didn't hear no answer right away, I did it again.

Cal's whisper, when it come, was so close to my elbow it startled me, even though I was lookin' sharp and knew what to expect: "You found him. Good. This way."

When I'd led Ole Roan down to the river where we could see Cal's boat, I made Luke dismount and climb aboard, figurin' there wasn't no sense gettin' him any more wet an' chilled than he already was, seein' the shape he was in.

I swam the roan across, and after we'd joined up with Cal an' Luke on the other side we took a couple minutes hidin' the boat. Then the Injun led us back in amongst the trees with a quick whispered, "Come. Half mile further, and there's fire, shelter, —and a visitor to see you!"

A visitor? Well, I was so wet an' tired an' miserable by this time I couldn't even speculate on who it was he might of meant. I just followed along leadin' the roan, whilst he took Luke into the woods and down this narrow little windin' trail what even a deer might of missed if it hadn't been lookin' close.

We finally stepped around one more big stand of titi bushes, comin' into a small clearing with a palmetto lean-to at one end and four mules grazin' amongst the trees beyond.

Marty was waitin' in front of the lean-to, where I seen a small but invitin' fire burning, its smoke thinned an' hid by the palmetto thatch and the limbs overhead. When she set eyes on Luke, she hurried up and put a arm around his shoulders, leadin' him back towards some blankets that was spread out on the ground close to the flames.

Me, I just stood there for a minute, gawkin' at the squatty, bald-headed gent in the stove-pipe hat who'd been conversin' with Marty as we arrived.

"Highdy, Tate! Fancy meeting you out here in the middle of nowhere!" Monk was grinnin' like his face was set to bust wide open. "Coffee's on. Come on to the fire and grab a cup!"

I reckon I couldn't say or do anything right then but just shake my head. When I'd got through strippin' my saddle and gear from Ole Roan after picketing him on t'other side of the clearing, I joined Monk an' the rest under the lean-to and took a steamin' mug from his hand with a grateful nod.

"It's good to see you, Tate. I'd a feeling we might meet again down this way. But at the time we parted I couldn't afford to take the chance of telling you why." I sampled my coffee, still not sayin' nothing while the little gent took a swallow from his own cup.

"A lot of men would have given up the chase after they found out the facts about Ravenant and the odds against them. Others might have had trouble keeping certain facts to themselves in the course of conversations with the locals. And we'd only known each other a couple of days." Monk paused and cocked his head to one side, lookin' past me to Luke. "—Of course, like you, I'd no idea your brother would turn out to be a prisoner here . . ."

"Monk," I interrupted quiet-like, blinking at him over my coffee with heavy-lidded eyes. "I've had a long, wearisome couple days, and a even longer night. Curious as I am to know what it was that brung you south and what you couldn't tell me up the country, I'm afraid if you can't get to the meat of things in the next fifteen, twenty seconds, I'm liable to miss ever bit of it in favor of a nice, long nap."

"Oh." I almost thought Monk seemed embarrassed there for a minute. He shrugged and glanced past me to Marty. Luke was already snorin' softly with his head on the young gal's lap.

"Okay. The long and the short of it is, being a traveling peddler isn't my real livelihood at all. It's what we in the business call a 'cover.' Actually, I'm a private investigator. On special assignment from our home office in Chicago."

19 ☀

"A PINK?" I stared at him, not knowin' whether to smile or what. "—Uh, I mean, a Pinkerton agent?"

"Yes."

Whilst Monk took another sip of coffee, I made a effort to re-draw that earlier picture I'd had in my mind of Monk Drucker, ex-rassler an' snake oil salesman. I knowed about the Pinks, of course. In them western lands where I'd lived they mostly worked for the railroads, and they wasn't always too popular with locals, outlaws nor lawmen either one. They'd a kind of a reputation for takin' the bit in their teeth and makin' up rules as they went along, which naturally rubbed some the wrong way.

But all of 'em was one hundred percent professionals, and mighty good at what they did. I never knowed a Pink to come away empty-handed once he set hisself to fetch somebody. Ever one would dog a man's trail like a hound worryin' a coon, from now till doomsday if need be.

"Our agency was employed by Mr. and Mrs. Burton Hamilton of Boston," Monk went on, "to look into the disappearance of their oldest son, Burton Hamilton the fourth. His last known stopping place was the boarding house of a Mrs. Alice Sheehan in Fort Dade. It's believed he rode east from there, alone, into this wilderness."

I recalled what that ole hostler back at the settlement had told me, about some Yankee tourist who'd disappeared into the swamp three, four months earlier. He was the one who'd left all his goods behind at the boardin' house, together with a heap of cash money. I reckon it wasn't no surprise that somebody'd come lookin' for him, or it, sooner or later.

I wondered why Ravenant hadn't figured on that too. Or was he gettin' so sure of hisself he didn't no longer care?

"The Hamiltons are a very old and wealthy family," Monk said, drainin' the last of his coffee. "They were known to Mr. Pinkerton through mutual acquaintances during the war. When they wired and personally asked him to investigate, he selected me as his representative."

I squinted at my little bald-headed companion with a new kind of respect. Al Pinkerton's personal rep? From what I'd heard, it wasn't a job the old man was apt to lay on any run-of-the-mill agent. He was a right prideful gent, and when his reputation was at stake it stood to reason he'd send the best that he had.

"Well, after a long hard night like you've described," Monk rose from the fire and waved toward a pile of blankets at the back of the lean-to, a sort of a half-smile touchin' his lips, "you and your brother could both use some rest. When you've slept we'll talk again. 'War talk,' as I've heard you call it."

War talk? I unbuckled my gunbelt and kicked off my boots. Well, mebbe. I wasn't feelin' much forgiveness about anything Lila and her uncle's people had done, and I reckoned Luke felt even less. But that was one heap of tough *hombres* to go warrin' against, without no more help than just who was in this camp.

I rolled up in the blankets and eased closer to the fire.

Luke was a free man now, same as me. I'd got a good horse, a bit of a outfit, and what was a heap more important, we'd both our whole hides to go with 'em. . . .

I closed my eyes.

'Course there was that sort of a promise I'd made to Marty about her brother.

It was the last thought I had for a good six, seven hours.

❖   ❖   ❖

When I woke the late afternoon sky was bright an' clear outside the lean-to. The fire had burned down to nothin', and Monk, Marty an' Cal was nowhere to be seen. After a minute I sat up, huggin' my knees and sort of watchin' and listenin' all around.

Luke stirred, kind of caught hisself in mid-snore, and opened his eyes.

"Mornin', sunshine." I grinned at him. Then when I'd got my hat situated on my head, I tossed off the blankets and reached for my boots. "Or good afternoon, I guess I should say."

"Mmmm." Luke blinked an' stared at me with red puffy eyes. Then he pulled his covers more tight around his shoulders and rolled over to bury his face on his arms.

I crawled out in the open where there was room to

stand up and stamp into my boots. Little brother could prob'-ly use the extra rest, considerin' all he'd been through this past couple weeks. But from what I could see by daylight he weren't so much the worse for wear. He'd filled out consider-able in the years since we'd been together, and didn't none of it appear to be fat.

I reckon we had got to where we favored one another like everbody said. Though some of it likely had to do with the fact we hadn't either of us had no exposure to barberin' for nigh onto a coon's age.

When I'd finished bucklin' on my six-shooter, I stepped out into the clearing and took a good look around in the late afternoon sun.

We was in the midst of a hardwood hammock, with turkey oaks an' hickories growin' so dense a little ways from the camp you couldn't hardly see fifty yards without strainin' your eyes. I reckoned it was Cal who'd chose this place with such special care. All the dead leaves on the ground and the thick forest everwhere about meant there wasn't no white man alive goin' to sneak up an' catch us unawares. And dog-gone few Injuns.

I could just make out the shape of Monk's wagon amongst the trees some thirty yards off. How he'd got that rig so far out here in the wilderness was a wonder to me. But I guess them out-sized wheels an' the boat-shaped bottom, what made such a humorous appearance on dry land, had more'n a little to do with it.

It looked different in some way. But it wasn't till I'd walked closer an' scratched my head a couple times that I realized what the difference was. All them hangin' pots an' pans an' what-all that made such a racket when they banged together was absent now. Monk must of packed 'em inside or got rid of 'em someplace along the road. That made sense too.

It's all well an' good for a rovin' peddler to advertise his-self by makin' noise as he travels about in public view. But it's a genuine drawback if he means to take a little private detour without lettin' the whole world in on it. Besides, in these deep woods them hangin' thingamajigs is just a disaster wait-in' to happen. Whatever ain't fetched off by branches is liable to get itself twisted round an' tangled up into some kind of a mess like you never did see.

Monk come out from the back of the wagon about the time I got close enough for conversation. I saw he'd shucked his fancy duds for a hickory shirt, canvas trousers and laced-up huntin' boots, which was a heap more sensible if he meant to spend much time traipsin' through this here swamp. He'd kept on his black top hat, though. Prob'ly as a matter of form.

His sawed-off shotgun was shoved through the belt of his pants at the moment. And in his arms was what looked to be a entire arsenal of six-shooters an' Winchester repeaters, with a big heavy croker sack full of boxes an' what-all slung over his shoulder for good measure.

When he seen me the little gent grinned an' waddled acrost the few yards between us, turnin' round backwards so I could take holt of the sack.

"Just in time! If you'll carry this lot of supplies to the lean-to I'll be obliged. I think we can handle the rest." When I looked up after liftin' the sack off his shoulder, I seen Marty comin' down the steps from the wagon with a couple fry pans and a fair-to-middlin' load in her own arms. Most of it appeared to be food, which had a sight more appeal to me right then than any number of shootin' irons.

It had been nearly two days an' nights since I'd had anything approachin' a decent meal.

I let Monk go on ahead, and I stepped up to help the gal with some of them cans an' sacks an' such-like that she was carryin'. I seen a side of bacon in the lot, along with flour an' lard for biscuits, several tins of them good Georgia peaches, and more besides. I had to say somethin' then, just so Marty wouldn't hear all the noise my stomach was makin':

"You 'pear a tad more pert than last time I seen you." I guess that weren't so tactful as it ought to been in light of her worry over her brother an' everthing. But I plunged ahead anyway. "I reckon a night's sleep and a fresh new day can put a little different complexion on any situation."

"Maybe." Marty's mood got sober and serious mighty quick. "It ain't so easy though, when somebody you love is standin' at death's door and nothin's happening to change it."

Well, I buttoned my lip, figurin' anything I'd been fixin' to say next would only make matters worse. We walked a few steps closer to the lean-to in silence, our elbows almost touchin'. Then I took a chance an' glanced down at her.

To my surprise, she was grinnin'!

When she saw my look her grin got broader. "You're right, Tate. I do feel better about things than I did yesterday. And you know why?" She stopped and half turned towards me. "'Cause somethin' *did* happen to change things. And that somethin' was you."

"Me?" I just stared at her.

"Oh, it wasn't only you." Marty paused an' shifted the load she was carryin' a mite. "But it all started with you. You tyin' into them bad men at Naomi's place, and tacklin' Jube afterwards. Then we discovered Luke was your brother and he might still be free. And finally, after Monk joined us last evenin', you an' Luke both come back here in one piece . . ." She paused again, starin' up into my eyes. "Tate, don't y'*see?*"

I'd a idea I was beginnin' to.

"Yesterday, it seemed like me an' Cal was alone against all the evil in the world. And as good a man as Cal is, even with me helpin' I couldn't see much hope. But today, —today they's four Hell-for-leather fightin' men here and me besides. From now on that Ravenant bunch ain't hardly got a *chanct!*"

Well, there wasn't much I could say to that. Or to be more truthful, I couldn't bring myself to say it, since Marty'd got her hopes up so sky-high an' all.

But five of us against fifteen or more of them was mighty poor odds, any way you cut it. I'd of felt a heap more comfortable with a duly-elected sheriff along, together with his duly-sworn posse of say, thirty or forty men, when and if we decided to take Ravenant on.

Monk had set his load down and was beginnin' to put together a fresh fire by the time me an' Marty reached the lean-to. Luke was awake, settin' up amongst his blankets and blinkin' his eyes in wonderment at all the hardware an' other truck the three of us brung out from the wagon.

"Doggone if it don't appear like Christmas come a month or two early this year," he said, shakin' his head as he turned from me an' Marty to our bald-headed companion. "I don't suppose you got any shoes or boots hid in with all them toys an' sweet-sops, do you?"

"As a matter of fact," Monk replied, not botherin' to glance up from his fire-makin', "if you'll peek in that sack Santa Tate is carrying, you'll find a pair that might even be big enough for a Barkley's feet."

I dropped my armload of food near the fire an' swung the heavy sack off my shoulder. "We'll have us a look-see in a minute," I said, squattin' on the opposite side from Monk and pickin' up two cans that I'd had along with the rest. "First I mean to break my long fast on some of these Georgia peaches." I grinned and tossed one of the cans to Luke. "Help yourself, little brother. I reckon it ain't the only time I've shared grub with you this tri . . ."

My grin faded, and the words caught in my throat as I watched Luke catch the can in mid-air.

He wasn't missin' just one finger off his right hand. He was missin' two! Nothin' but a big ugly gap was there between his pointin' finger and his pinkie!

Luke saw me lookin', and he kind of half-shrugged while droppin' the hand to his side.

"Ravenant's callin' card," he said, not meetin' my eyes. "His way of tellin' the world he owns a body. Sort of thinks of it like his personal brand or earmark."

I'd all of a sudden lost my appetite. When I tossed my opener to Luke he turned a shoulder to hide what he was doin' while he used it.

"Second finger was for gettin' caught after escapin'," he went on. "Would of been one or two off my left hand if he'd fetched me again." He got the can open, and then smiled without humor. "He's right careful not to cripple anybody so bad they can't use a spade or a hoe."

"But for a man who deals cards for a living . . ." Monk's voice was cold and grim. He'd stopped short of lightin' the fire, and like the rest of us was watchin' Luke.

"I reckon I can still manage it, though I ain't had a chance yet to try. Nothin' fancy, o' course." He chuckled dryly. "Anybody plays me from now on can be certain of a honest game!"

Luke started eatin' his peaches, while the rest of us just sat there in silence. After a minute he lifted up his eyes. "Quit actin' like you're all at some kind of a wake, damn it! I get along fine." He paused to pluck another peach from the can and pop it in his mouth. "See?

"This here Ravenant ain't half so smart as he thinks he is," little brother went on as he chewed. "'Fact, it's his pure-out pride an' stupidity that's goin' to cost him dear."

"How you figure?" I asked, curious in spite of myself.

"He still left me my trigger fingers. One on each hand!"

Well, there wasn't no more doubts on my part about seekin' out a reckoning with Ravenant. And if anybody else there had 'em, I didn't hear it. This had got to be a right personal matter now, not only for Marty and her brother, but for me an' Luke too.

We'd some old-fashioned ideas when it come to family and fightin'. One of 'em was that whoever shed one Barkley's blood had done shed it from all of us. Another was that any such debts has got to be repaid, in blood.

I might still of welcomed a few more troops on our side, a posse or regulators or whatever. But as Monk explained later over dinner, there just wasn't much help to be had out here in the deep swamp. The citizens was few and far between, besides bein' more'n half buffaloed by tales of ghosts an' Ravenant's men. And since his home place sat real close to the borders of three Florida counties, it'd be mighty easy for any sheriff who didn't want to get involved — and they'd all got plenty other troubles to occupy 'em — to claim this here was somebody else's job.

None of us was much mind to waste around another week or longer gamblin' on the chanct of roundin' up help. 'Specially not with Marty's brother close to death an' Luke nursin' thoughts of gettin' some of his own back. I reckon I was near-'bout mad enough now my ownself, to ride through Ravenant's tater patch a-kickin' and a-smokin'.

'Bout the time I'd got through pourin' a big can of tomatoes in with the bacon grease to heat, and Marty was layin' coals on top the pan lid to brown the biscuits, Cal come in from the forest where he'd been scoutin' for sign of Ravenant's riders. He allowed that there weren't nobody closer'n a couple miles at least. So we all hunkered down to enjoy a leisurely supper.

Afterwards, with the fire down to coals and the shadows growin' long behind us, we sat pickin' our teeth and swappin' plans an' information till it was pure-out dark.

Luke done most of the talkin' there at first. He said Marty's brother was still alive the last time he seen him, and might even be growin' a little bit stronger. That was welcome news, but I noticed as he mentioned it Luke kind of lowered his eyes, so the issue must of still been in doubt.

Mr. Burton Hamilton the fourth, who Luke knowed only as "Burr," was makin' out good as could be expected. He was a right tough man to hear little brother tell it; and the two of them kind of hit it off while penned up in them barb-wire corrals together. 'Fact, they got to causin' so much trouble between 'em that the guards kept 'em separate ever chance they could. Weren't for that, Luke was a mind to take Burr with him this last time he escaped.

I asked about that Yankee gent and his woman, but they must of arrived some time after Luke took his leave. Said he thought he might of heard a lady scream whilst he was hidin' out in the woods yesterday. But for all he knew at the time it could just as easy been a bird or a painter.

We got into some serious discussin' after that. 'Cause just exactly how the four of us — five if you counted Marty — was goin' to ride into that armed camp, free the prisoners, and ride out again all in one piece was a thing none of us could see very clear right away.

I reckon Monk had a idea or two. But he kept his thoughts to hisself for the time bein', till the rest of us all had our say.

Luke an' me, we wasn't neither one much on the fine art of plannin'. You give us a reason to fight, and a place to do it, an' we'd just soon walk right up, toe the line, and get in the first lick. Maybe it ain't always the smartest way, but it's the surest. And though we'd each took some hard knocks over the years, we was both still breathin'. An' that was more'n you could say for some other, more clever gents we'd met.

Right then Marty was pretty much the same mind as us. She'd a brother who was ailing an' needed help, and she did-n't have a awful lot of patience for calc'latin' and goin' at things in a round-about way.

20 ✺

Cal, he kept mostly silent like always, only puttin' in a observation or askin' a question now an' again, what tended to make it clearer to everbody what kind of task we was facin'.

Like where Ravenant's men was apt to be at different times of the day. Or if the prisoner pens was situated so that a body could sneak up on 'em without bein' seen. And how much help we could expect from the captives if an' when we was able to set 'em free. Questions like that.

It become obvious pretty quick from how Luke answered, that no head-on attack was goin' to accomplish much besides givin' Ravenant a few more slaves or maybe some extra corpses to bury. His men stayed too spread out for us to come after 'em all to onct.

Durin' the day there was a couple men with rifles on look-out from the top floor of that log block-house up on the hill; plus three, four others watchin' the prisoners as they worked in the fields below. The rest might be takin' it easy in the second cabin what served as a bunk house, or they might

224

be ridin' picket 'round the country — which somebody done pretty near ever day, but without no regular pattern or schedule Luke could guess at.

At night there was at least three men on guard: one for each of the prisoner pens and the third just kind of rovin'. But Ravenant could easy enough increase that if he expected a attack. And he surely wouldn't tell us where an' how if he done it.

The upshot was, we couldn't never be certain where more'n half them gunmen would be at any one time. Even with surprise on our side and the extra firepower offered by Monk's Winchesters, them wasn't very hopeful odds. Like as not we'd be the ones who got surprised, and ballasted down with lead along in the bargain.

Monk just sat there cross-legged by the fire, frownin' and noddin' like some kind of a Hindoo fortune-teller whilst all this come to light. Then finally, with the deeper shadows closin' round us and Luke an' Marty an' me runnin' low on steam, he stretched and yawned real broad. Then he reached for a stick to poke up the coals.

"It seems our task is like a two-edged sword," the little gent observed mildly. "On the one hand, we'd like to give Ravenant and his men a reason to stay close to the homestead so they can all be attacked together. . . ." He paused, seemin' to study the fresh licks of flame at his feet. "But on the other, if we somehow manage to accomplish that, they'll be at their maximum strength and ready for any attack we mount."

Monk toyed with the coals a moment longer. Then he looked up at me an' grinned. "Fortunately, Mr. Ravenant himself is faced with the same dilemma!"

"Huh?" Up to there I thought I'd been followin' him pretty good. But somewhere on that last turn he lost me.

"If he concentrates his men in one spot," the little Pinkerton agent said patiently, "he gains strength but he loses flexibility. So long as they stay dispersed, they make a concerted attack more difficult, but they must also pay the price of being weaker at every point. One man alone, or even two, can be taken by surprise and overcome." Monk glanced at Luke. "If not for that, you couldn't have escaped even once, let alone twice."

Right then I begun to get a glimmer of what he was drivin' at.

"Since you two brothers are so anxious to take the war to the enemy," Monk continued, smilin' when he seen my look, "I think you ought to get started right away. The plan will be to approach their camp in secret, take out any isolated guards or stragglers you find, set the prisoner free if possible, and cause any other confusion you can without getting killed or captured yourselves." He glanced at our Cherokee companion. "Cal can go with you, if he's agreeable."

The Indian nodded, reflected firelight glitterin' in his eyes. I'd a notion this here was beginnin' to look like his kind of a war.

"You three set out tonight, then," Monk went on, "as soon as you're armed and ready. Marty and I will break camp and leave in my wagon at first light."

"Where to?" the gal asked, soundin' a mite testy it seemed. I reckon she'd got the idea she was bein' kept from the fightin' because of her sex, and maybe I'd been thinkin' somethin' like that my ownself. But it didn't take Monk long to set both of us straight:

"We, my dear, are the cavalry. Once these three have harried and weakened the enemy so they dare not leave their compound, we arrive and complete the gather." He turned from Marty to the rest of us. "I figure it will take the better part of two days to bring my wagon around to where we can approach Ravenant's place from the south, even using both pairs of mules for the pulling. You'll be on your own until then. So do what you can, but don't get captured. And above all, stay alive! We'll need every gun for the final showdown!"

"What about that log blockhouse of Ravenant's?" Luke asked. "If even half that bunch stay holed up inside, we'll play Hell roustin' 'em out."

"Leave that to me," Monk said calmly. "Or us.—I've got a plan."

He shifted round and emptied out the croker sack onto the blankets in front of us. "All right, there are Winchesters and pistols here for everyone, with ammunition and some other items you might find useful. Help yourselves to anything you want."

Luke an' Cal didn't waste no time armin' theirselves to the teeth, though I noticed Cal didn't give up the bow an' arrows he'd had with him at the start of things neither. Me, I was pleased enough with the shootin' irons I'd already got. So I contented myself with a likely-lookin' sheath knife, a pair of wire cutters Monk was thoughtful enough to include, and a couple, three boxes of cartridges what I emptied into my pockets. I took an' looped a hundred-foot coil of hemp rope over my shoulder as a kind of a afterthought. You never could tell when somethin' like that might turn out to be useful.

Each of us shoved some cold biscuits and other bits of

grub in our pockets too, though not near enough for steady nourishment. Somethin' told us travelin' fast an' light on this here expedition was goin' to be a heap more important to our health than full bellies.

The swamp we'd be movin' through wasn't no country for ridin', even if we'd had more'n one horse for the three of us. Monk would have to bring Ole Roan on hitched behind his wagon. Once I'd got my other truck together, I crossed the clearing to fetch my Winchester from its saddle boot, and to say a couple words of farewell.

On my way back to the lean-to I recollected somethin' I hadn't yet mentioned to Monk, but what I thought he better have the knowledge of before he went traipsin' all over the landscape with only a young gal to watch his backside. If they was a joker in this deck, what might discombobulate our plans unexpected-like, I figured them two hired killers I'd met on the street in Fort Dade would prob'ly be it.

Monk, he agreed. And he seemed right thoughtful at the news.

"Professionals, you say? Not just paid fighters like the others, but hired killers?"

"Uh-huh." I nodded in the faint glow from the camp-fire. "Back-shooters, more'n likely. I seen their kind a time or two before."

"And you say Lila set them on your trail?"

"When she met me there in town she did. But till then she didn't have no idea I'd be comin'. So I figure they must of been sent for earlier, with some other job in mind."

"Some other target, you mean. Like a Pinkerton agent who was getting a little too close for comfort?"

"The thought has crossed my mind."

"Okay, Tate. Thanks for the information." Monk gripped my hand by way of so long. Luke and Cal was already waitin' at the edge of the woods. "I'll be watching my back from now on. And you do the same!"

❖ ❖ ❖

Even with Cal an' Luke knowin' the country from their earlier travels, and with us usin' Cal's flat-bottomed boat to sneak upstream past Naomi's cabin on the first leg of our journey, it still took the better part of the night before we come close to Ravenant's homestead.

Time we'd grounded the boat an' hid it a little ways from that first row of barb-wire fencin', the moon was past its high point and droppin' toward the trees again. When we'd cut fence and picked our way through dense woods for maybe another mile to where we come up on the second line of wire, I figured there prob'ly wasn't but a hour or two of darkness left.

"How much further you reckon it is?" I whispered, clippin' the final strand and foldin' it back to let Luke pass.

He shrugged in the near-dark and glanced around at the forest.

"'Nother couple miles prob'ly, as the crow flies."

"Well, we ain't crows. You figure one more hour of walkin'? Or closer to two?"

Luke shrugged again, and Cal, who'd been hangin' back to listen and keep a eye on our back trail, come up to find out what the delay was.

"We're mighty near to usin' the entire night just gettin' where we're goin'," I explained. "If we ain't careful, we're liable to embarrass ourselves considerable by stumblin' into

Ravenant's camp just about the time him an' his boys are stir-rin' round lookin' for their first cup of coffee."

The Injun nodded. "Better use what time is left to find a good place to hole up for the day. Somewhere we can watch from, but not be seen."

"Uh-huh." I turned to Luke. "You got any ideas?"

He was thoughtful for a minute. Then he said, "Best spot I can think of's maybe a hundred yards south and east from that hill where the house sits. There's a kind of a boggy slough, not real big but mighty thick and uninvitin'. I never saw anybody go there, and can't imagine a reason they would." He paused. "Trouble of it is, that's all the way on the other side of the homestead from here. We'd have to circle round to reach it, and hope we could make it before it's light enough to see us."

"Anywhere closer you can think of?" I figured I'd already guessed the answer.

"None that's near as well hid. Or as off the beaten track."

"Then we'll have to chance it. Go on an' lead the way."

We moved out at as fast a clip as we dared, what with Luke tryin' to keep his bearin's in the dark and all of us tryin' not to make no more noise than necessary. The woods thinned out as we got further from the river, and that helped some.

The moon was down and it was near pitch dark when I heard Luke cuss all of a sudden under his breath. I dropped to one knee and my Winchester swung to my shoulder in a sin-gle movement.

"Dad-ratted wire! I plumb forgot that last stretch of it!" Little brother added a couple more deep-felt observations in a throaty whisper, whilst I lowered my rifle and moved forward with the cutters in my free hand. But before I got close enough to snip, I felt Cal's fingers tighten on my upper arm.

"Wait. They find the wire cut here, they'll know somebody's inside."

"Makes sense," I said, speakin' almost in his ear. "But how do we get acrost it? —Climb?" I didn't favor the prospect. They was six strands on this partic'lar fence, from a few inches off the ground to some five foot up.

"Or go under. But let's follow it first and see what we find. Any guards are prob'ly on the inside, so we'll stay outside for now." Without waitin' for Luke or me to answer, he started movin' along the fence, quick an' silent as a ghost.

We knowed there was openin's in the wire, scattered here an' there without no obvious system except what Ravenant and his men had marked in their minds. The problem for outsiders like us was tryin' to find one when you needed it. Luke had told us they was reg'lar gates sometimes, an' other times just a sort of a zig-zag layout that was too narrow for a horse or a cow or anything but a man on foot to weave its way through. Most was mighty well hid amongst brush or scrub trees or whatever.

The fence kept curvin' round to the left in the general direction we wanted to go. And Cal, he seemed to have almost second sight the way he managed to follow along a few feet outside without never runnin' into it. Or hardly ever. I noticed how he 'peared to reach out now an' again to be sure of the wire's location. And once I seen him wipe his hand on the leg of his trousers, like maybe he was wipin' off blood.

Luke an' me followed behind him for what must of been

the better part of a mile, movin' pretty fast considerin' the trees and the dark. Even so, I could see the sky had growed paler than the leaves overhead when Cal suddenly raised up his hand to call a halt. It wouldn't be long now till it was light down where we was too.

None of us spoke. Cal placed a finger on his lips for silence before kneelin' to point at somethin' on the far side of a big ole long-leaf pine. It was a second or two before I could make out what he was pointin' at. Then I seen the gray outline of a gate, almost hid behind the tree it was hinged to and a thick wax myrtle bush on its far side.

I begun to take a step forward, but Cal, he gripped my arm and pointed again. That's when I caught sight of the dark figure with a rifle just beyond the gate.

The Injun was already un-slingin' his bow an' arrows. But Luke shook his head and stabbed a finger at his chest. He wanted this one for hisself.

When Luke begun movin' hunched over an' silent toward that wax myrtle bush, he signaled me with a wave of his hand to the pine tree closer by. I nodded to show I'd got his drift.

Crawling on hands and knees, I reached the bole of the tree just about the time Luke was gettin' into position. When I snuck a peek round the near side to see where everbody was, Cal had disappeared amongst some bushes on my right. I unlimbered my sheath knife just in case. Then I stood up slow with my back against the tree trunk.

"Ssst!" I hissed, kind of soft an' under my breath. It was a sound I knew would draw attention, without bein' real easy to identify the first time you heard it. I pictured in my mind's eye what the man with the rifle was thinkin', and I let him have four, five more seconds of silence to ponder on things. Then I went "Ssst!" again.

When I heard a slight creak as the guard started to unlatch the gate, I smiled to myself. After I'd counted up to three real slow in my head, I stepped around the tree.

He was primed an' ready for trouble, I'll give him that. Soon as he seen me move his rifle jumped to his shoulder and his finger tightened on the trigger. I had me a nervous moment or two, standin' there like a cut-out in a shootin' gallery, wonderin' if he'd ask questions or just blaze away.

But before either one of us could catch our breaths, little brother was all over that feller like a turkey on a June bug. First he jammed the cold steel barrel of his Winchester underneath the guard's left ear. Then, after he'd got his undivided attention, Luke reached out with his left hand an' yanked away his shootin' iron, followin' it up in nearly the same instant by a mighty blow of his rifle butt to the skull.

The guard dropped like a rock, uttering a faint sighin' moan on his way to the ground. I couldn't tell right off whether Luke had kilt him or not, and I don't guess either one of us would of shed too many tears if he had. I recognized him now. It was that Henri, the gent with the knife who'd been a mind to appropriate one of my fingers for a souvenir back at Naomi's cabin.

Whilst we was strippin' his weapons off, unloadin' 'em and tossin' everthing back in among the trees, Henri's chest heaved up and he commenced to be sick. I let him finish what he was doin'. Then I laid my own razor-sharp knife up under his chin.

"You holler out now," I whispered, "and it'll be the last sound you make before your craw fills with blood." I seen him blink a couple times, tryin' to make his eyes focus on me. Then he opened his mouth and closed it, lookin' for all the world like a fresh-caught bream in the well of a boat. The next thing he done was faint dead away.

"What'll we do with him?" I asked, keepin' my voice down to barely over a whisper.

"You loan me the borry of that toad-sticker a minute," Luke said, "and I'll show you." I could tell he was more'n half serious.

"No." Cal had come an' joined us whilst the guard was bein' sick. "Strip off his clothes, use 'em to hog-tie and gag him. We'll hide him for now. May have a use for him later."

Well, I reckon I looked at Cal kind of funny when he said that, and I think Luke did too. But we done it, and we didn't waste no extra minutes on the task neither. By the time we'd got finished stashin' that feller under some leaves in a thicket fifty yards away, there was a pale, hazy light fil-terin' through the trees and it was just nearly comin' on to sun-up.

"We best be makin' some tracks," I told Luke, prob'ly needlessly. "How much further is it to that slough you was talkin' of?"

He paused inside the gate to have a look around, whilst Cal an' me finished scatterin' leaves an' pine needles to hide the signs of our recent activity. Luke didn't answer till we'd got right up next to him. And before he did, he pointed out in the open past them little scrub trees where we was standin'.

Not five hundred yards away was Ravenant's block-house, settin' up on a grassy hill for all the world to see!

Luke bent closer to speak in my ear: "Slough's 'bout another quarter mile on our right. I think. Maybe a little more, maybe a little less."

"Let's hope for less," I whispered, closin' the gate behind us. "This here time of the mornin', that 'maybe' could get a feller kilt!"

21

WE MOVED OFF RIGHT SMART through the bushes an' scrub along the inside of that barb-wire fence, steppin' careful so's to keep from makin' any sounds we didn't have to, but not wastin' no extra time about it neither. There was light enough to see where we was headin' now, though the ground at our feet was still pretty dark.

'Course a feller in or close to that block-house who was lookin' sharp might of noticed three man-shaped shadows a-ghostin' through the woods about then too. We all kept glancin' over our shoulders and listenin' mighty alert for any sign we'd been discovered, holdin' our weapons ready and plannin' how to beat a quick retreat in case we did.

Only there wasn't no place to retreat to, what with the barb-wire at our backs and Ravenant's company of cut-throats in front. I tried not to dwell on that whilst I plodded along in Luke an' Cal's footsteps for what prob'ly seemed a heap further than it was.

As it turned out we reached the cover of that swampy place in fairly short order, without ever bein' seen or noticed.

I expect it was a right long while since anybody up to the house there had give much thought to folks sneakin' in on their compound. What few concerns the guards had was more along the lines of prisoners sneakin' out. And accordin' to Luke, we was on the opposite side of the house now from where them captives was held.

We took our time scoutin' the thick woods around us, what didn't amount to more'n fifty or a hundred yards on a side. Then after we'd found what we reckoned was the best place to keep a secret eye on Ravenant's block-house and its surroundin's — a big ole live oak that rose up on the far side of a shallow creek — Cal, he climbed up in the branches to take the first look-out while Luke an' me settled in to make what promised to be a long an' tiresome day of it, just watchin' and waitin'.

The way Ravenant's place was laid out, there wasn't much we could accomplish in the way of causin' trouble for anybody in the wide-open daylight. We was prob'ly safe enough here in this dense ole thicket. But gettin' close to the house or the pens with the prisoners was another matter entire. There weren't hardly any trees in that direction for somethin' over a mile.

We discussed ideas an' plans for a time, Luke or me tradin' places with Cal off an' on so he could put his two cents in. Then we made a lunch out of cold biscuits an' sweet potatoes, and I settled more comfortable against the tree trunk where I could think about a little snooze.

"Y'know," I said to Luke, who was airin' his toes after a all-night trek in his new pair of boots, "that Ravenant's a pretty clever feller when you think about it. I mean, take his notion of pretendin' him an' his men is haints an' all. It's not a story everone might put stock in, but it does offer a explanation for all them disappearances hereabouts. And it has a way of discouragin' your garden-variety busybody from lookin' into the situation too close as well."

I eased my hat lower to block out a stray sunbeam what had worked its way down through the leaves overhead. "Just makes a feller wonder how anybody comes up with ideas like that."

"I expect the thought come natural enough to him," Luke answered dryly, "if you got any notion a-tall of the French tongue."

Well, I just waited for little brother to explain, knowin' he meant to use the opportunity to show off some of that learnin' he'd got on them Mississippi riverboats.

"The word *revenant*," Luke went on, swallowin' the *r* like he was fixin' to spit, "is just the way the French have of sayin' 'ghost' or 'spirit.'"

"Uh-huh." I answered from under my hat, like I'd more'n half expected it all along. "That do make a kind of sense, don't it?"

Then I closed my eyes an' went to sleep.

❖   ❖   ❖

Since there wasn't much else to do, the three of us mostly just traded off sleepin' and watchin' through the long afternoon. In between times we talked a bit, 'specially Luke an' me, startin' to fill each other in on what we'd been up to durin' the past fifteen years.

Like anybody else, we'd both had some good times an' some lean times. But Luke, he 'peared to of took more to the high road than me — hobnobbin' with the Quality on them riverboats and in the fancy saloons of Denver an' San

Francisco, while I'd spent my evenin's by a open fire in the company of cowpokes an' miners and your occasional rustler or stand-an'-deliver artist. You couldn't always tell it from the way little brother spoke when just us two was together, but now an' again he'd let somethin' drop what showed he'd picked up more'n a tad of learnin' from bein' round all em rich folks an' furriners an' high-falutin' women. 'Specially the women.

I guess maybe we'd each had a few more'n our share of difficulties an' altercations during our travels. Six-gun difficulties and knuckle-an'-skull altercations, I mean. Not that we ever went huntin' it. But if they's one thing could be said for all our clan, from Great-grandpappy down to Pap an' us, it's that there ain't never been much back-up in any Barkley.

When we'd done comparin' notes I figured Luke an' me was pretty close to even on that score, 'spite of any differences in the circles we run in. Might be I was a hair quicker to get my feathers ruffled an' take up the challenge. But I wouldn't make no bets a-tall on who was more dangerous once the lead started flyin'.

Finally the shadows started gettin' long and the sun dipped behind the trees, and Cal slipped down from his perch to take part in one last council of war.

"They're all sittin' down to supper now, except the guards over the prisoners and one look-out on the top floor of the blockhouse." Cal glanced from me to Luke an' shrugged. "Doesn't appear like they suspect anything. Ravenant got a little perturbed this morning when he found out the man at the gate was missin'. They spent some time beatin' the bushes. But then he just posted another guard and things went on as usual."

Luke smiled kind of grim-like. "It isn't the first time it's happened. Even among hard cases like that, not everybody has the stomach for loppin' off fingers and keepin' folks slaves. A couple others hauled their freight while I was prisoner there." His smile faded. "One of 'em made it. The other one didn't."

"We'll have 'em all mullin' it over 'fore this night's done," I said. "Monk's plan was to rile 'em up, spoil their sleep, and make 'em so all-fired jumpy they won't leave them cabins tomorrow for love nor money." I glanced at my *compadres*. "I reckon we're just the gents who can do it."

Cal, he'd took off his hat and was settin' out some things from a little pouch he'd had with him on top of a fallen tree trunk. "War paint," he said when he noticed me watchin'. "Can't hurt. Might help." He moved a little to one side as he begun doctorin' his face, pointin' to the fixin's with a free hand. "Help yourselves. It's not generally our custom to share with pale-skins, but I was never one to stand on tradition. Anything that'll advance the cause."

Well, I figured, what the Hell? I dabbed a mite on my cheeks an' forehead just to make any of them owlhoots I come acrost in the dark wonder what it was they was up against. Luke was a tad more conservative, knowin' he'd got to talk to them prisoners in the stockades before too long an' not wishin' to stir up any more excitement than absolutely necessary. He just took a little of the charcoal black an' smeared it on his nose an' cheekbones, so's to cut down on any reflection from the moon or a guard's lantern.

Before twilight slipped entirely into dark, little brother climbed up to have one last study over Ravenant's layout, whilst I snuck off with the wire cutters and made a couple good-sized openin's in that fence what run along the back side of the woods we'd been hidin' in. That was to make movin' around a mite easier, and give us a quick way out in case worst come to worst.

Cal, he followed along behind me to the fence-line, waitin' till I'd made my cuts before raisin' up a hand and disappearin' into the forest beyond it. The plan was that he'd take care of any guard what might be watchin' the gate we come in by this mornin', while Luke an' me slipped past it to the first stockade of prisoners. We knew he'd some kind of idea for usin' our captive to create a distraction later on. But neither of us was much mind to question that redskin 'bout how he meant to do it.

When I'd made it back to the live oak tree, Luke was easin' hisself to the ground. "All's quiet," he said, his voice scarcely over a whisper. "They just got through sendin' out fresh guards so the others could come in and eat. No more'n three outside now that I could see. One for each stockade, and the third seemed like he weren't in no hurry to go anyplace partic'lar. He stopped to light up a smoke in front of the bunkhouse, and I couldn't tell where he got to after that."

"We'll need to be lookin' out sharp for him, then." I loosened my knife in its scabbard and took aholt of my Winchester with my left hand. "You go ahead an' lead the way to that first stockade. I'll keep a eye on your back."

We'd in mind to try settin' all the prisoners loose first, before any general ruckus got started. Otherwise them folks would be in serious straits, penned up like they was under the guns of their guards. Besides which, Luke figured some of the more hearty might like a opportunity to get a mite of their own back, once they was free and had a chance at some weapons.

When we got close to where I recollected that gate in the fence to be, I put a hand on Luke's shoulder and we hunkered down amongst the low-growin' scrub, watchin' and listenin'. There wasn't no sign of the third guard, nor of Cal neither. I cupped a hand to my mouth and give out with my bob-white quail, real soft an' low. A couple seconds later I heard the Injun's answerin' barn owl, maybe fifty feet to our left an' front. I figured he'd prob'ly seen us, so I motioned for Luke to go on the way he'd been headin'.

I wasn't too certain what Cal would do, since the man he was meant to take out wasn't nowhere around. But I expected it'd be somethin' thoughtful and needful. 'Cause that's the kind of warrior that Cherokee struck me as bein'.

In another couple minutes we was close enough to hear the prisoners movin' about and talkin' amongst theirselves in low, weary voices. Luke an' me pulled up behind a little patch of high grass an' palmettos maybe forty feet away, huggin' the ground and raisin' up our heads just a hair to look over the situation.

A second later Luke nudged me an' pointed. But I'd already seen the guard, movin' round leisurely outside that double row of barb-wire fence, with a coal-oil lantern in his left hand and a old Colt revolvin' shotgun under his elbow.

That shotgun was enough to make a feller cautious. But since one charge of buckshot can kill you just as dead as four, the thing was not to let him have no chance to use it a-tall.

I nodded my head to let Luke know I'd spotted him. Then I begun snakin' through the grass on knees an' elbows till I'd put a dozen yards between us. When I come to a little dip in the ground I took a long careful breath, laid my Winchester down beside me, and waited. If the guard kept on the way he was goin', he'd pass almost in arm's reach of me in another couple minutes.

Well, he took his sweet time about doin' it. But finally I seen the flicker of his lantern movin' closer. And pretty soon he come amblin' past, his head turned so he could watch over them helpless prisoners without a thought in the world for anything else what might be hidin' in the shadows.

I didn't give him time to think better of his carelessness. I just rose off the earth in a mighty lunge, throwin' my left arm across his Adam's apple to crush his voice box whilst the fingers of my right hand closed down on the cylinder of that revolvin' shotgun.

I mean, he was some perturbed. He couldn't holler out, and he couldn't get off a shot with me grippin' his piece real tight so the cylinder wouldn't turn. And when he twisted his head around an' caught sight of me scowlin' over him in my war paint, I thought he was 'bout to lose it entire.

But Luke put a end to his misery with the butt of his Winchester, and I let him down to the ground, keepin' holt of the shotgun till his fingers sort of melted away from the action.

Some of the captives closest to us was payin' attention now, and I tossed the wire-cutters to Luke so he could make hisself useful whilst he was explainin' the situation to 'em. Meanwhile I doused the guard's lantern and went about collectin' up my own an' his hardware, feelin' through his pockets mighty thorough for hide-outs an' what-all else I could find, just like Miss Lila showed me how to do a week or so back.

It wasn't till I'd rose to my feet to go join Luke that I noticed this little dot of orange-red light movin' round on the other side of the stockade. I dropped my other goods and started bringin' my Winchester to my shoulder maybe two, three shakes of a hound's tail after I'd seen it. 'Cause that's about how long it took me to recognize what it was.

It was our missin' guard. The one what favored cigarette smokin' whilst he was out skulkin' round in the dark.

He made a mighty pretty target whenever he took a draw on that butt. Ten inches underneath it ought to put a ball dead center of his brisket. But as my finger tightened on the trigger, I hesitated.

A glance toward Luke an' the prisoners told me they wasn't near finished cuttin' through all that barb-wire yet. And even if they was able to get it done an' make a dash for the woods before my shot brung Ravenant's men out of their cabins, there was still that second stockade a little ways past this one. Them folks wouldn't have no more chance than a mess of fish in a barrel.

But the guard was too far away for me to do anything 'bout him shy of a rifle shot. And if I didn't dust him now, the game was goin' to be up no matter how the rest of the cards got dealt. I took in a deep breath and held it, my finger takin' up slack again on the trigger.

All of a sudden there was this kind of a low, gurglin' moan, and I watched the cigarette tumble end-over-end to the ground. Cal's second arrow made a nice solid 'Thunk!' what meant it must of struck right about that same place in the brisket I'd been aimin' for.

I didn't waste no time in collectin' up the hardware I'd dropped an' hot-footin' it over to where Luke stood with a couple gents what 'peared to be more scarecrows than men. They was bendin' the last of the barb wire out of the way so the others could get through.

"Hurry 'em ever chanct you get!" I whispered harshly. "Cal bought us a little extra time, but I got a feelin' our luck won't hold much longer. They's been too many peculiar little sounds out here, along with missin' guards and a missin' lantern, for somebody not to start gettin' curious."

"We're doin' the best we can," Luke answered, soundin' a mite testy his own self. "Some of these folks are so weak an' sick they'll have to be carried."

"Let 'em carry each other for the time bein'." I shoved the revolvin' shotgun at one scarecrow and thrust the guard's spare pistol in another man's hands. "If we get that second stockade opened up in time, we can come back to help. If we don't, they'll be some blood-lettin' down yonder what'll make the fever seem like a welcome change of air!"

Luke knew I was right, though it grated in his craw to leave these people behind weak an' near helpless like they was. He handed his Winchester to a tall man who 'peared a little more sprightly than the rest, then he started off towards that next stockade without another word.

I was close on his heels, both of us movin' now in a low, crouchin' run. The place we was headed for was over a little rise, out of sight of the first stockade but in plain view of the bunkhouse and the main cabin, maybe two hundred yards on our right.

I kept glancin' thataway, my heart thumpin' and ever sense alert for signs of a general hue an' cry. But so far we'd got luck, or so it appeared. Lights was burnin' behind the closed shutters of both buildings, but only because it was early yet. A card game was prob'ly goin' hot an' heavy in the bunkhouse, and it was anybody's guess what kind of doin's in Ravenant's private quarters.

With Luke in such a big hurry to get where he was goin', and me glancin' over my shoulder ever couple seconds while tryin' not to trip over my own feet, I guess neither one of us was payin' as good attention as we could of been regardin' the man who stood watch over that second stockade. First time we noticed him was when his lantern started bobbin' up the hill towards us.

Fortunately, he couldn't make us out worth a hoot there in the dark neither. And we hadn't made so much noise yet that he'd reason to expect trouble. Him comin' to meet us was more curiosity than anything else.

Luke, he didn't even slow down. He just lowered a shoulder an' barreled into that gent full steam ahead. By the time I got to where the man lay sprawled out on the grass, little brother was comin' up on the nearest row of fences with the wire cutters in his hands.

I stopped to kick the guard's shotgun away, then went to stompin' out some little streamers of burnin' oil what spilled from his lantern as it smashed on the ground. That didn't take more'n two, three seconds. But it was all the guard needed to collect his wits and claw a six-shooter from his belt. When I glanced in his direction he was thumbin' back the hammer with a mind to air out my shirt with .44 caliber holes.

22 🌓

I DIDN'T HAVE TIME TO THINK. My Winchester just swung up and I fired into him one-handed, like I was shootin' a pistol. As he cussed an' grunted, his gun spouted flame, and I felt the whip of a bullet close by my ear. I worked the lever and took aim so I could put another in his brisket where it'd quiet him a mite better. Then I spun 'round on my heel to see what effect our noise an' commotion was havin' on them men in the cabins.

There was shouts from the bunk-house, and I seen somebody in the big building blow out a light. A instant later a rifle cracked an' flashed from the second story, but I figure whoever it was hadn't been watchin' the way he was supposed to be. 'Cause his bullet didn't come anyplace close.

When the door to the bunk-house swung open I levered three, four quick shots at its rectangle of light, movin' out lively in the direction of the stockade soon as I let go the last one. The door slammed shut again and lanterns were doused amidst general cussin' an' pandemonium. But the rifleman up to the big house was payin' attention this time. Two well-aimed shots split the air where I'd been standin' a couple seconds earlier.

Luke was makin' fair-to-middlin' progress with the wire as I dropped down on one knee a little distance away, tryin' not to draw no fire in his direction or the prisoners' if I could help it.

"Sorry, little brother," I said, thumbin' cartridges into my Winchester. "It couldn't be helped. That feller was bound and determined to see one of us kilt. Only choice he give me was which one it was."

"Then I guess you made as good a choice as you could." Luke cut an' pulled another strand aside, then one more, and the prisoners swarmed out. These 'peared in a little better shape than the first batch. The strongest was already helpin' the weakest as they started through the wire and off toward the forest a hundred yards behind us.

Luke an' one other big feller separated out from the crowd and moved in my direction. "Where'd you leave that guard?" the big man asked when they was close enough for whispers.

"Tate, this here's Burr Hamilton. The gent your Pinkerton friend was huntin'."

"Pleasure," I said, pointin' with my rifle. "Over yonder where you see that dark little mound. You goin' after his guns?"

"Yes. The shotgun was mine anyhow, when I first rode into this swamp. It's a valuable weapon and I'll be glad to have it back."

"Your funeral." I thought I could see movement now from round an' about the dark bunkhouse. I levered a couple shots thataway, mostly to slow 'em down and make 'em cautious. Then I skittered to one side, slappin' Hamilton on the back when I did to hurry him along. "Go on and make your play. I'll cover you."

He hadn't made it twenty feet when a half dozen guns opened up from the direction of the cabins. Luke fetched his six-shooter and begun slingin' lead back at 'em, whilst our new acquaintance hit the ground in a stumblin' dive. I held up for a second till I could get a bead on one of them owlhoots by his gun flashes, and then I dropped him clean as a whistle. As I was movin' afterward so they couldn't do the same to me, I seen Hamilton on his hands and knees, scurryin' towards that dead guard like a fox flushed from cover.

"He's got grit," I said, sendin' a couple, three more shots toward the cabins while Luke reloaded. "Might turn out to be right helpful if he lives long enough."

"He's a one like us, Tate, for all that he was reared up North with a silver spoon in his mouth. Don't count that gent out till you see 'em chuck dirt on his face."

Hamilton hit the ground again as we spoke, usin' the guard's body for cover. I watched him take up the dead man's pistol and shove it into his britches, along with what I guessed was ammunition from the other's pockets. Then he peered out from his hidin' place, tryin' to learn what direction I'd kicked the shotgun. I wanted to holler and tell him, but that would of only give them boys up on the hill some better place to shoot at.

Finally he seen where it was, maybe six feet off on his left. An' while me an' Luke blazed away at the cabins he made a scramblin' dive, rollin' over and comin' up in a crouch with the piece cradled in his arms. By that time I was pullin' so hard for him to make it that I caught myself mutterin' little encouragin' words under my breath, like some gent with his life savings ridin' on a horse race.

Hamilton made a wild dash for us an' the woods, with all Hell bustin' loose on that hillside behind him. I winged another shooter, lettin' out a Texas whoop afterwards in spite of my better judgment. Then I seen Luke's big friend go down on one knee, and I was certain the game was up.

But a instant later there was this huge flash an' roar from one barrel of his shotgun, and in the sudden light this gunman we hadn't spotted yet threw up his arms and sprawled on the grass. He'd been sneakin' alongside the stockade wire, not more'n a dozen yards from Luke an' me.

Hamilton didn't spare no more time about completin' his run, and we all three lit out for the woods with gun-flashes an' lead balls stabbin' the night behind us. When I turned at the edge of the trees to catch my breath an' glance back, I seen Ravenant's men had begun to come closer, spread out in a ragged line now and movin' as they fired so that it was near impossible to find a steady target.

"Take them wire-cutters and see 'bout gettin' the prisoners past that next row of fencin'," I called to Luke, "where they'll have a better chance of losin' theirselves in the woods an' the dark! I'll fort up here an' try to hold 'em off a tad longer!"

I weren't too hopeful about how long it'd be, 'cause them gunmen was gettin' nearer with ever second that passed. But I found me a good thick oak tree for cover, hunkered down amongst the roots, and begun dustin' lead back an' forth in hopes of at least makin' them boys a little nervous whilst they closed in around us.

Burr Hamilton took up a place some twenty feet away, addin' his two cents with the guard's captured six-shooter. They was bullets flyin' ever which-way through them trees, kickin' up bark and whippin' amongst the leaves like a reg'lar hail-storm. But neither side was doin' no real damage that I could see. And Ravenant's hard cases just kept movin' nearer.

My Winchester was empty and I'd reached for my Smith an' Wesson to take up the slack, when all of a sudden there was this spine-shiverin' scream from somewhere away off on my right. It was like ever single person for a half mile around just froze in their tracks. The shootin' died down to almost nothin'. And then that scream come again, cater-waulin' and keenin' along on the night air.

"Come on!" I hissed to Hamilton, whose gun had fell as silent as the rest. "Let's git whilst the gettin's good!" I took up the empty Winchester in my left hand and begun fadin' back into the forest, watchin' sharp for any sign of pursuit. But near as I could tell, there wasn't none a-tall.

"What the Hell was that?" Burr Hamilton asked, after we'd joined up an' put another forty, fifty yards behind us. For a big, tough man, he sounded more'n a little spooked. And I reckon I understood how he felt.

"Injun customs," I answered, not slowin' my pace as I led us deeper into the swamp and away from Ravenant's lay-out. "If you don't ask no more questions, I'll stop tryin' to guess."

It took a mite of doin', but after while we located Luke's break in the wire and found him there waitin' for us, along with maybe half a dozen of the men prisoners. Three of 'em was armed with weapons took from the guards, whilst the others had tree limbs an' what-not that they'd picked up along the way. One carried a evil-lookin' six-foot whip of barb wire, what he'd wrapped the end of in cloth torn from his shirt.

"These gents wanted to help," little brother said, "so I allowed they could watch over the back side of the homestead in case anybody gets it in their heads to try and sneak off that way. Prob'ly be most useful tomorrow, after Monk gets here and we start our gather."

"Sounds good to me," I agreed. I still weren't too clear on what the li'l Pinkerton agent had in mind. But we could likely use all the help we could muster. "Meantime they can rest a mite, standin' watch in turns. Us an' Cal has had our sleep, so we'll see can we arrange it so none of them gunslingers gets any of their own."

"A couple more of them pitiful cries of torment like we heard earlier," a tall rangy gent said, who I recognized as the prisoner Luke had lent his Winchester to, "an' won't none of us have to worry about sleepin' sound for some weeks to come!"

"I expect there'll be more," I replied, "'cause that was our Injun friend's plan from the git-go. Was I you, whenever the noise started to fret me I'd just recall all the fingers what's been lost amongst this here company. Especially the women."

"What about them?" Burr Hamilton asked, glancin' from me to Luke an' the men with him. "And the other captives?"

"Safe enough for the time bein'." The rangy gent jerked his head toward the dark shadows behind them. "We got 'em hid back in the trees a half mile off. Everybody's already used to sleepin' out without no fire or shelter, so I reckon another night won't make much difference. If worst comes to worst an' they got to run, 'least they'll have 'em a head start on whoever comes lookin'."

"We'll do our best to see it ain't needed," I said. "Which reminds me, little brother. What you know about how them boys' horses is kept? You think we might have a go at them some time before mornin'?"

"Maybe." Luke was thoughtful but not especially hopeful. "They got 'em penned in a corral right back of the bunkhouse. Could be with the right kind of a distraction. . ." He shrugged. "But there's a lot of hours till daylight still. Let's see what opportunities present theirselves."

We left it at that, biddin' the men from the stockade farewell and startin' back along the fence line toward where we'd last seen Cal and his prisoners. Burr Hamilton wouldn't have it no way but he'd got to come with us. So it was a party of three what begun light-footin' it through the brush an' the leaves, each one of us keyed up and loaded for bear.

We hadn't gone more'n a hundred yards when we heard ole Henri start in to howlin' and screechin' again somethin' dreadful. It was a sound what made ever hair on your head stand on end, an' give you the shivers down to the soles of your feet. I tried not to imagine what kind of heathen tortures that Injun was usin'. I just followed my own advice an' reminded myself there wasn't no more deservin' feller in this whole big swamp — unless it was Ravenant hisself.

I'd reloaded my Winchester whilst we was havin' our conversation back yonder, so the Smith an' Wesson was in its holster again, with a good sheath knife on t'other side for any quiet work needed to be done. Luke had his six-shooter and a good-sized Bowie too, and with Hamilton's shotgun an' a pistol for spare, I'd of hated like the dickens to be one of Ravenant's boys meetin' us there in the dark by his lonesome. Or even with a couple friends for company.

But that's a kind of thinkin' can cut both ways. So the further we went the more I found myself wonderin' where all them hired guns had got theirselves to, and what they was doin'.

Each of us kept up a mighty sharp look-out as we made our way alongside that fence-row. But I reckon it was Luke who first heard the voices an' called a halt, crouchin' sudden-like behind some low-growin' bushes. Me and Hamilton followed suit about a half a second later.

". . . You heard me! Go on an' get your tails back to the cabins now, and no further foolishness!" This first gent sounded angry, and maybe a tad scared.

"Damn it, Joe, we trailed them shouts from all the way t'other side of the hill yonder. It ain't but another fifty, sixty yards out past this fence here."

"I don't care if it's in them bushes right under your noses!" I'd a idea he meant the bushes where Luke was hidin'. And if he took another half dozen steps that way, he wasn't goin' to care about much of anything any longer. My Winchester and Hamilton's shotgun was all set to blast his friends an' him to doll rags the minute one of 'em made a move to show hisself.

Only they didn't. Joe just went on explainin' from somewhere off in the dark, soundin' more an' more irritated as he went along:

"You don't know who-all or what-all's out yonder in the night. Could be a hundred men within the sound of our voices. Ravenant told everbody to congregate on the cabins an' fort up till daylight. Me, I say that makes a heap of sense. Maybe tomorrow, whenever we can see what it is we're up against . . ."

"But that's ole Henri's been doin' that hollerin'. You know it the same as us. Likely he's been hurt an' needs help, — or else . . ."

"Or else?" There was a bit of a pause before Joe went on in a grim voice: "Leave him. He's a growed man, and he'll have to fend for hisself. No sense any more of us gettin' took by whatever it was got him. Besides, like I told you, them's Ravenant's orders!"

I reckon the other two finally seen Joe's point. 'Cause we didn't hear nothin' else except a little scufflin' through the grass. And then they was gone.

Luke an' Hamilton an' me hadn't hardly started movin' again when I heard the hoot of a owl close by. Soon as I'd answered back, Cal stepped out from the shadows to join us.

He was grinnin' ear to ear, like he hadn't had so much fun in a entire month of Sundays!

"What you think, men?" the Injun asked soon as he was next to us. "Are we giving them Hell, or what?"

"I reckon." I studied his war-painted face in the pale light from the stars. "'Pears like you been causin' a fair amount of consternation anyhow. You an' your prisoner."

"Oh, that's just the beginning. I figure it's time we moved him now. I'll set him to howling from some new place. Then we can pick up that other guard I hog-tied after you dented his skull, and start to work on him. Before morning they'll think there's a dozen men bein' skinned alive out in these woods!"

"You expect you'll be able to keep 'em alive long

enough for all that?" I avoided his eyes. Ravenant or no Ravenant, I wasn't sure I'd got the stomach for a full night of this kind of work.

"Why not? That one ain't hurt, 'cept for the knot you put on his head 'long about first light yesterday."

"Huh?" For a minute I couldn't find no words. I just stared at him whilst Burr Hamilton took up the slack:

"But those screams we heard . . ."

"Spiders." Cal's grin got broader.

"Spiders?"

"Yeah. The man's got a mortal fear of spiders. Took a little experimentin' to find out, since he wasn't inclined to talk about it. But most everybody has somethin' sets 'em off like that — snakes, rats, leeches, spiders. . . —Just a matter of findin' out what it is, and then collectin' enough specimens to keep him occupied while he's all bound up and helpless!"

Luke run his fingers through his hair an' shook his head. "Well, I'll be a . . ."

"Me too," I agreed. "You got any idea the kind of bloody imaginin' we was all doin' when we heard them screams?"

"You," Cal said. "And Ravenant's men too, I hope. — Though you ought to know better."

"Why's that?"

"Didn't anybody ever tell you us Cherokees are one of the five *civilized* tribes?"

❖　　　　　　❖　　　　　　❖

Well, we left things more or less peaceful for the next couple hours or so. With the exception of Cal an' his prisoners, I mean. We moved Henri like he suggested, and after a little bit he managed to get the second one bawlin' too. Then he kept 'em both at it by turns, until they was so plumb tuckered they couldn't hardly croak.

Luke an' Burr Hamilton an' me rested in the meanwhile, keepin' a eye on the homestead from our live oak tree by the slough, and talkin' things over whilst we was doin' it.

We'd already accomplished most of what Monk said he wanted. The bad men was holed up in one place, and I reckoned they'd stay that way at least till morning. With the help of them armed men we'd posted out back, maybe we could keep 'em boxed until Marty an' Monk arrived later on.

Only I didn't feel altogether confident about it. We hadn't hurt their numbers near as much as I'd of liked to in preparation for a final show-down. And 'long as they still had their horses, they'd be a reg'lar caution if they chose to attack instead of just sittin' tight. 'Specially since us an' their former captives was on shank's mare our ownselves.

I'd a mind to do somethin' about that, whilst we still had the dark an' the night on our side.

23 ✺

Luke an' Burr was game. So after discussin' things a tad longer we roused ourselves an' begun driftin' through the trees to our right, easin' toward where we could have us a good look at that split-rail corral behind the bunkhouse.

I'd gone to find Cal an' have a word with him first, lettin' him know it'd be helpful if he was to throw some lead from his Winchester at the opposite side of the cabins ever now an' again, just to keep them boys kind of thinkin' and lookin' in that direction.

We followed along the nearest barb-wire fence for a good part of our trip, cuttin' holes in it ever fifty or a hundred yards so's to give them horses a good choice of ways to leave. By then I reckoned we'd got maybe two, three hours left till sun-up.

When we finally come to this dry creek-bed at the bottom of the hill, all growed up in weeds and snakin' its way to within maybe thirty feet of the corral, things had been kind of quiet for some little time. Cal's songbirds had long since run out of steam; and now he was doin' like we agreed, movin' about and takin' pot-shots at the far side of the homestead ever ten, fifteen minutes — just enough to be sure them boys inside was awake and thinkin'. Pretty soon they got to where they didn't even answer him back, prob'ly realizin' that in this dark they was only wastin' ammunition.

I crawled out amongst the tall grass of the creek-bed on my hands an' knees. And then I laid there for awhile, studying the situation.

They was two guards inside the corral, one on the far side away from me and the other closer by. 'Peared like each was doin' his best to stay watchful, but with the moon mostly hidin' amongst the clouds overhead there wasn't too much to watch. Now an' then one would shift his weight or take a couple steps in this direction or that, so's to look over the surroundin' trees, and more'n likely keep hisself awake.

I figured there was prob'ly one or two more look-outs on the second story of the big house. But it was some several minutes before I seen a little glint of moonlight on a rifle barrel and one gent showed his face for a instant, peerin' out from a narrow window a couple feet to one side of the stick and clay chimney.

Now, when I got to lookin' up at that chimney it made me thoughtful. Not that it was any different from most other cabin chimneys you'd see in the Florida wilderness, made out of stacked-up green twigs lined with clay. Bricks was costly and hard to tote, so most folks just done with what was free and close to hand.

But of course that kind of chimney wasn't half as sturdy as one made from bricks. And that's what made it interestin' to me right then.

That an' the fact I could see a faint plume of smoke trailin' out from the top of it now. Which meant somebody inside had a fire lit against the night an' the damp, or maybe the skeeters.

I eased back to where Luke an' Burr was waitin' in the deeper shadows of the trees, and we held a short whispered pow-wow. Then I handed my Winchester to Luke before startin' to unlimber the rope I'd been carryin' coiled around my left shoulder.

Whilst the other two begun to Injun through the grass of that dry creek bed toward the corral, I built a loop in one end of the rope and counted up to a hundred before followin' after. By the time I figured Luke an' Burr ought to be gettin' in position, I'd made my way on chest an' belly to a place just opposite the chimney and some dozen yards away.

I was pert' near to bein' out in the open here, but I forced myself to stay put and study my surroundin's. The two guards in the corral didn't seem to of noticed nothin'. They was still at their posts, kind of half restin' an' half payin' attention. When I glanced up at the window where the other man had been, I couldn't see no more sign of his rifle or him. I hoped he'd moved on around to some other window by now.

Finally I took in a deep breath, eased a mite closer to the building, and stood up, swingin' the loop wide over my head. I prob'ly wouldn't get but one chance, so I done my best to make the first throw count. The loop sailed up an' over the chimney, an' quick as I seen it drop I begun backin' up and haulin' on that rope for all I was worth.

As things turned out, it was some easier'n I'd thought. The chimney crumbled an' give way with a dull Crack! And before I knew what was happenin', I'd landed flat on my tail in the grass. In the process I reckon I finally managed to get the full attention of them two guards.

Bullets begun buzzin' round my ears whilst I struggled to fight shy of the rope and make a dash for the forest. I slithered a few yards, rolled over an' unlimbered my six-shooter, then let fly a couple in the general direction of the corral before skitterin' a dozen feet further on my hands an' knees. I come up on the run, and didn't slow down till I'd found me the cover of a nice solid water oak.

They was shouts inside the house, what told me somebody was startin' to notice the smoke from that tumbledown chimney. And when I chanced a peek out from where I was hidin', I seen one of the men from the corral had jumped the fence and started in my direction. The other was zig-zaggin' amongst the horses, tryin' to get close enough to where he could back his friend's play.

I didn't wait for him to make it. I took aim an' drilled my pursuer through the third button of his white cotton shirt. Then I let him have another one a couple inches lower before steppin' back to let his partner waste lead on that stout ole oak.

Cal must of knowed from all the racket we was up to somethin'. 'Cause he begun leverin' rifle balls at the far side of the cabins so fast it sounded like a army. There was a heap of frustrated men inside there now, shootin' in both directions. But near as I could tell they wasn't hittin' nothing except grass an' night air.

When the guard who was takin' pot-shots at me held up to give a shout, I figured Burr an' Luke had finally managed to pull down a section from that split-rail fence. I dropped to my knees an' risked a peek, just as Burr's shotgun let out a huge double blast. And them hosses flat begun to migrate.

The man by the rail was starin' at 'em slack-jawed, blinkin' from the shotgun flash, when I put a ball in his side to remind him I was here. A instant later Luke's Winchester spoke, and that feller begun clutchin' air on his way to the ground.

I kept throwin' lead at the cabin windows till my pistol was empty so's to buy Luke an' Burr enough time to make their getaway. When I hunkered back behind my water oak to re-load, everbody in the cabins had got my range and it 'peared like bark an' twigs was flyin' everwhere. For a second or two after I finished slidin' fresh cartridges into the cylinder I just huddled against the trunk and tried to catch my breath.

Burr's scatter-gun roared again from someplace on my right, and they was a couple rifle shots closer by. Then Luke's voice come from one of the trees at my back, soundin' just a mite concerned:

"You doin' okay, Tate? You didn't go an' get yourself hurt, did you?"

"Not yet, little brother. Though it ain't from any lack of effort on them owlhoots' part. I just had a mind to lay low an' take a breather for a spell."

"Well, let's see can't we do that together some deeper in the forest. Give me a second to change position here, and I'll draw their fire while you make your move."

I opened my mouth to say somethin', then closed it again and held my peace. Luke prob'ly wouldn't pay no atten-tion to my words anyhow. And besides that, he was makin' sense. When I heard him start leverin' rifle shots toward the cabins I jumped up an' hot-footed it back amongst the trees.

Then I found another spot of cover from where I could return the favor. After a couple, three such leap-froggin' moves we was both out of sight from them muzzle flashes at the cabins.

"Whew!" Luke allowed as he finally come up beside me in the dark. "That there was a exhilaratin' piece of work."

"I reckon. Did you an' Burr manage to get all the hosses out from the corral?"

"Ever one. They seemed to feel pretty much the way you an' me did about hangin' round after the shootin' got fierce. By now I expect they're scattered to the four winds."

"Or at least to that second row of wire fence. Been nice could we of made a couple holes in that too whilst we was about it."

"There's a hour or so left till sun-up. And I still got the cutters." I felt more than saw little brother shrug in the dark. "I doubt those boys'll take a chance on chasin' after 'em before daylight. They still don't know how many or who we are out here."

Well, that part was true enough. We'd got 'em discombobulated and afoot now, an' made a little dent in their numbers besides. I tried askin' myself what I'd do next if I was in Ravenant's place.

If he'd got vittles enough, and the grit to keep a tight rein on them hired guns of his, it 'peared like the smartest thing was to just stay forted up where he was and see what he could discover come sun-up.

Our edge so far had been surprise and the night's dark. Tomorrow could be a different story. We was still outnumbered, even countin' the addition of Burr Hamilton and whatever help them prisoner gents might offer. And I was havin' trouble convincing myself the arrival of one young gal and a snake oil salesman — Pinkerton agent or no — would make enough difference to turn the tables.

We surely wasn't goin' to have no luck rushin' them log buildings, not with eight or ten armed men inside all primed an' ready to meet us. The best we might hope for was a case of who could out-wait who. And even then, if for some reason Ravenant got a notion he couldn't hold out, it was them'd have the advantage come nightfall. They could sneak off into the swamp by twos an' threes with mighty little chance of us stoppin' 'em.

I let Luke go ahead with his wire-cuttin', whilst Burr an' me made it back to our look-out place at the live oak tree. I hadn't mentioned none of my thinkin' to 'em yet. But the more I mulled it over, the more I wondered if we might not of already done the best we could hope for.

We'd set the captives free, though it'd still take a mite of doin' to get 'em all back to civilization safe an' sound. And we'd gone a fair way towards upsettin' Ravenant's apple cart in the process. Maybe we ought to just fold our hands now, and skedaddle with our winnin's.

Maybe. Only it left a bad taste in my mouth to do it. Us Barkleys still owed a debt to that crowd, Luke a heap more than me. Besides which, it wasn't neighborly or decent to just walk off an' leave a nest of vipers like these where they could strike at the next unsuspectin' traveler who come along.

So I kept my lips buttoned for the time bein'. And I told myself that if a clever gent like my friend Monk said he had a plan, he prob'ly had one. And a better'n average plan at that.

Luke made it back just as the sky was turnin' from charcoal gray into a robin's egg blue. Cal had already joined us some time before. And now we all settled in for a good, long wait.

There wasn't much else we could do, in the broad daylight with only us four facin' all of them men behind log walls. We couldn't risk a shot without givin' away our position, and in a exchange of lead they'd more chance of hittin' one of us by accident or design than the other way around. So we'd just got to sweat it out until Monk made his play, or it come on to dark again, whichever happened first.

'Course, we kept a mighty sharp lookout the entire time, one of us always up amongst the branches of that live oak, turn an' turn about. But for the time bein' it seemed like Ravenant and the others was content to let things stay as they was too.

I imagined there was a good deal of talk an' discussin' going on amongst 'em, about what they was facin' and what they'd ought to do. But they was safe enough 'long as they sat tight an' didn't show theirselves. It was outside in the open where a feller could get hisself hurt.

Time to time we'd notice somebody at one of the windows or loop-holes with what appeared to be a spyglass, searchin' the woods for whatever he could see. We done our best to make sure it wasn't anything except trees an' tall weeds.

In the meantime we tried to catch a little rest an' shuteye, though speakin' for myself that didn't come easy. It weren't in my nature to set doin' nothing whilst armed enemies was about. And like any old soldier'll tell you, waitin's the worst part of war.

I reckon it wasn't no easier for them up at the cabins, though. By the time the sun had reached its high point an' begun slidin' down the other side, they hadn't seen hide nor hair of us for better'n six hours. I expect some was beginnin' to wonder if we hadn't pulled our freight entire. After all, it was what I'd been a mind to suggest earlier.

When I mentioned that kind of quiet-like to my companions, we agreed we'd go on lettin' 'em think so if it was in their minds. 'Long as they didn't get ambitious an' start nosin' round this here patch of woods, we'd leave 'em be even if they showed us a target we couldn't hardly resist. It might put 'em off their guard for whatever Monk had planned, or for a second night's skirmishes if it come to that.

About midway through the afternoon we begun seein' little signs of movement here and yon outside the cabins. First this one feller made a dash from the big house to the hired hands' quarters. And a few minutes later another made the same trip in reverse. Then after maybe a half hour longer two gents come out an' Injuned along the lee side of the split rails of the corral, crouchin' there watchful as a couple long-tailed cats in a room full of rockin' chairs.

Burr, who was up in the live oak at the time, reported all this down to Cal in whispers, who passed it on to me an' Luke. We took holt of our shootin' irons just in case, with Luke givin' me back the Winchester he'd borrowed, knowin' I favored it. Then we sat tight, lettin' them boys have all the time they needed to come to the conclusion they was alone.

I reckon they finally started to convince theirselves, though Ravenant was mighty cautious about how an' where he'd let 'em move. He kept three, four rifles at the windows all the time, and it was the better part of a hour before them men by the corral appeared to let their neck hairs down enough so's they could breathe normal again.

We just left 'em be, knowin' there wasn't no urgent need to start anything whilst it was still light and Monk hadn't made his appearance yet.

I was startin' to worry over the little gent an' Marty now. I knew they'd a long way to travel, bringin' the wagon round-about an' all. But the day was gettin' late, and there was them two hired guns what could of took scent of 'em. . . .

❖   ❖   ❖

I guess it was somethin' after four in the afternoon when we finally heard this wheezin', whoopin' almost-but-not-quite-musical shivaree come squawlin' through the woods behind us. It like to spooked ever man there plumb out'n his boots, myself included!

But that was Monk of course, with the wind-up music box in his wagon runnin' full bore so's to let everbody in the neighborhood know he was comin'. From the sound it 'peared he was headed for that gate in the fence a little distance west of where us four was hidin'.

Sure enough, a few minutes after Luke and me had left Cal an' Burr to begin sneakin' through the trees in that direction, we heard Monk call out "Whoa!" Then there was a pause whilst he let hisself in, followed by another "Whoa!" as he stopped on the far side to close the gate behind 'em — just like any proper visitor would do.

Before I was close enough to spy the wagon I seen Ole Roan tied to some bushes outside the gate. Monk must of left him there as a kind of insurance against anything goin' wrong after they passed inside. But we'd scarcely time to nod Howdy to one another before Luke was wavin' for me to join him at the edge of the trees and have a look.

When I knelt down beside little brother, our Pinkerton friend was swingin' his mules around and headin' straight for Ravenant's homestead. He was on his feet handlin' the reins, dressed to the nines in his black suit an' top hat, with Marty beside him grinnin' and wavin'. I almost had to look twice to recognize the gal, all painted up like she was and decked out in this fancy satin outfit what showed nearly as much as it hid. Minded me more'n a tad of them fancy sportin' palaces in Denver.

I heard Luke cuss softly under his breath. And I'd a notion it was as much because of the way his lady-friend looked an' acted just then as from the pure-out nerve it took to ride up on that nest of vipers without so much as a "By-your-leave."

I didn't hardly know what to make of it my ownself. But I meant to be ready for anything Monk had in mind. So I dropped down on my belly with the Winchester at my shoulder, sightin' through high weeds at the closed door of the big house.

Luke, he kept on past me for another dozen yards or so, comin' to rest finally behind a low tussock of earth where he'd have him a different angle to shoot from.

"Hello the house!" Monk hollered out in a big cheerful voice above the creakin' of harness and the noise of his music-box, whilst he pulled his team to a halt. "Call in the hands from the fields and the women from the hearth; free the children of their chores and the father from his labors! Everybody gather round, and prepare to make merry! Professor Maximilian and his world-famous medicine show have arrived!"

Soon as he'd got through loopin' the ribbons around the

brake lever, Monk took up his long cane and give three, four boomin' raps on the side of his wagon. "Come one, come all! Witness the incomparable terpsechorean interpretations of Mademoiselle Martine of Paris, followed by an interlude of music and humor, and an educational discourse on the latest wonders of medical science! Edification and entertainment for the entire family!"

Marty had slid to the ground an' gone back to shut off the nickelodeon whilst Monk was talkin'. And the way that gal flounced her skirts when she moved, pretendin' all the while that she didn't have no idea they was two full cabins of menfolk watchin', was plenty enough wonder for me.

24 ⚜

When Monk said "Ma'mselle Martine," Marty stopped to pull a silk kerchief out from the open top of her dress, bowin' real low towards the windows of the house. Right then I got to wonderin' how long it'd been since those men inside had seen anything besides cold-hearted Lila to remind 'em of what they was missin'.

I reckon it was long enough. 'Cause not more'n a minute later the door to the bunk-house opened an' two hard-eyed gunmen poked their unshaved faces out, grinnin' like a couple young-uns what just sneaked under the edge of a peep-show tent.

The men by the corral had started driftin' towards the wagon right after they first seen Marty up on the box a-wavin' at 'em. Before you knew it they'd been joined by those from the bunk-house. And then the door to the main house opened an' two more stepped out.

I'd a idea this was pretty close to all the hired help what was still able to stand upright, though I couldn't be entirely sure. I noticed Ravenant an' Lila hadn't put in a appearance yet. Nor big Jube neither.

I shifted my rifle barrel up to the top floor window what overlooked the wagon, just in case. But I couldn't see no sign of movement there.

"Gather round, friends!" Monk jumped down an' strutted a little ways off into the open, totin' a carpet bag in his left hand. "Gather round, and say hello to the lovely Mademoiselle Martine, fresh from sold-out performances before the crowned heads of Europe!" When he stopped some forty, fifty feet from the house an' beckoned for Marty to join him, them boys all made a crowd. They was nearly stumblin' over one another tryin' to see who could get up closest to the gal and have the best view.

About then ole Jube come amblin' out of the house. And I seen Ravenant framed in the door behind him, starin' at all the doin's with narrowed eyes. He didn't look very pleased over what was happening. But it appeared like there wasn't much he could do to stop it. Them hard-case men he'd hired weren't about to let no opportunity like this pass 'em by.

Me, I breathed a mite easier when I set eyes on him an' Jube. This had to be pert' near the lot, and now they was all wide-open targets for the four guns I knew was sighted on 'em from out here in the brush.

Not to mention Monk and Marty, who it turned out was just on the verge of makin' their own play.

When I glanced from Ravenant over to where the others had congregated in a tight half-circle, Marty was smilin' real wide an' sassy. She flounced round with her back towards 'em and bent down, liftin' up her skirts like she was reachin' for a garter. Ever one of those gunslingers leaned forward to onct, their eyes nearly poppin' from their heads.

The next thing they knew they was starin' into the cold, black barrels of two Colt Pocket .44s, one held steady in each dainty fist.

Surprise ain't even close to the word for what was on them men's faces now. And it weren't helped a bit when they looked acrost at her partner an' seen the sawed-off shotgun Monk had slipped from his satchel whilst they was moonin' over the gal.

"Pinkerton agent. Nobody move." The little gent's voice was mighty sharp now, nothin' a-tall like the cheery perfessor of a couple minutes earlier. "Drop your weapons and undo your cartridge belts. You're all under arrest."

I watched them hard cases glance at one another, wonderin' about their chances. But even leavin' aside Marty's six-shooters, a scatter-gun filled with double-ought buck tends to make a feller mighty thoughtful an' cautious.

In another second Burr Hamilton liberated 'em from any last naggin' doubts. "You're surrounded into the bargain!" he hollered from his hiding place, "so hurry up and put your iron on the ground!"

Well, they done it without no more hesitatin', keeping their movements slow and easy with one eye on Monk and t'other on the dark forest around 'em. Jube shucked his pistol — my ole Dragoon — along with the rest. But then he started slewin' crabwise round in back of the crowd towards his right an' Monk's left. It caught my attention because he was the only one gettin' closer to the Pinkerton man whilst everbody else was sort of driftin' the other way.

I already figured that black feller was a tad more'n half crazy. And I was afeared he might have somethin' crazy in mind. So I was just about to holler out a warning to Monk, when this flash of sunlight on metal at the upstairs window took my eye instead.

Monk seen it the same time I did, and his shotgun begun to lift almost of its own accord. But my Winchester was already pointin' where it needed to be, and quicker'n you could spit I put a ball through the openin' three, four inches up above where that rifle barrel showed itself.

There was a shouted curse mixed with surprise an' pain. But I worked the lever and fired again without takin' time out to listen to the man's words. The rifle barrel in the window tilted towards the sky. Then it slid out the opening an' dropped to the ground with a dull Thunk!

When I swung my Winchester round on them men in the yard, they was mostly where they'd been 'fore the shootin' begun. Marty was seein' to that. Her pistols was both still steady an' level, though her green eyes seemed to of got mighty big of a sudden. A glance at the hillside beyond her was all it took to find out why.

Monk was nearly hid from view under Jube's huge body as the two grappled amongst the weeds an' the sandspurs. I could see the Pinkerton agent's shotgun on the ground a dozen feet away, where it must of fell after the big man attacked.

They was rollin' over and over now, clenched up tighter'n the iron band on a wagon wheel. There wasn't no question of riskin' a shot at this distance. Nor prob'ly from anywhere closer either, even if Marty hadn't got her hands full holdin' them others at bay.

Luke was already on his feet, closin' the distance between us an' Monk's wagon with long, reg'lar strides. Me, I didn't waste no extra seconds risin' up to go join him.

Burr an' Cal had broke cover and started for the cabins too. When I seen 'em, I hollered over my shoulder, "Look sharp, men! They's still one gent and a gal what ain't in attendance at this here party!" Ravenant had managed to disappear inside whilst my attention was elsewhere.

Them boys caught my meaning and slowed their steps, closin' in cautious-like with rifle an' shotgun at the ready. I kept glancin' up at the windows of the blockhouse my own-self as I followed Luke to where the wagon was parked.

But I couldn't see no trace of Ravenant or Lila. And it was mighty hard not to let my attention wander time to time, over to the sweatin' bodies of Jube an' Monk as they clutched an' throttled an' clawed at one another for all they was worth. It was pretty clear that my little ex-rassler friend was havin' the battle of his life.

'Course big Jube wasn't goin' noplace afterwards, even if he won this fight. But that didn't 'pear to make a whole heap of difference to his thinkin' at the moment. And it sure-ly wouldn't make none to Monk if he got his neck snapped an' wound up dead in the dirt.

It was somethin' to see, an' that's a fact. I already knowed more than I needed to about Jube's power an' quick-ness. But the longer I watched, the more I got the notion Monk hadn't been as serious as he might of been when me and him had our own li'l set-to up the country. The little per-fessor was givin' back good as he got now. Ever time it seemed like the big Negro had him pinned an' hog-tied, he'd make some kind of a twist what slid him free like a larded-up shoat. An' put him on top where he could do some damage too, often as not.

They was both wheezin' and snortin' like a couple bull

gators, and after they'd been at it maybe five or ten minutes the sweat was pourin' off 'em in rivers, mixed with blood where a hard knuckle or a fingernail had made a cut in somebody's skin. But there wasn't no quit nor back-up in either one. The longer the scrap lasted, the harder each seemed to go at it, tooth an' claw.

Them boys of Ravenant's had got almost as caught up in the fight as me and my *compadres*. Cal an' Burr had herded 'em a little ways off from where they'd dropped their weapons. And now, strange as it sounds, the entire crowd appeared to be pullin' for Monk. With them under our guns it didn't make no nevermind to their situation who won or lost. So being fightin' men theirselves, I reckon they admired the little gent's grit.

A couple of 'em even managed to let out with a sort of a cheer when Monk rolled free and hunched up on his back, catchin' Jube under the belly with his feet after the big man tried to fall on top of him, and then flipping that huge body into the air, high, wide an' handsome.

Jube landed with a grunt and a crash, and I guess that could of been the end of it if Luke or me had been ready an' quick enough to put lead into him whilst he was down. Only we wasn't. And anyhow it wouldn't of seemed right, after the battle that big feller'd put up.

No matter. 'Cause Monk didn't hardly wait long enough to give us the chanct anyway. He rolled to his feet an' sprung on top of Jube before a body could hardly blink. Next thing you knew he'd done scissored his stubby legs around the big Negro's neck and was clampin' down about it tighter'n the jaws of Hell.

Jube, he still wouldn't quit. He thrashed an' bounded all

over the place, fierce as a gar-fish caught in a net. But Monk just clamped down harder an' stayed with him, eatin' dirt and spittin' it out ever twist an' turn of the way.

"Give it up!" the little gent managed to gasp at last. "Or by God, I'll break your neck!" There wasn't no doubt in anybody's mind he could of done it, and Jube knowed it too. He closed his eyes and strained his huge muscles one last time, hollerin' out with pain and rage as Monk forced his head almost back in between his shoulder blades. Then he sighed an' let hisself go limp, wheezin' and puffin' like a locomotive at the top of a ten-mile grade.

I took a couple, three steps forward and laid my rifle barrel up next to Jube's ear, not wantin' to give him no hope a-tall of a second chance whenever Monk turned him loose. Way I figured it, he'd already give us enough excitement for one afternoon.

"Thanks, Tate." The little Pinkerton man let go an' backed away on his elbows. Then he just kind of laid there, gaspin' for breath and not hardly movin'. I noticed his face had got all red and splotchy.

"You okay?" I asked, kneeling beside him whilst keepin' my Winchester pointed at Jube.

"Fine," Monk sighed. He looked in my eyes an' grinned weakly. "Just fine. For an old out-of-condition wrestler who hasn't been in the ring with anything that large since a brief — and peaceful — introduction to Mr. Barnum's pachyderms a few years back."

After a minute I lent him my free arm so's he could climb to his feet. He was a mite rubbery 'round the knees. But then he steadied hisself and took holt of my Winchester to look after Jube, whilst I went to fetch the sawed-off shotgun he'd dropped. I turned my back on everbody for a second as I bent down to pick it up, so the first I knowed about our latest visitors was when I heard this sharp voice behind me:

"Just leave it lay, son. Then turn around real careful and slow."

Well, it weren't a voice what left much room for argument. And I'd a notion the man behind it had somethin' more than words to back it up. So I done like he said.

And there beside Monk's wagon, with a Colt Peacemaker in one gent's hands and a cocked an' leveled shotgun in the other's, was them two hired killers I'd met in Fort Dade.

Marty was on the ground a little distance from the first one's feet, rubbin' her fingers and glarin' up at him with a angry expression on her face. It looked like the big *pistolero* had stripped her of her hardware whilst she was watchin' the fight, prob'ly throwin' 'em back out'n the way somewhere behind the wagon. He was aimin' the long barrel of his Colt square at Monk's back now, though his eyes kept flickin' ever so often towards Luke, who was closer but whose pistol was still in its holster.

Ever single one of us was flat out of position for any shootin' difficulty from that direction. And them two professionals knew it. Burr an' Cal had let their long guns relax so the muzzles nearly pointed at the ground. And my Smith an' Wesson was in its leather to boot.

The man with the scatter-gun, whose name I seemed to recall was Pete, stood well back so that he could cover all three of us together, with me a dozen yards behind the other two. It was him who was doin' the talkin':

"All right now, everbody just take a nice, deep breath

and relax. We only got business with one man here today. The rest of y'all just let go your weapons and leave 'em drop. If you stay peaceful there won't be no trouble amongst us. We'll do our job, climb back in the saddle, and you'll never set eyes on us again."

I glanced at Monk, bein' pretty certain he was the one Ravenant had paid 'em to kill. The little Pink was standin' like a statue with his back to the gunmen and my borrowed Winchester still pointed in the general direction of Jube. The big Negro had raised hisself off the ground on one elbow now, takin' in the proceedings with a evil grin on his lips.

"What about me," I asked, shiftin' my gaze back to Pete and his shotgun. "They was a time outside Fort Dade when you-all seemed to take more'n a casual interest in my hide too."

"I reckon you could mostly chalk that up to a case of mistaken identity," Pete's partner put in. "Ravenant's niece tried to make us believe it was you we'd been brung here after." He half-shrugged, his pistol still holdin' steady on Monk Drucker's back. "'Pears like she had some kind of a private score she wanted to settle, and figured she'd get us to handle it for her whilst we was here. Didn't make her no nevermind that we wasn't bein' paid to take on any extra work."

Pete was lookin' at me through narrowed eyes. "'Course it mattered to us. But who knows? Maybe some other time."

"Maybe." I grinned at him.

"There's only one man's got to die here today," Pete's partner declared, stickin' to business. "And right now that man ain't you."

Well, by their own standards I reckon they was bein' awful generous, givin' me an' the others this chance to not get kilt. It almost made me feel guilty and ungrateful for what I'd made up my mind to do.

My eyes met Luke's for a instant, and he halfway nodded.

"Are you boys certain-sure you want to do this?" I asked mildly, easin' a couple steps to my right so that Burr an' Cal wasn't directly between me and Pete.

I figured I knew the answer. But it was still worth a try whilst I improved my position. "All that's left of Ravenant's gang is them empty-handed gents over yonder." I jerked my head in the bad men's direction, movin' a tad further to my right as I done it. "His niece and him have both lit a shuck. . . ." That was pure bluff on my part, though I hoped it was true. "—So now his entire operation ain't nothin' but some barb wire and empty cabins." I risked one more casual step to my right.

"None of that's anything to us," Pete said matter-of-factly, "one way or t'other. Me an' John already took the man's money, so we've hired on for the job. Only question is whether you-all mean to shuck your shootin' irons in the next three seconds, or join this little Pinkerton runt in Hell." When John eared back the hammer of his Peacemaker, I saw the time for talkin' was close to bein' over.

"Okay," I said. "'Pears like you ain't give us no choice. —Burr, Cal, drop your pieces."

They both looked at me, hesitatin' like I'd more'n half expected they would. I met their eyes and spoke again in a loud, sharp voice: "You heard me, DROP!"

My hand was fannin' leather before the words was out of my mouth good. The Smith an' Wesson come up spittin' lead whilst Cal an' Burr hit the ground and Pete's shotgun blasted flame, all in what seemed to be the very same instant.

I felt the sear of hot metal take me in the leg an' shoulder, but I'd been expecting it. I managed to spread my feet apart and put two more holes through Pete's faded cotton shirt before glancin' over to see how Luke was farin'.

I reckon he done all right for a three-fingered man. John lay stretched out face up in the grass, with his Colt a inch or two away from his cold, limp fingers.

When I looked back at Pete he was still clawin' for the pistol in his belt as he dropped down on both knees. But his hands seemed to of gone all clumsy of a sudden, and he couldn't fetch it out. He peered at me acrost the fifty feet what separated us and opened his mouth to say somethin', but his tongue wouldn't work neither. Finally he give a kind of a wheezin' sigh, pitched forward on the ground, and was still.

Me, I didn't feel so sprightly as I had earlier my ownself. I couldn't be sure how many pieces of lead from Pete's scatter-gun I was carryin', but it was enough to weigh me down so my knees wouldn't hold me. I decided I'd just set there on the soft grass and take a little rest, whilst Burr an' Luke an' them finished corralin' the prisoners and goin' through Ravenant's cabins an' all.

I'd been countin' on the distance between us to take some of the force out of Pete's blast, and I guess it must of worked since I was still alive to suffer the hurt an' misery of it. But another fifty yards or better would of pleased me more.

Seems like I must of nodded off for a minute or two. It was some kind of a loud noise in the distance what brung me around. The next thing I knew Marty an' Monk was kneelin' beside me, both lookin' concerned as all get-out.

25 ☀

Luke come up a minute or two later, and between 'em they managed to get me inside the blockhouse, where they laid me out on this big soft bed they found in one of the rooms. I guess it belonged to Ravenant hisself, or maybe Lila. It was a bed the like of which I'd never even saw before, much less stretched out upon, with this satin canopy overhead and mosquito-net curtains all around, and enough pillows an' comforters an' such-like to pacify the Queen of Sheba.

Mind you, I wasn't in too much mood to enjoy the luxury of it just then. I'd lost a deal of blood, and now the shock was wearin' off so them wounds was painin' me somethin' fierce. I guess I kind of drifted in and out of wakefulness for a time there, not always able to recognize who or what was around me.

I recall vivid enough when Monk started cuttin' the lead out of my flesh, though. 'Least the start of it. He hadn't nothin' to ease the pain except that fire-water out'n his canteen. And before it took holt to where I could pass out, I near bit clean through the hickory handle of Cal's skinnin' knife — in between yellin' my fool head off and takin' swings at him an' Luke, who was holdin' me down.

After it was over I was grateful enough for what turned out to be the li'l Pinkerton man's considerable skill at doctorin', on top of his other talents. At the end they was six pieces of buckshot in a whiskey glass on the bedside table that he'd managed to fish out of me.

But I didn't know nothin' about them till later, when I'd woke to see Marty standin' over the bed with a bowl of hot broth and a spoon in her hands.

"You reckon you feel up to takin' some nourishment?" she asked. I nodded, noticin' the shutters was closed now and it was dark outside. A coal-oil lamp was burnin' on the wash stand acrost the room, castin' a warm homey glow over everthing that wasn't swallowed up by shadows.

'Bout the time Marty'd got the bowl put down so she could lift me into a sittin' position, Luke come through the door and finished the job for her. Me, I helped all I could. But it seemed like them perforations in my hide had left me weak as a kitten.

"You ain't so full of ginger as you was a couple hours earlier," little brother observed, swingin' a chair around to let the gal sit next to me. "Couple times while Monk was operatin', I thought I'd have to knock you upside the head just so you'd be quiet an' lay still."

"It was that ole bayhead augerdent of his," I said, pausin' to accept a spoonful of broth from Marty, "what brung the blood to my eyes. That, and the pure-dee agony of a steel blade pokin' round my innards. You ought to try it sometime, whenever you ain't got enough misery in your life to keep you satisfied."

I took a bit more broth, and Marty leaned forward to wipe my chin. "Still, I'm right appreciative for what the little gent done. I feel a whole heap lighter now than after Pete got finished loadin' me down."

"You ought to, considerin' it was a full half pound of lead Monk plucked from your hide." Luke shook his head. "Dangdest thing I ever did see, you drawin' square in the face of a cocked an' loaded twelve-gauge."

"I had it to do. We both did, or lose the company of a mighty fine friend." I glanced past Marty toward the door that led to the rest of the cabin. "Speakin' of which, where's that li'l rascal got hisself to? And Burr an' Cal? They ain't still huntin' after Ravenant are they? Not in this deep ole swamp with it come on to night and all?"

"No. There isn't any need for that." Luke shrugged. "I expect they'll be pokin' their heads in directly. Everbody just figured you could do with a little peace an' quiet whilst you was recoverin' from your hurts."

"Well, I ain't never been so bad hurt that I couldn't spare a 'Howdy' for my friends. You go tell 'em . . ." I fell silent, realizin' what Luke had said. "There isn't any need . . . ?"

"*Monsieur Ravenant* isn't with us any longer," little brother said soberly. "He tried high-tailin' it into the woods after them hired guns got the drop on us. Only before he could make it to the first row of fencin', he run across Mr. Petrie and a couple others of his former captives."

"Dead?"

"And then some. Ravenant weren't a one to go easy, nor quick. He was still tryin' to crawl off into the brush with two bullets in him when they finally run him to ground." Luke shook his head. "It wasn't a pretty picture, though I guess maybe I can understand what some of those men were feeling."

"And Lila?" I halfway held my breath, waitin' for his answer. There wasn't no love lost between me an' that gal, and I'd be hard-pressed to think of much to say in her defense. But I'd of still hated to hear about any woman dyin' thataway.

"Nobody's seen her since some time before the shoot-out. Prob'ly snuck off and made her run for it without Ravenant or the rest of 'em knowin' it." I'd a idea Luke had some of the same mixed feelings about that as I did.

"And them men out back?"

"Never caught sight of her. Near as anybody can tell, she got away clean."

Well, clean into the swamp, I thought to myself. Which weren't exactly what I'd call scot free. But then, who knew? If I was a bettin' man, and it come down to choosin' between Lila and a moccasin or a gator, I wouldn't risk all my stake on them reptiles.

❖　　　　　　❖　　　　　　❖

We spent the night there at the cabins, and a few more days besides. There was plenty of food an' supplies laid by for the use of Ravenant and his men, though they hadn't been much inclined to share with their captives who done all the work. We just switched the scheme of things around a mite, so the former prisoners got to build up their strength on good, substantial vittles whilst the hired guns made do with cold taters an' greens.

There was a deal of cash money too, what Ravenant had salted away after first robbin' his captives and then sellin' the fruits of their labors. It come to pretty near five thousand dollars, which was little enough for all the sufferin' them poor souls had been through. Everbody agreed the fairest thing was to just divide it up amongst the survivors, share and share alike.

Me, I didn't want nothin' of Ravenant's 'cept the forty-odd dollars Lila had stole from me back up the country. After payin' Monk the sixteen I owed him and settin' aside twenty for my earlier debt, I'd enough left over to make out till I found a payin' job.

Marty an' Cal wouldn't take nothin' either, nor Burr Hamilton who allowed his family had plenty without it. Luke was a mind to turn down his share too, until I threatened to club him upside the head with a iron bedpost if he kept on refusin'. Even so, I'd a idea he didn't get back near what he'd lost.

The second day I spent layin' there abed recoverin' from my hurts, I finally got a introduction to that Yankee and his lady.

I'd speculated more'n once on everthing I meant to say when this meetin' finally come, about not helpin' folks when they needed it, and makin' too hasty judgments about people you didn't know, and all like that. But they was both so all-fired thankful an' gracious — having come to my room a-purpose just to tell me how much they 'preciated what I'd done — that I couldn't bring myself to say hardly anything except, "Pleased to meet you" and "You're welcome."

Luke, who'd come into the room along with 'em, had a couple more questions that he wanted answers to:

"What in the world were you thinking, travelin' into this wild country in a little city rig with a woman and hardly

285

no outfit a-tall? Didn't you realize it might not be no Sunday picnic?"

The Yankee shrugged. "I guess we didn't plan for our journey as carefully as we should have. But the agent in Hartford from whom we purchased our land gave us the impression that citizens of the North were relocating to Florida by hundreds and thousands. Naturally, we assumed there would be roads and other improvements . . ."

"You bought land here?" Luke asked. "I mean, you bought land *here*?" He glanced around at the rough walls of the cabin, and then he tried to meet my eyes. But I was keepin' my own counsel, and I'd turned my face to the pillows, tryin' my dangdest not to look at either one of 'em.

"East of here, actually," the Yankee said a tad stiffly. "We purchased a full section of six hundred and forty acres between the villages of Orlando and Kissimmee."

He pronounced the second town's name like he was askin' for a smooch, and I could tell from Luke's sudden fit of coughin' and throat-clearin' that he was havin' a time holdin' his feelings inside.

"You got any idea how far it is to those places from here?" he managed finally. "It must be better than thirty miles, through swamp and scrub ever bit as rough as the twenty miles you covered after leavin' Fort Dade. Why in the world didn't you just come up the St. Johns like everone else who has a notion to visit that part of the state?"

"We wanted to look over the surrounding country. And as I said, we were given to believe . . ."

". . . that there would be Yankee settlements and roads all along the way. Well, sir, I'm sorry to be the one to tell you, but far as I know the only settlements you'll find in that entire thirty miles are colonies of bears and wild hogs, an' scrub cows and alligators — ever one a natural-born Florida native."

Luke paused, and I'd the idea he was beginnin' to feel a mite of sympathy toward our visitors now. "Oh, there's new folks movin' in all the time," he said, tryin' to sound encouragin'. "But so far they've mostly set up housekeepin' near the coast or along the rivers north of here. Anything might happen, but I expect it'll be a good many years before this part of the state has settlers." He hesitated, then added under his breath in spite of hisself, "If ever."

Our Yankee acquaintance didn't seem to take the news too terrible hard, and I had a notion he'd prob'ly already guessed it. What he said next led me to believe he hadn't exactly sunk his very last dime into that section of Florida land neither:

"It's a pity, so many uninhabited acres just going to waste. You know, if a few enterprising gentlemen like myself were to form a corporation, we might dredge out canals and drain these lowlands. The cut-down timber from clearing the land would help defray our costs, and if we imported industrious farmers and tradesmen from New England, along with free Negroes to do the actual work instead of relying on the indolent natives . . ." He looked at his wife, who smiled an' nodded like she'd heard all this before. "—Who knows? In time mid-Florida might become a seat of commerce to rival our own fair state of Connecticut. With good roads, sturdy villages . . ."

The lady led him outside to finish his daydreamin', whilst I looked at Luke an' shook my head.

"You think he means all that?" I asked. "'Bout turnin'

this parcel of swamp and low hammock into another New England?"

Little brother just shrugged. "I hope not. Mis'able as this country can be sometimes, I feel mighty attached to it just the way it is."

"Me too," I agreed. "But I was thinkin' about the Yankee's own health an' welfare when I raised my question. For his sake, I hope he don't ever get close to makin' this country over accordin' to his personal plans an' specifications."

"Why's that?" Luke asked, lookin' at me kind of curious and suspicious.

"'Cause once he'd got it all exactly how he wanted it, there wouldn't be a solitary thing left for him to complain about. And I'd be afeared that any Yankee who had to stop complainin' might just waste away an' die!"

❖   ❖   ❖

Well, that's pret' near the end of the story, far as Ravenant and his "haints of the swamp" is concerned. Them folks what was held captive rode out pretty much the way they rode in, in twos an' threes an' family groups, each takin' along what livestock they come with or compensatin' their losses out of rounded-up outlaws' mounts. Some of 'em said "So long" an' "Thanks" when they left. Others didn't say nothin'. I reckon each one was in a hurry to put this sorry business behind 'em an' get ahead with their lives.

Me, I stayed with Monk as far as the county seat at Bartow, helpin' him an' Burr to guard their prisoners whilst takin' advantage of the chance to spend a couple more days in a wagon 'stead of up on the hurricane deck of Ole Roan. I was mendin' fast, though. And I figured I'd be ready to take to the leather again just soon as this li'l task was done.

Marty an' Cal come with us that first day, along with Luke an' Marty's brother Harry, who was almost over his fever and better fit for ridin' than me, time we left that place in the swamp. We took it easy anyhow, havin' no partic'lar reason to hurry. And besides, with everbody in our party ridin' captured horses, there wasn't enough left over for all them out-of-work gunslingers. So we tied 'em behind the wagon and just let 'em travel on shank's mare.

We spent the night on the shore of a little lake, with wild orange trees growin' everwhere and fish splashin' in the shallows so you almost didn't need a line to catch 'em. After supper Luke an' me talked a bit, him tellin' me 'bout his plans to visit North Carolina and then prob'ly come back to Florida afterwards — if Marty'd come with him. I didn't have no plans of my own, as usual. So I just congratulated little brother on his, and allowed as how I'd come callin' just soon as he got hisself situated.

With everthing that can happen to a body in this world, I hoped it wouldn't be another fifteen years till that all come about.

Later on, whilst I was takin' off my boots and gettin' set to roll up in my blankets under the clear Florida sky, I reached down and felt for that gold double eagle I was holdin' back to pay off a loan from this lady on the Gulf coast. I reckoned it was time I rode back yonder an' settled my debts, 'fore anything else untoward had a chance to get started.

After that, well, you never could tell . . .

THE END

Historical Notes

ALACHUA LAKE — The large wet prairie south of Gainesville, first known as the Alachua Savannah and by later generations as Payne's Prairie (after the Creek war chief King Payne), has filled with water to become a lake at least three times in recorded history, most recently in the late 1800s. Steamboats transported passengers and cargo between Gainesville and Micanopy from 1871 until 1891, when flotsam blocking the sink at the northeast corner became dislodged and the lake drained dry in a matter of days.

AUGERDENT — A corruption of the Spanish *aguardiente*, referring to the same high-octane "white lightning" still favored by many natives of the Caribbean and Latin America. Those who overindulged to the point of stupor were said to be "augured in. (See "Bayhead.")

BARBED WIRE — In 1873 Joseph F. Glidden of Illinois developed an improved twisted-barb type of fencing which he placed into production the following year. Despite adamant (and sometimes violent) resistance on the part of cattlemen everywhere, barbed wire found an early market in the American West, where timber was scarce and traditional fences caused problems with drifting snow. Florida itself remained an open range state until 1947.

BAYHEAD — Cracker term for rough backwoods moonshine.

COLT REVOLVING SHOTGUN — Some 20 years old at the time of this story, it was still a formidable piece of artillery as long as the shooter could manage to avoid the ever-present danger of discharging several loads at once. The revolving cylinder employed basically the same action as Colt's revolvers, but was divided into four 10- or 20-gauge chambers. A side-mounted hammer offered partial protection from "accidents."

CRY OF THE WHIPPOORWILL — Widely regarded in Southern folklore as an omen of impending death. As with all such portents of course, whose death is never exactly specified.

THE DADE MASSACRE — On December 28th, 1835, Major Francis Langhorne Dade and two companies of soldiers on their way from Fort Brooke (Tampa) to reinforce the garrison at Fort King (Ocala) were attacked by Seminole Indians near present-day Bushnell. Of the 111 troops engaged, only 3 survived, two of them dying afterward of wounds. Together with the assassination that same day of Indian Agent General Wilie Thompson and Lieutenant Constantine Smith near Fort King, this marked the beginning of Florida's Second Seminole War. It was to be the longest and most costly war in American history (in percentage of casualties and contemporary dollars) prior to Viet Nam.

FORT DADE — The first fort of this name was built in 1837 on the south bank of the Withlacoochee River, seven miles north and east of present-day Dade City. During the Third Seminole War (1856-58), a new fort was constructed some four or five miles south of the original, and the community which grew up nearby was known as Fort Dade for a number of years afterward.

THE GREEN SWAMP — A modern term, used to describe more or less that vast area of wetlands between present-day Bushnell and Kissimmee which also encompasses the headwaters of the Withlacoochee and Hillsborough rivers. At the time of this story the place had no name. "That big swamp" was deemed more than sufficient.

HAINTS — Ghosts, or "haunts."

HERNANDO COUNTY — Partitioned from southwestern Alachua county on February 24th, 1843. At the time of this story it included present-day Citrus and Pasco counties, with a total population of slightly over 5,000.

HOPEVILLE — An early settlement on the Gulf Coast, later to be known as New Port Richey.

MR. BARNUM'S PACHYDERMS — Elephants were an important feature of P. T. Barnum's "Greatest Show on Earth" almost from its inception in 1871, although the world-famous "Jumbo" did not arrive until 1881.

MOSQUITO INLET — A passage through the barrier islands north of present-day New Smyrna Beach and an important navigational landmark that also lent its name to a Florida county in territorial days. (Mosquito County became Orange County in 1845.) The name of the passage itself was changed by image-conscious public officials during the land boom of the 1920s. It is now known as Ponce de Leon Inlet.

NEWNANSVILLE — County seat of Alachua County from 1828 until 1854 (with a few brief interruptions when boundary changes put the town in Columbia County). It was located about 2 miles northeast of present-day Alachua. All that is left today of the once-thriving community are a historical marker and a cemetery.

OLD LENO — Located near an earlier settlement known as "Helltown," this village west of the Natural Bridge of the Santa Fe River was first called "Keno," after the gambling game. The name was changed in 1876 at the urging of local ministers and business leaders. Nothing of the town remains; its former site is now a part of O'Leno State Park.

PAINTER — Cracker term for the Florida panther. A wide-ranging predator which some recent "experts" have had difficulty identifying.

PANASOFFKEE — At the time of the story this lake in western Sumter county was surrounded by wild orange trees that had grown there without cultivation for more than two centuries. (The Spanish were in the habit of planting oranges wherever their ships made landfall, as a future prevention against scurvy.) There was a small settlement on the lake's south shore, also named Panasoffkee.

PINEY WOODS ROOTER — Cracker term for Florida's fierce native wild boar.

POLK COUNTY — Where the climax of this story takes place, was separated from Hillsborough County in 1861. Its population in 1870 was 3,169. By 1880 there had been a net gain of twelve inhabitants, to 3,181.

SETTLEMENT — One of the difficulties of attempting to locate population centers (such as they were) with any accuracy in frontier Florida, is that most of the state's independent and agrarian inhabitants preferred to live as far apart from one another as was economically feasible. A "settlement" was nothing at all like the Northern or Old World concept of "town"; many of these extended for miles, yet consisted of only a handful of families. One classic example is the early settlement of Wacahoota, which included parts of Alachua and Levy Counties encompassing an area of some 100 square miles.

SMITH AND WESSON ARMY REVOLVER — Model 1875 (Schofield). Caliber .45, six shot, single action. One of the most accurate handguns of its day. At two pounds, eight ounces, it was substantially lighter than the old four-pound Dragoon Colt Tate formerly carried.

SUMTER COUNTY — Created on January 8, 1853, from southern Marion County. At the time of this story it also included most of present-day Lake County. The county took its name from General Thomas Sumter, a Revolutionary War hero of South Carolina. (Many early settlers originally migrated to north and central Florida from that state.)

SUMTERVILLE — Established in 1857 to serve as the county seat of Sumter county. At the time of this story the county government had been moved to the more recent (and smaller) settlement of Leesburg. It would be returned to Sumterville in 1881, and would remain there until 1911, when a public referendum declared Bushnell the new county seat.

TUCKERTON or **TUCKERTOWN** — An early settlement near present day Richland, four miles southeast of Dade City on the old Lakeland Highway.

YANKEES — From Tate's point of view, any of that strange, foreign breed who came from north of the Pennsylvania-Maryland border. As for the author, some of his best friends are Yankees. But it does strike him as a peculiar quirk of human nature that so many who have uprooted their lives in order to relocate permanently to our state spend so much time afterward grumbling about how different it is from the place they abandoned.

Other Books by Lee Gramling

Ninety-Mile Prairie

Riders of the Suwannee

Thunder on the St. Johns

Trail from St. Augustine

Trouble in the Everglades

War Clouds Over West Florida